GYPSY BONES

CHRISTIN LORE WEBER

Cyberscribe Publications
9700 Sterling Creek Road
Jacksonville, Oregon

This book is a work of fiction. Names, characters, incidents, and the town of Cold Creek are products of the author's imagination and are used fictitiously. Any resemblance to actual events, locale, or persons, living or dead, is entirely coincidental. As with all novels, though, the more real the fiction appears, the better read it is.

Cover photography by Sandy Rubini
http://www.vintimo.com/

ISBN 978-0-9835500-7-5

DEDICATION

In Memory of Liz

ACKNOWLEDGMENTS

After many revisions of a book over as many years, it would become virtually impossible to mention all the people who provided encouragement. Though I am grateful to all of them, I am compelled by a special gratitude to mention the names of a few. Bill Cunningham: You believed in this book from the beginning and never ceased wanting to see it in print. Sandra Scofield: you picked me up at my lowest point and sent me forward. Sheri Reynolds: you laughed and wept with me by email almost every day and in the middle of countless nights. Kathleen Jesme: You provided a critique as only a gifted poet could. Shiloh Sophia and Sharon Trent: each of you saw the promise in these characters and called *Gypsy Bones* a contemporary women's mythology. And finally, the members of Gather.com honored me by their winning vote for the excerpt on "James." If such a talented community of writers could believe in this book, there could be no question but that I must continue right up to this moment.

And John: you arrived in my life at exactly the moment to say, "The time is Now."

PART ONE

1

James Olson figured the wife would be back by sundown. That day she left with the girl, he figured she had to get it out of her system, whatever it was, whatever made her harden to him like the crusts of January. He woke that morning and reached out to her. He wanted to lay his hand on her belly, to feel the round curve. He imagined her sensing the weight of his presence and his awakening. It must have been the storm got her up, he thought, as his hand touched the rumpled sheets and then the pillow with the smell of her hair still lingering. She must be curled on the couch downstairs or already in the kitchen getting coffee.

He opened every door, even the closets. In the girl's room he parted the clothes hanging there. Did he expect to find his daughter huddled in a corner, her little knees brought up to her chin, her hair hiding her eyes? His blood felt suspended in his veins. He couldn't feel his heart beating. Did he breathe? He didn't seem to breathe, but that would be impossible. He walked around the house three times before going to the barn. Nothing. He stood looking at the spot where his old black 1938 Ford was supposed to be parked and he squinted as though something must be wrong with his eyes. In just a second the car would appear. But the car was gone.

James walked back toward the house. He opened the kitchen door and went inside. He walked to the center of the living room. He just stood there facing the big front window that looked out over the fields. He didn't know what he was feeling, or even if he was feeling. The house was empty; that's all there was to it.

Maybe she left because he wouldn't call her by her name. He could think it but not say it. He couldn't get it off his tongue. Yarrow. The word slit him down the front and laid him wide open, a thing too womanly to be tolerated. Like a furrow or a slaughtered calf. Women, they can tolerate such a rending and live afterwards. There's a saying, women are the strongest, and when it comes to being intimate with words, that's certainly his experience. Names hold a danger. Oh, he could say names like Fred or Frank; no problem. He could even say Mrs. Anderson and Granny Shea. But "Yarrow"? No. He couldn't. "I take you, Yarrow, to be my wife." He said it then and that had to stand for all the days to come. He made his promise. He stood by his promises. But even with his daughter, James couldn't say her name.

"Do you love me, James?" Yarrow asked him again the night before she left. He told her once. She shouldn't ask him anymore. "Just take it that I do," He said when they still were on their honeymoon in Minneapolis. "If I ever change my mind, I'll let you know." By this he meant to secure her in the knowledge and the promise of that love. He meant to let her know she needn't worry ever again for her entire life. He meant the cocoon his silence made, the protection of a love too tender. He'd seen what can happen to a love unguarded. He would show her in the strong ways, in the working of the land, the security of this home. And he would be faithful to his promise.

"Can't you just say you love me?" Then she cried. He took her in his arms as he always took her in his arms. He smoothed back her hair and kissed away her tears. What was this if not love? She lay there, her head turned, her eyes open. Outside the wind came up and the rumble of thunder far away.

He wanted to say this will make you feel better, but he stopped himself. Better to let the actions speak. He lifted her gown and she allowed this. He took some comfort in that small fact, that redeeming detail. He held that fact up as proof against guilt. He lifted her gown and admired how her breasts caught the pale shimmer of lightning through the window. He found her nipple with his mouth, touched the tip with his tongue and it sprang to life. She can't deny it sprang to life. He sucked and she groaned. She groaned through sobs, but women are complex, their emotions flow in opposite directions at the same time. He's always been aroused by this complexity. He reached his fingers into the cave between her legs and rubbed that shining spot inside of her, that silken space. She gasped as he knew she would. She grabbed the pillow and cried out.

Afterwards he had lain back, secure in this demonstration of his love. Her quiet moaning and the rocking of her sobs put him to sleep.

~~~

When James's mother left, back when he was a boy, he didn't speak for two weeks. His grandmother, Adeline, told him this. He remembered nothing of her. Not a smell, not a sound. He can't remember her eyes or her arms holding him. The first memory he has is of the barley, crushed, broken on the ground by hail. He was twelve. His father lifted his fist to the sky and yelled. "First Lily, now this, who the hell do you think I am?" That was the last he said of it. He never said her name again. To James's knowledge his father never called on God again either. The man died cursing, sitting at the breakfast table. "What the hell is going on?" He looked confused. He started to stand up and fell over dead. His coffee cup arced into the air, hot coffee trailed behind it, a splash of brown and copper, stopped midair, or so it seemed whenever James remembered it. Everything stopped. James just stood there. Then all of it crashed to the floor.

"You're the man of this family now," Gran told him. She said the farm was up to him. It was back in 1934. James had turned sixteen, and she was right.

James Olson's world consisted of fields and silence and the wide sky, a white sun in winter with its dogs hunting the horizon line. His was the feel of earth beneath his boots all seasons, the melting earth of April, thick, sticky, sucking at his feet. His, the loam rich like a woman, the musk scent of earth inviting seed. Midsummer earth cracked around the barley stalks while rain held off for yet another day. August always came with dust-devils, chaff of the spent fields.

His were the fields, the silence, the wide sky and home.

You can't just sit still no matter what happens. There's plowing. There's irrigation. There's always something to be mended--doors off their hinges, tractor gears not working smooth. James opened cans the first week after the wife left him, cans of baked beans, Campbell's chicken noodle soup. Ate it all straight from the tin, cold.

~~~

After the first week passed and the wife didn't come back, James went looking. He drove the pickup out in spokes from the farm. Down towards Grand Forks, first, and even crossed the river into Minnesota. Women like to shop and it had been years since she'd even bought herself a new pair of shoes. He spent one whole afternoon visiting shoe stores hoping to catch a glimpse of her.

He didn't ask after her. Asking is a form of confidence he couldn't bring himself to give to strangers. It's like turning over and showing your underbelly. He developed a system, a map in his head, for searching. He crisscrossed the town like a weave, every street— east and west, north and south—keeping his head to the front like he knew perfectly where he was going. A man with a purpose. And he watched for her. The slim back of a woman with a girl in tow could make him turn his head. But the sight of a face with features laid all wrong raised an anger in him that he didn't expect. He swallowed, clamped his fists around the steering wheel and kept on looking.

Once, in Roseau, he thought he saw her turning up a sidewalk to enter a house. His heart tensed. "Hello, there! Missus!" He called out the window but she didn't hear or else she didn't know it was herself he meant. She would have recognized his voice, though, wouldn't she, if it had been the wife?

Nights at home James watched dust settle on the curtains. He watched the light dim on the horizon. He listened to the sound of crickets in the cut grain. A field mouse nested in the wife's yarn basket and he let it stay. North Dakota winters can raise a deep terror in prairie creatures. He'd seen their bones in spring. And besides, he felt a companionship with the tiny thing as he watched it go about its daily tasks. It gnawed a ragged hole in the flour sack, which he let be. He was willing to share his abundance with whatever companion given him, in whatever form. He had no need of flour anymore. If he had need of anything, it was of this tiny creature. After it grew accustomed to his presence it would sit on the edge of the yarn basket and look at him. He looked back, and in those wee eyes he thought he saw what only could be an intelligence or an intention about life from which he determined he would learn. By winter's end the mouse sat on his shoulder. It ate peanut butter from his spoon.

No one came to the house. If they had, he wouldn't have let them in. How could he let them in? Such an embarrassment for the wife if she'd been there, the way her house had turned without her keeping it the way she did before. He kept the barn. He kept the garage and the tool shed. He kept the fields. Her flowers went to seed and in May they sprang up along with the weeds. Her house thickened with dust. Her curtains sagged under the weight of it and began to shred. Mouse droppings littered the kitchen floor and the wife's yarn basket smelled. The sheets on James's bed turned gray and her pillow no longer held the scent of her hair.

James began to talk to the mouse.

"Mouse," he posed. "It's about time we planted the west field, don't you think?" The mouse held a bean in its delicate paws. It sat on the kitchen table. What a miracle it was, the life of it, the perfection. "The wife will be back soon. She'll expect planted fields." We love the ones we can. We give ourselves to whatever will share our path.

After that he began once more to look forward to returning to the house at noon after a morning of planting.

"I'm home, Mouse!"

Sometimes it burrowed deep in the yarn. Sometimes it scampered from the pantry and climbed up his pants leg to his shoulder. He made a cup of Postum and fed the mouse a bit of whatever he might be eating by letting it nibble from his fingers.

From time to time he wondered if he should give the mouse a name, but thought better of it.

~~~

Somebody had to visit Gran now that the wife was gone, and who could it be but himself? He let it go as long as he could, but she was calling him on the phone asking was the wife back yet, and saying wasn't it just like his mother had done? Just up and leaving the family. A true Olson woman never would consider such a thing, she went on and on. It was a sin to take a child away from her father like the wife had done. Gran's voice crackled like straw.

Mondays James always drove to town anyhow to get the few supplies he needed, so he started stopping by Gran's room at the old folks' home.

"You ought to go to church, son." Gran smoothed her afghan with her claw of a hand.

"Never had much time for it."

"Still and all, it'd help to get yourself out of that house." She sounded just like when he was a boy.

"I get out fine."

"Alone, though. You get out alone, but you need people. At church they have those fellowships," she said, and he wondered what she was doing talking about fellowships when she never went to church herself. Not once that he could remember in all those years.

"Never had much of a knack for people."

When he looked at Gran, she reminded him of Mouse, her beady eyes trained directly on his face. Maybe she could see something he didn't know and even if he did, he wouldn't want it seen.

"Your mother's fault. Shame. Shame on her."

He kept his mouth shut.

"You ought to go to church." She continued to look straight at him though he wouldn't meet her eyes.

"I'll think about it." Words to put the discussion to an end.

They sat a few minutes in silence.

"And the house. Can you keep it up?" A softer tone of concern and maybe loneliness put a slight tremor in her voice, a thing almost unbearable.

"It's fine." He wished they could talk about planting or about politics even.

"A mess, I'll wager. None of you men ever could keep a house, not your grandfather, not your father. Why would you be any different? I expect you're no different at all." She'd recovered her voice, put that brittle edge on the tone that stopped the tremor.

Again he kept his mouth shut, picturing the dust, the dirty dishes, droppings of the mouse.

"I expect that house is a complete mess."

Over the years you learn when not to talk.

"You'd best get somebody in there now and then who knows what to do with a mop and broom."

"It's not necessary, Gran." He told her and hoped that would put an end to it.

"Ha! I don't even like to imagine how that place looks by now. I can see by the clothes you're wearing. Do you even know how to operate the washing machine?"

Silence.

"You need hired help. Ida Gunderson, maybe. We've a family connection, there, you know. Her husband. Might say he'd be your uncle if the truth be told."

Not Ida Gunderson. Not anyone, family connection or no family connection. The wife would be back, if not this summer, then by fall for sure. Women make too much of cleanliness.

"I'll think about it," he said.

"You do that. Otherwise you'll just fold up and die out there. You mark my words, James Olson. You just mark my words!"

He went back to see her on the first Monday of every month. The conversation continued pretty much the same except he had less and less to say. What he did have to say he told the mouse. Then one evening he came in from the fields and couldn't find the little thing. He looked all through the yarn, the pantry, even in the upholstery of his big chair. He called out. He searched for three hours before he could admit that the creature was gone. Then James sat down in his chair and looked at the tattered curtains and listened to the crickets in the field and stared out the window until almost ten that night when the sun finally set. After that he cried. He sobbed like he couldn't when the wife took the girl and ran away. He yelled out in his empty house like he couldn't when his own mother left so many years ago. His heart felt like a melon in his chest, split and running out, and nothing James could do anymore, and nothing he could say from now on would be able to change that.

2

Hannah liked to draw her name. Before her mother took her away, she sat at the table in the old Olson farmhouse kitchen, two Sears catalogues under her on the chair to raise her to a proper height. Her skinny ash-brown braids hung over her shoulders all the way to the sheet of paper, and she held her wooden pencil like a sculptor's tool.

HannaH.

She pressed the "H's" hard into the lined paper of the tablet. They must be strong, to hold the Anna, like a mother's bony knees are strong, or like mountains on each side of a wide plain.

Hannah's mother, Yarrow, had brought her into this world on a hot August day back in 1938, in the upstairs room of the same farmhouse where Hannah's father, James, also had been born, and his father before him. "I never saw such a serious baby," Yarrow recited to Hannah the story of that day. "Such blue eyes, and they never turned. A seafoam color, your eyes, like they say about the ocean. But we wouldn't know about that, would we now?" Her mother would pull one of her braids; it was part of the story. "And your hair, it was the color of ash wood in spring, so fair with just a touch of green. Too bad it darkened like it did."

To Hannah's way of seeing, she entered the world one summer afternoon at the edge of a barley field. A whirl of barley chaff and dust woke her, and she cried out from the shock of it. Barley chaff and the roar of the threshing machine swirled in a circle around the basket where she lay, seeming the only sound, until the night she heard something keening.

The keening dissolved the boundaries of Hannah's world She heard strains of it across fields of winter wheat in spring and when the barley turned gold in mid-July. She heard its sharp edge in the cry of the red-winged blackbird, poised impossibly atop a barley spine. Her mother told her that the original people of their land, the Indians, had a story about the red-winged blackbird's cry. "Those birds protect us," her mother said. There was a story she'd learned when she was a little girl in the Cold Creek school, an Indian legend about how the red-winged blackbird got its name. A fire, set by an enemy was approaching the village. Seeing it the blackbird cried out, "*Ku nam wi cu,*" which means, "The world and everything in it is going to burn." Hearing this warning, the enemy threw stones to silence the bird. The stones hit it on the wings and they bled, but still it cried out, "*Ku nam wi cu,*" and had been protecting the people that way ever since.

Her father told her that the keening must be wind across the Great Plains, and the girl imagined that the wind collected sounds as it passed, and that its song was made tender by the breath of newborns and poignant by the final rasp of old women and men crumbling toward death. When first she heard the song, she thought leaves sang it as they fanned the wind. Later, when the song truly did become one with the music of earth, she learned that some people on the prairie never heard the song at all, though it sang all around them. These buried their dreams in the rich black loam of the plains and stood guard over the whispers that lingered above the grave. These turned to stone and their bones could not be hollowed out. Wind keened against them like a banshee's cry.

~~~

"Mommy?" Hannah had just finished a perfect drawing of H's and Anna. She lifted her pencil. Her feet dangled from her perch on the Sears catalogs.

"Let's pretend you are all grown up--maybe a girlfriend of mine. Then you could call me Yarrow." Hannah's mother had her back turned, busying herself at the stove in the farmhouse kitchen, frying freshly laid eggs in hot bacon grease. They cracked and sizzled as they slid from shell to skillet.

"I don't want to play that game, Mommy. Come see what I made." She wanted her mother to raise her eyes, to see her where she sat on the Sears catalogs, to leave the eggs and bend over her shoulder, to look at the H and the Anna on the paper where she'd drawn it so fine. Her name. Her self. Hannah. But the mother didn't look up. She fried eggs. She inserted the spatula under an egg and flipped it over on its sunny side.

"It's my name, Hannah, the prairie flower name my mother gave me. Don't you want me to call you by your name?" Her mother murmured. She sprinkled salt. She sprinkled pepper.

"I want to call you Mommy." A field rock seemed pressed down on Hannah's chest.

"Please, Hannah." Yarrow reached for a potholder and lifted the iron skillet from the flame. She didn't turn around. With her other hand she brushed dark strands of hair away from her face.

Hannah imagined a tiny green leaf floating inside a tear on the mother's eye, but couldn't say for sure that it was actually there, because her mother kept herself busy with the skillet and didn't look at her.

"Why?" Hannah asked again.

"I like to hear my name once in a while; that's all." Yarrow set the skillet on the butcher block and thwacked the potholder down beside it. She grabbed a plate.

Hannah disappeared for a moment into the crackle of eggs and the sizzle of bacon grease. She stared at the limp bow tied in Yarrow's apron strings and hanging down the back of her wrinkled cotton skirt. She looked back at the drawing of her own HannaH. Her head was a room filled with echoes of her father's voice breaking the house silence, a voice advancing ahead of his feet, stamping, knocking away gumbo stuck to his boots during a long day in the fields, "Hello, there. You here?" And then his muttering, "Can't never find the wife when you need her."

"Daddy doesn't call you Yarrow." She reminded her mother over the sizzling grease.

Yarrow slid eggs onto the plate. She poured hot bacon grease into the copper jar that she kept on the warmer.

"That's what I mean, Hannah. Wouldn't it be nice if he would?" Her voice--a breeze through a back door on a summer afternoon, the haunt of a mourning dove.

At other times her voice sounded thin as dishwater poured down the drain, but not when she sang her lullaby. Then Yarrow bent over Hannah who lay in her narrow bed, and Yarrow's thick, molasses colored hair fell over her shoulder onto the pillow beside Hannah's head. "Blow, blow, the grasses blow," she crooned in tones of barley and cottonwood leaves. "Wind in our hearts, child, singing low. Song of our lives, forever free, will bring us home, far though we be."

~~~

The Olson family's land ended at the sky. At their meeting Hannah conjured mountains. On a hot afternoon Yarrow shelled peas while she sat on the swing in the relative shade of the farmhouse porch. She offered a taste of peas to Hannah, her palm a cup of crisp green sweetness.

"Is that a mountain, Yarrow?" Hannah pointed far off to the horizon. Yarrow looked up, examined the place toward which the child gestured, as though it could be, perhaps, a mountain.

"Those are clouds." She popped a sweet pea in her mouth. "Did you try those peas, Hannah? They're extra sweet and plump this year."

"But it could be a mountain far away." Hannah limited herself to one pea at a time to make the sweetness last. Her teeth closed, and the pea burst.

"I'm afraid we can't see mountains from here, Hannah."

"Not even with a spy glass?"

"No, not even then. The mountains are beyond the earth's curve."

"Is that far away?" Hannah squinted into the distance where heat waves distorted the cottonwood tree alongside Cold Creek so that it appeared to be floating from side to side like a ghost.

"Very far." Yarrow snapped a peapod to run her thumb along the inside, and Hannah listened as each pea dropped into the bowl.

"Will we go there someday?"

"I don't think so."

Hannah could imagine how the earth would look, curving down and away from her, and she wondered if, traveling beyond the curve of earth, she might see the sky beneath her feet.

"We have to grow the crops and then it's winter." Yarrow sighed and snapped another peapod.

"I want to see the earth's curve where the mountains are."

"Tonight we'll watch the mountains of the moon."

"With a spy glass?"

"With your father's binoculars." Yarrow looked at her and smiled.

Those mountains wrinkled the light along the moon's curve and that was all. Afterwards Yarrow sat with Hannah on the porch swing and sang about the wind in our hearts. Behind her voice, crickets in the cut barley fields tore the night to shreds of sound. Hannah tried to knit it together. She tried to take the curved light, the wrinkles, the crickets, and Yarrow's lullaby, and weave them with the night into one song that maybe even her daddy could learn to sing.

The light that shimmered across the prairie passed right through her father as though his skin were made of brown cellophane. In deep summer his white undershirt with its sleeves rolled almost to his shoulders was a flag waving over a gold lake of barley. The blue denim farmer cap covered his dark hair, not exactly brown and not exactly black, and with no highlights so that it seemed to absorb rather than reflect the light. All day long he sat on his tractor or tossed hay bales and by evening he'd soaked up so much sunlight he was almost invisible. His edges wavered like a tar road off in the distance. At the end of the day he came in the back door, issued his ritual call to the inhabitants of the house, and walked through the kitchen to the bathroom. He seemed to be looking at something inside himself.

"Have a good day, James?" Yarrow inquired evening after evening, but he never answered other than to give a nod, and she went right on peeling potatoes or shaking chicken pieces in a bag of flour.

He filled the sink with water and shook Boraxo into the palms of his hands. The soap turned gray and oily as he rotated palms over fingers in a smooth and precise, almost meditative motion. Without refreshing the water, he cupped his hands and carried it to the tops of his arms where the tan turned to white, then he let it run down over the thick dark hair of his forearms. Afterwards, with fresh water and ivory soap, he scrubbed his face. He left the sink grimy with evidence of his toil and his humanity. Hannah ran her finger over the scum that stuck like glue to the enamel and wondered if, without the skin of earth that covered him during the day, he might, some evening when the sun went down, simply disappear.

"Is Daddy going to disappear?" She asked Yarrow who scrubbed the sink with Dutch Cleanser.

"What?" She scrubbed with a swirling motion, a scrap of Daddy's old winter shirt in her hand, boiled wool shrunken to the texture of felt. It had been a plaid shirt. Red and black.

"Will Daddy disappear?" He wore that shirt last winter, and when he took his jacket off and lifted her up into his arms she smelled the wet wool smell mixed with her daddy's sweat that poured from him when he worked even if the air was cold enough to make his eyebrows white with frost. His blue eyes, the color of summer skies reflected into the water of Cold Creek, looked into her own. They were the same, those eyes, father and daughter. The only blue eyes in the family.

"What do you mean?" Yarrow's eyes, looking at her, were brown, dusted with gold flecks.

"His edges wobble."

"They do?"

"Like a road wobbles before it falls off the earth's curve. Like the mountains of the moon."

~~~

The Olson farmhouse stood taller than it was square, but the covered porch skirting it gave the house an impression of being larger than it actually was. It needed paint. The white coat from several years ago had begun to peel, flaking off in little curls that littered the narrow flower beds, the peonies in the south and the ferns and lilies of the valley in the north. The front door faced the county road, a gravel road, but adequate to connect the Olson's to their neighbors and to town. The house, though, sat back from the road a ways and had its own driveway, straight from the country road to James Olson's barn. A path led from barn to house. Both driveway and path existed simply from being used. Back in 1875, James's great grandfather drove a covered wagon up to where the barn now stands and then he walked to the spot he planned to build a house someday. Neither drive nor path had changed position in all the years between.

Standing on the back porch and looking off to the left you could see Cold Creek snaking through the prairie, separating east from west, and running diagonally up towards the Red River of the North. The creek joined the river at Little Fork and continued flowing north into Canada. Both sides of Hannah's family, the Olson's and the Murdock's, homesteaded the creek's banks back when the prairie grass grew taller than a man, and the women bore their babies in houses dug from the earth itself. You could see the Murdock's big house way off across the fields to the east and a touch north of the Olson's.

It was Yarrow who collected family stories while sitting with Gran, which was what they called Hannah's great-grandmother, Adeline Olson. Gran's stroke had left her bedridden. A rag doll, she said, that God took out his anger on. That plus the arthritis was enough to do anybody in.

Gran smiled crooked at the child but her dusty brown eyes were kind. Her hands bent like the claws of birds and her feet hung useless, stuck into fuzzy blue slippers as best they could be, considering their deformity. Yarrow and an aide lifted her from bed and settled her on an old oak rocker covered with a sheep's wool throw. Her room smelled of urine combined with baby powder. Her voice cracked like a radio during a lightning storm.

"Your daddy treating you well, girl?"

"Yes, Gran."

"He was a funny boy, your daddy."

How strange for Hannah to think of her father as a boy.

"He was my grandson." The old woman cackled.

"Yes, Gran." Hannah stood, hands clasped behind her back, and spoke with all the politeness she could muster.

"He never was right after his mama left."

Hannah's father never spoke of his mother and she would have dropped into a crack in time and disappeared entirely had it not been for Gran's stories.

"She went off with the circus." Gran watched for Hannah's reaction and then she cackled again. "Abandoned that boy. Left him on the floor of my kitchen. I found him there when I came in from hanging sheets. Just standing there in his Sunday clothes. Just standing with his little fists clenched and his tear-stained cheeks and dirty nose. And it was his birthday, too. Can you fathom that? Running off and leaving your own little boy on his birthday? I had to raise him myself, every bit of the way."

"Did she really go off with the circus?" Hannah guided Gran back onto the track of the story, the circus. The elephants and tigers. The two-headed men.

"Certainly did, girl. She was a crazy one."

"Did she ride elephants?"

"How should I know what she did? Do I look like a person who goes to the circus?"

"No, Gran."

"Well, then." Gran's claw fingers hooked the yarn of the afghan lying across her knees, lifted it, let it fall. The activity absorbed her. Hannah waited, hands still clasped behind her back.

"She couldn't abide the prairie. You have to be hardened to it." The old woman lifted an eyebrow and skewered Hannah with her eyes like a chicken hawk, swooping down.

"Maybe she walked the tightrope." Hannah's imagination swerved, resisting capture by things more real, more everyday. This circus grandmother rose above the everyday tasks of farm life. She didn't wash the grime from sinks. She didn't can peas. She wore feathers in her hair and walked ropes high above the ground while all the people gasped.

"I doubt she had the balance for that sort of thing." Gran snorted and clicked her false teeth.

"Maybe she told fortunes."

"She had the craziness for it!" Gran cackled again.

"I wonder where she is now." Hannah conjured exotic lands and flying carpets like the one on the radio each Saturday morning. "Let's Pretend" started with all the children climbing on that Persian carpet and flying off into that week's fairy tale.

"Probably went all the way to the end of the world." Gran reached over to her bed-stand for her jar of hand cream, fastened her bony fingers around the lid, opened it, and dipped her index and middle finger into the goo. "She'd be getting old." She turned her hands over and around each other to rub the oily cream into her transparent skin. "I got too much. Here." She opened her hands to the small hands of the girl. "Give me your hands."

Gran's hands felt cold and the cream, slick. "Can old people stay in the circus?" Hannah said to refocus her great-grandmother's mind on the important topic.

"She's probably a beggar by now."

"A beggar?"

"A crazy beggar." The old woman let go of the girl's hands and reached for her glass of water. Her fingers closed around the glass like fleshless bones. She put the other hand underneath to keep it from slipping. "Fell into the ocean for all I know."

"Didn't you like her?" It seemed a shame.

"She shouldn't have run off like that." Gran took a long drink and gave the glass to Hannah who set it back on the stand.

"And left my daddy." That part could be understood. What if Yarrow went off, leaving her behind? She automatically reached for one of her braids, twisted the end in her fingers twice and then put it into her mouth.

"Children need their mothers." Gran's bony hand reached for the braid and pulled it from Hannah's mouth. "Don't suck on that, girl."

"He had you, though." Right that minute Gran didn't seem a good substitute for a mother. Hannah liked the taste of her hair and the comfort of its wet thickness on her tongue.

"It wasn't the same."

Gran's given name, Adeline, sounded far too musical and curved for the stark life she hardened herself to. Hannah never heard her sing, not once. Of course by the time Hannah came into the world Adeline's vocal cords had likely turned to tough vines in her throat. Adeline had been born within the earth itself, in a house made of prairie sod, her link to Hannah so nearly prehistoric that it felt tenuous as a dandelion chain.

"Someday I'll go find her," Hannah said.

"Who?"

"My grandmother."

"She's no one, girl. She left the family and she pulled her roots up from the land. She's nothing to you."

But Hannah couldn't make her nothing, and she dreamed her grandmother gazed into her palm, tracing her life line with an enameled fingernail. A candle flame wavered on its wick and end of the world winds tore at the grandmother's canvas tent as she whispered secrets. Hannah woke trembling from the sensation of that finger in her palm like a spider spinning her destiny.

~~~

Wind keened its song, haunting Hannah's childhood. On deep summer nights, she awoke to the wind's minor melody. Softened by distance, its tones traveled from the edge of the narrow woods alongside Cold Creek across her father's fields. From the song's melody, Hannah conjured a woman clothed in silken capes woven of stars who sat alongside her bed playing a flute carved of bone. Hannah leaned against the flute of night winds and fell through its music into sleep.

"God sings to me when you're sleeping, Yarrow," she told her mother in the morning.

"That's not God singing, Hannah."

"Who is it then, the wind?"

"Not the wind. It's old Sarah who lives on that plot of land between us and the Murdock's is playing her flute."

"The fortune-teller?"

Yarrow laughed. "People say she is. And they also say she plays a magic flute that can charm you into running off from home. A fairy tale, I'd say, made up by folks with not enough to keep them busy. Not something I'd know a thing about." She brought a bowl of oatmeal and set in on the table in front of Hannah. "Anyway she's made her own way on land she bought long ago from the Murdocks. Bottom land, down by the creek. But she grows what she needs and keeps a few chickens. She's no one a little girl like you might know. Now eat your breakfast."

After her mother's discouragements, Hannah began to wonder if she only dreamed the nighttime music because the distance between old Sarah's place and the Olson house spanned the entire length of Murdock's wheat field. Could wind carry a tone so far? Yet it seemed near as though it played on the little bones in her ears, each one a flute. Far/near music, she began to call it but only to herself, because even though it sounded real and coming from outside of her, she might have made it up. Perhaps she only conjured the haunting melody she heard sometimes even on clear afternoons while wandering by the creek, when the flute tones hung on the air like smoke.

"Where did she come from?" The child's curiosity about the woman would not be quenched easily.

"No one knows, but her people lived all around here one time. This was their tribal land."

"Does she live all by herself?"

"I guess so, Hannah. My, but you ask a lot of questions."

And so she left her questions to be answered by her dreams. But one day Hannah saw the old woman coming out of the woods and through the fields, disappearing finally along the road to town. She saw gray hair whipping around her head like storm clouds, so long that it stuck out on either side past her shoulders and created a constantly moving, electric frame for her face. After that Hannah came to believe that in the night the woman left her little house to stand in the open field, her wild hair flying, and lifted her flute toward the mountains of the moon. The song she cast upon the wind combined, subtle and intricate, with Yarrow's lullaby, so that even after Hannah lost the sound of both flute and voice it seemed her blood still remembered, and her body's pulse could recreate that song.

~~~

Hannah woke from dreams of wind to the sound of Yarrow's murmuring behind the wall that separated her room from that of her parents. Yarrow's sounds rose and fell like the branches of cottonwood trees such as grew beside Cold Creek. The girl drifted under her sound as under a thousand leaves like fans whirling the air. Yarrow moaned from time to time and Hannah wished to be her father, then, so she could rock her mother in big arms and sing "Goodnight Sweetheart," while she smoothed Yarrow's hair back from her face with her hand.

"Do you cry at night, Mommy?" She asked the next morning at breakfast.

"Sometimes I cry." Her eyes looked at Hannah through slits under puffy lids.

"Are you sad?"

"Sometimes."

"I don't want you to be sad."

Yarrow reached out and placed her hand on the girl's cheek. "Don't worry, Hannah. Even the earth is sad now and then."

"Even meadowlarks?"

"Everything." Yarrow's voice caught in passing over the word like sheep's wool catches on barbed wire.

"If you are sad, you can call out, 'Hannah,' and I'll come and dance for you."

"I'd like that."

"I'd like it, too."

Hannah danced at the graves of baby birds and of rabbits so small she could hold one in the palm of her hand. They died under the blades of her father's work.

"Look, Daddy." She lifted the small rabbit, still warm, still soft though bloody.

"Don't pick up dead animals, Hannah, they have germs," he said as he continued calmly with his cultivation.

When the blade sliced the earth, turning up a shining black clump of soil, he showed no compunction. A smear of red upon the black, what was that but the prairie, living and dying to become our food?

"It's a rabbit, Hannah. Hawks kill them every day."

Hannah buried it. Yarrow found one of Great Uncle Ancil Murdock's cigar boxes and they lined it with a swatch of flour sack printed with flowers muted blue. The girl dug the hole under the cottonwood that leaned over the creek and Yarrow stood beside her when she laid the box on the wet soil.

"Do you have a prayer, Hannah?"

"I could say 'Now I lay me…'"

"That would be nice, I think."

"Now I lay you down to sleep; I pray the Lord your soul to keep. If you should die…" She stopped because the rabbit had died already.

"What's wrong?" Yarrow put her hand on Hannah's shoulder. Her apron lifted in the wind.

"Maybe I should sing." Hannah looked up into her mother's face.

"That would be nice, too." Yarrow gave her shoulder a little squeeze.

Yarrow's lullaby was for real live babies. Yarrow waited. Old Sarah's song could not be sung for it required a voice too piercing and too dark for a child to produce.

"Maybe I could dance."

Mother and daughter joined hands and circled the small grave. After the dance Hannah picked flowers and scattered them on the tiny mound of earth.

"Ring around the rosie," She sang as the petals floated onto the grave. "A pocket full of posies. Ashes, ashes, we all fall down."

Summer and winter winds tore at the Olson farmhouse. In summer the winds tasted of chaff. They swirled like devils dancing. Hannah's hair whipped into her face and if she opened her mouth to speak, hair stuck to her wet tongue. Winter winds carved the snow into waves across the prairie. She walked them as fairies walk upon the sea. She bent into winter, opening a path through the wind with the crown of her head. At night the house groaned and her mother cried. Hannah heard her through the walls. The wind moaned in her as she became its body.

"I can't tolerate this, James."

The sounds of wind are many and complex. It moans and screeches. It cries out like the banshee. It can be low as lullabies.

"You'll meld to it."

"I'm not talking about the prairie."

"What else is there?"

When summer came again, Hannah watched him in the fields, a red farmer's hanky tied over his nose and mouth, sun glinting off the gold chaff that encased him like a genie. She wished on him for her mother's happiness.

3

When Yarrow was a child in the small grade school on old County Road 8, she barely noticed James. He blended with the colors and movements of his surroundings, like those pictures all the children liked, the ones with ten different animals camouflaged among the trees and in the walls of houses. Only later, when both of them attended Cold Creek High School, did she begin to distinguish his separateness as her vision matured and she developed the skill to focus on the still point in any changing pattern.

Yarrow abandoned algebra and studied James. The quiet eyes of James. His tall, strong body. He sat bent over his books at the table next to hers in the library during sixth period study hall. She memorized the contours of his face, the way strands of his dark hair escaped his careful combing to wisp across his tanned forehead. She cast a spell, willing him to raise his eyes, but his composure surpassed her magic.

When he left school in junior year after his dad died and he needed to run the farm, Yarrow created fantasies of joining him there. At night, her bedroom door closed against the voices of her parents in their eternal conflict with her grandmother Murdock and Uncle Ancil, she transported herself into the house of James where silence wrapped her in a secure cocoon. Silence is love, she concluded as she tried to close her ears to the violent words that tore at her family and left her mother exhausted in her tears.

The summer she was sixteen—they both were sixteen—she rode her bicycle down the dusty gravel road to the Olson farm, James's farm, his house. His grandmother was still home then, though she was already old, and she served Yarrow cookies and ice-cold milk at the kitchen table.

"James is a good boy," Mrs. Olson—Adeline—said from across the table where she sat upright on the tall-backed wooden chair, looking hard at Yarrow. The woman's hair, then, was just turning the color of fresh cream. Her large brown eyes reminded Yarrow of oak leaves in October.

"We miss him at school." Yarrow took small bites of her cookies, careful with the crumbs, careful not to smear the lip of the glass.

"He knows enough to run the farm. He has to be a man now. School's for children." She broke off a small piece of her cookie, put it into her mouth, and wiped her lips with her napkin.

Yarrow turned her head to look out the kitchen window, listening to Adeline Olson while watching James stack bales, his hair bleached by summer to the color of bark on the cottonwoods.

"He is a man, isn't he?" She said more to herself than to James's grandmother.

"He has to be." His grandmother stood. She stacked the plates with the remaining cookies on top and carried them over to the sink. The visit was over.

Some realities are indisputable.

After a week of visits Yarrow moved closer, from house to barn or field, wherever he was working. Light filtered through spider webs and straw into the barn, enhancing the glow of sweat on his arms as he examined a maze of engine parts in the tractor.

"Can I help? Hand you tools or something?" She asked. She sat on the topmost rail of a stall, watching, memorizing him.

"Sure. Why not?" He said.

After that, from time to time he let his eyes meet hers. "You know which one the socket wrench is?" A flicker of humor in those eyes.

"I think so." Of course she knew perfectly, but this delicate business required finesse.

"I need the three-quarter inch socket." He held out his hand like a surgeon.

She discovered how to make mistakes so he would laugh at her.

Strange how she went to him for silence only to seduce him into words.

On a July afternoon a cloudburst drove them running into the barn from the creek where he'd been staking up a young maple tree his father planted there before he died. Yarrow was holding the trunk straight as he pulled the rope taut, when lightning struck right alongside the old cottonwood. He grabbed her by the hand.

"Come on!"

They abandoned his father's tree and ran.

In the barn they murmured to the animals to quiet them, and then sat together on a hay bale. You don't exactly listen to rain like that rain. Its sound contains you like glass. You're enclosed in one of those globes you shake until snow falls on the farmhouse within. A world made of rain.

James reached over what must have been for him a distance wide as life itself and took Yarrow's hand. She held her breath, not wanting to frighten him away.

"Why do you come here?" He asked. Their fingers barely touched.

"It's quiet." She whispered.

Then lightning and a crack of thunder struck so close they both jumped. They laughed at the irony. James tightened his grip on her hand.

"I mean, no one's fighting here." She said, once nature had steadied itself to a quiet rain and James's grip on her hand had loosened again.

"I like it quiet, too" He said.

He didn't ask what she meant by fighting. Maybe he assumed it was none of his business. Maybe he just didn't want to get any closer than he was already.

It rained for half an hour before it let up enough for a dash down the path to check on James's grandmother. In all that time together, those words and the squeeze of his hand were as close as he came to her.

The winter Yarrow was in twelfth grade, James's grandmother had the stroke that made her an invalid for good and all. He couldn't care for her. Who could expect it? She herself chose to go to the rambling blue house, the Pioneer Nursing Home, on the edge of downtown Cold Creek. It was best for all of them, or at least Yarrow always found it comforting to think so, since she never did offer to reverse the decision and bring Adeline back to the farm, even after she James and were married.

Adeline recovered just enough to keep getting into other people's business with her wisecracks and her advice. But she seemed a burden on Yarrow only much later, after Hannah was born and James gave her the duty of those weekly visits. At first, his grandmother's stroke simply opened up a clearer road to James and the fulfillment of Yarrow's plans.

Most days Yarrow rode the school bus beyond her own stop on to his farm. She helped him in the ways men need, the ways of food and the comfort of a home. He never asked for her help; she didn't expect him to, or else she thought he might not ask at all.

Yarrow's mother, cornered her at the Murdock farm one night just before she went to bed. She came into the bedroom without knocking and stood in front of the door so there could be no escape. She wore an apron with a spaghetti stain running down the front of the bib, and her hair escaped a fine net to feather, the color of a cedar waxwing, around her face.

"What do you think you are doing with that Olson boy?" Agnes Murdock Harris doubled her hands into fists and held them at her hips, her elbows jutting out.

"I don't know what you mean." Yarrow had been brushing her hair, sitting on the edge of her bed with her head down between her knees, hair hanging almost to her toes. She tossed her head back and the hair tumbled into place.

"Don't spar with me, Yarrow. You go there every day after school. You're there on weekends. Are you playing house over at his farm?"

"Playing house?" She barely dared breathe. She could hear the ticking of the alarm clock on the stand beside her bed.

"Don't act innocent. That boy's alone there. If you get pregnant, there's not a thing I can do. I hope you understand that. I've enough with my own problems; don't you add another." She sat down, or more accurately, collapsed alongside Yarrow on the edge of the bed. Her words had transformed the woman into a stranger who, to Yarrow's mind, knew nothing of her and had no right to judge her.

This reaction came to Yarrow first, followed by the odd sensation that the harsh words didn't match the voice her mother used to say them—a bleating voice, like a trapped lamb.

Yarrow chose to react as though her mother were the stranger. "Well, don't worry! If I get pregnant, you can be rid of me which seems to be what you've wanted all along." She wouldn't turn her head to meet her mother's eyes. Her teeth felt too big for her mouth as she clamped down on them.

"Yarrow!" Whatever energy her mother had garnered for this encounter, now drained from her like starch from a shirt in a June rain. She bent over like an old woman. "All I want is happiness for you--to have a better life than..." Her voice caught.

"I suppose you're going to cry again." The sharp edge on Yarrow's voice surprised both of them.

Her mother did cry, long ragged sobs. Yarrow sat beside her for a minute and then left the room. When she returned from the bathroom her mother had gone.

Chores she complained at having to do at home came easily at James's house. Dishes. Washing clothes. Sweeping floors. Making supper. His kitchen became her own. In Home Economics class at school she sewed new curtains for its windows, bright curtains with a pattern of ripe cherries and green leaves.

On Sundays that winter, when light slanted off the horizon, she and James walked together in the snow down to the creek as far as the old cottonwood. A herd of white tail deer filed along the frozen creek each day at four in the afternoon, and the boy and girl sat unmoving in a clump of bushes almost near enough to touch them. They remained until the sun turned the winter sky a brilliant rose that faded to pearl and gray. Afterwards they walked back to the house by the light of the snow underfoot. Winters never darkened totally. After supper James always drove her home in his grandmother's Ford truck.

In March, when the snow turned to crystals from alternate thaw and freeze, and last year's leaves began to appear under pools of ice, preserved as red as when they fell, Yarrow and James came in soaked to the bone following their Sunday visit to watch the deer. Yarrow wore an old bathrobe of his grandmother's while her clothes dried, and James heated up some Campbell's soup. They ate together at the kitchen table.

"James, I feel so cold." Her shivers started deep inside her chest.

He led her to the sofa in the living room and covered her with his grandmother's afghan.

"Please James, sit close to me." She reached out to him, motioning. She leaned her head against his shoulder. He smelled like damp wool. She raised her hand and touched his face, turned his face until he looked at her.

"James, look into my eyes." He lowered his. "No. Don't look away. Let's just see how long we can look at one another." Her mother would have called her childish, said she was courting danger, but the moment belonged to Yarrow. Her mother wasn't there.

He turned those serious blue eyes of his to look into the complex amber-brown of her own.

She kissed him. A moth-wing of a kiss.

They were watching the fingernail moon, its thin curve above the fields when he touched her chin and turned her face toward his to return the kiss, his lips cool and smooth.

"I don't know why you come to see me here." He broke the silence they both had kept, the silence like an incubator for their attraction. .

"It feels like home." She wanted to place her hand on his hair, to bend and kiss him again, kiss the dark shine of his hair, wet, curling at his temple.

Silence enclosed them again for a long time. She did kiss his hair and then reached her hand out to touch his leg, the one that touched her own under the afghan. She felt a tremor.

"My grandmother never touched me much." He attempted to explain. "I think I remember my mother touching me. I used to miss that." It was a lot for James to admit to anyone and Yarrow knew that, even then. Inside her something moved, something large, a generosity of being, a kind of fundamental womanhood. She seemed to know exactly what James wanted and every cell in her moved to satisfy his need.

She opened the folds of his grandmother's robe and took his hand to her breast. She heard his swift intake of breath. She felt her nipple harden at his touch. They seemed to have memorized this choreography. He turned and laid his head on her lap, his eyes looking into her eyes. Yarrow leaned over him and her nipple touched his lips. He took her into his mouth. She felt his tongue moving soft and then his sucking, gentle as deep breaths that travel all down the body and fill a person totally. She stroked his face, his hair. Tears came to his eyes. Seeing those tears, she felt the brimming of her own, and she knew she never could be satisfied with any kind of love that would be less.

"I'm here," she murmured as she ran her hand down the length of his body as far as she could reach.

"Don't leave me." His voice emerged, ragged with something she couldn't identify nor maybe even understand.

"I'll never go away. Ever." She promised him.

The day Yarrow Harris left her Grandmother Murdock's farm to marry James Olson she felt freed from a tether holding her since birth. Her mother, Agnes Murdock Harris, and her Uncle Ancil Murdock fought that morning, their voices sharpened to a keen edge on the whetstone of their mutual rage. Until that day it had not occurred to her to ask why they lived with such intent to destroy each other's happiness. But on her wedding day she concluded that families must have cultures of their own, and violence formed hers, while James Olson had been nurtured in a sweet and enviable atmosphere of silence.

James picked her up at the end of the road. She wore her pale yellow graduation dress and a white straw hat with silk daisies circling the brim. She carried her mother's small suitcase, stolen from her closet the night before. His truck smelled of hay with just a faint mixture of silage and manure.

She climbed into the front seat and closed the door. She looked back at her grandmother's farmhouse and wondered when her mother would discover she had eloped.

"Fields are looking good." James gestured toward the greening crops. He'd worn his father's second-best suit. They'd buried Joseph Olson in the best one. This one was brown and double-breasted. The white shirt contrasted with James's dark skin in a way that made Yarrow want to touch that skin right above the collar where his hair curled because he hadn't thought to see a barber.

"Yes. The right amount of rain." She responded ritualistically.

"It'll be a good year." He completed the ritual.

She didn't touch him. They didn't talk of themselves, not of their lives, not of their future. They moved in a current of necessity away from the hollow spaces of their young lives and toward all they couldn't yet know of the future they had chosen.

James drove to Grand Forks where they finally located the courthouse and were married by a Justice of the Peace. It went so fast. He put his mother's ring on Yarrow's finger.

"She left it behind." He told her later when she asked where he'd come on such a lovely thing.

"Your mother?" The ring encircled her finger with intertwined silver leaves and vines of gold.

"I guess when she left she figured she wasn't married anymore."

"Your dad told you this?"

"He kept the ring in her jewelry box on the dresser in his room as if she'd come back to wear it any day. But she never did. And now it's yours."

Yarrow gave up her virginity in a third floor room at the Grand Hotel in East Grand Forks. She expected the tenderness of those nights on the sofa, the soft wet tugging at her breasts. She expected the softness of his whimpers. She lay with him in the hotel bed and caressed his body down as far as she could reach. She expected to feel the rush of something large, the greatness inside her containing him. They fumbled a lot. They were so young. He pushed himself into her, hard and swift when he finally could, and she cried out with the burning of it. When, afterwards, she asked James if he loved her, he couldn't say he did, and though she wondered if she had just made the biggest mistake of her life, she also understood not to expect those words from him.

But later in the night when Yarrow heard him whimper, she turned to him in that strange bed.

"James?" she whispered and touched his shoulder.

He moved towards her, and she offered her breast to him.

"You won't leave me, will you?" He sounded like a child.

"I'm here." She never would be able to forget how she felt at that moment. Round. Immense. A world for him. Something enough.

He took her nipple into his mouth. They fell asleep like that on their wedding night, with James clinging to Yarrow's breast, while she curled around him, grateful for what she couldn't quite define.

~~~

Between the Olson farm and the Murdock farm someone had constructed an invisible wall that Hannah was forbidden to cross. She knew its position exactly, and from time to time it rose up in her imagination just as though its stones and mortar could be felt if she were to put out her hand, or stop her if she attempted to step through. A section marker and an old road ran alongside the imaginary wall, and in summer she sometimes hid in the barley on her side of the road, hoping to catch a glimpse of one of the Murdocks, it didn't matter which one. Great Grandmother Marcia Murdock sometimes sat in a rocking chair on the porch of the big house, but too far away for Hannah to see her face. She looked like a tiny stick-woman with a bright red afghan covering her lap. From time to time Great Uncle Ancil came from the house with another man who must have been Hannah's grandfather, Mark "Shorty" Harris. He'd moved in with the Murdock's thirty years before when he married her grandmother, Ancil's sister, Agnes. But distance smeared their faces—every one.

So it turned out to be exciting rather than sad news when Yarrow told her that her Grandma Agnes had died and Hannah should get out her best dress to be checked for stains and wrinkles, because she'd be going with her mother to the funeral.

"I hope you'll change your mind and come with us." Yarrow's voice split the silence. The three of them were sitting at the kitchen table. Hannah's father bent over and spooned soup into his mouth. The spoon traveled around just like the Ferris wheel at the country fair.

"I'd appreciate it if you'd answer me." Yarrow snapped.

The spoon stopped in the bowl. "I didn't know you asked a question," he said but didn't look up. Then, as if he assumed the discussion had ended, he lifted the bowl to his mouth and tipped it, in order to drain the rest of the broth and slurp the last of the noodles.

"James!" Her voice sliced the kitchen right down the middle.

"What?" This time he did look up. The soup spurted from his

mouth onto his shirt. "Damn!" He began to rub it with the corner of his napkin.

"Will you please pay attention? I'm asking you to come with us to my mother's funeral." Her hands made fists beside her plate.

"I heard you." His voice the edged blade of a saw.

"Well?"

There was a long silence. Hannah felt her legs begin to swing back and forth under the chair. She tapped her spoon on her soup bowl in rhythm with the *"Mairzy Doats"* song she'd heard on the radio.

"Hannah, be quiet!" Yarrow yelled, and Hannah dropped the spoon. More soup splattered onto the tablecloth.

"Now look at what you've done!" Yarrow grabbed her napkin and reached over to wipe away the stain. Hannah bit her lip to keep tears back.

Again the silence.

"James?" Both of Yarrow's hands gripped the edge of the table.

"Why do you want to go there anyway?" He finally said.

"Good Lord, James! It's my mother, for God's sake!" Her voice shook and she gripped the table even harder making ripples in the tablecloth.

"So, you go. Nobody's stopping you." He started to get up from the table.

"You stay right here until we're finished, James Olson." Now her hands and arms were trembling, and the harder she gripped the table the more they shook.

He continued to get up, and then he shoved the chair back under the table. It made a grating sound against the linoleum. "Look," he said. "I won't be in the same room as Ancil Murdock even if it's a church. You can go if you want. Can't see why you'd do it, though. Your mom's dead. She won't know one way or the other. And there you'll be, right in the middle of them." He turned and walked out the back door toward the barn. It was more words than Hannah ever had heard him say at once. Yarrow pushed her soup bowl out of the way and laid her head on the table.

"Don't cry, Yarrow." Hannah slipped off her chair and came around the table to stroke her mother's hair. But it was too late. Yarrow's upper body already was shaking with sobs.

~~~

The citizens of Cold Creek, North Dakota and its surrounding farms had three choices when it came to religion. Lutheran, Presbyterian and Catholic. The Murdock's more or less belonged with the Presbyterians since Marcia Murdock always thought of the Lutherans as being of a somewhat lower class, and the Catholics, well, Catholics were another story altogether. Besides that, the Presbyterian Church had the distinction of being better built, and also of possessing a superior location. It stood right downtown on the corner of Oak and Main, so when you dressed up for some occasion like a wedding or a funeral the town noticed the additional swirl of bustle and color.

Yarrow hadn't entered the church since before her courthouse marriage to James. She'd not even had Hannah baptized—a magical rite, in her opinion, giving human beings the illusion they controlled their destiny. God, if there was a God, took care of such things as destiny and the afterlife, and no amount of dunking babies in water and mumbling of words could change that.

She parked the car down the block from the church. The hearse already had arrived, and the Murdock's, including her father, milled around on the sidewalk with men in somber colors.

"Get out of the car, Hannah." Once she was out of the car, Yarrow smoothed the girl's skirt, crouched down in front of her at eye-level. "Now you be polite," she said as though speaking to her own heart that pounded with terrible abandon inside her ribcage. "You mind your P's and Q's."

"I will." But Yarrow could feel the pull of the girl toward this group of people whom she'd never met, but who, by rights, belonged to her.

Hannah stood small in the center of a circle of grown-ups who bent to her, one after the other, and took her hand. Yarrow sing-songed the names. "And Hannah, this is your Grandpa Harris. And over here is Great Grandma Murdock." Grandpa Harris patted her head and said how much her Grandma Agnes wanted to set eyes on her—close up.

"She used to watch you playing way across the field," he said. "It's too bad…" and his voice trailed off. He took out a big hanky and wiped his eyes.

Great Grandma lifted her white eyebrow and said how little she resembled the Murdock's. "More of an Olson, I'd say—or even back a generation to Aimee St. Germaine. She was a Brule, you know, with those seafoam blue eyes. The child's aren't quite that light—" She turned to the gaunt man standing at her right. "Except for the eyes, would you say she resembles Lily, Ancil?"

Yarrow put her hand on Hannah's shoulder. "Hannah, this is your Great Uncle, Ancil Murdock," she said.

"You sure are a pretty little thing," he squatted down on one knee in front of her. "Do you have a kiss for your old uncle?"

Hannah felt her mother's hand slide from her shoulder to the top of her chest, right under her neck, to pull her closer. "Goodness," she said to him, "the girl just met you."

Hannah explored his face. His eyes peered into hers like a spy's through a keyhole. Charcoal violet, her mother described them later, the color of a storm cloud. "Well then, next time." He smiled at her and stood up. "I think they're wanting us to go into the church," he said, taking charge of everyone, and paying no more attention to Hannah. She wanted to call out to him, to ask what he'd seen inside her, something that, by the way his eyes had narrowed, seemed necessary for her to know.

The pastor's voice droned. Hannah stared for a while at the amber-colored windows, the plain little altar with the brass cross in the center, the pulpit, and the black-clad man who kept talking. Yarrow whispered that Grandma Agnes was lying in the coffin right in front, but the lid had been closed. "I wish I could see her," Hannah whispered to her mother, but Yarrow said, "It's too late." And that's all there was to that. Hannah fell asleep.

Later, at the cemetery behind the church, the undertaker lowered the coffin into the ground, and Hannah watched her mother and the other Murdock's, including her Grandpa Harris, pick up a handful of earth and let it drop into the hole. It made a thud as it hit the coffin. Yarrow told her she should scatter earth for Grandma, but she didn't want to.

"I wish you'd come see us." Grandpa Harris took both Yarrow's hands in his own while Hannah waited beside the car. "It's been way too long."

"I can't, Dad. You know that." She brushed the side of his face with her cheek but didn't kiss him. "Anyway, the road runs both ways." She paused. "You don't have to stay there now, either. You know that, don't you?"

"It's home now, Yarrow." He held her hand as though he never intended to let it go. "We had our whole life there, your mother and I. And besides, where else would I go?"

Yarrow didn't say, "You can come live with us, Dad," and Hannah might have said the words herself, except that her mother already was hustling her off, away from Grandpa Harris, toward the car.

At supper that night no one said a word until, finally, during dessert as Hannah's father sliced into his apple pie and filled his fork to heaping, Yarrow said, "Aren't you going to ask me how it went?"

He just looked at her holding the fork suspended in front of his mouth. Then he put it in and began to chew.

"What is wrong with you, James Olson?" She brought her fist down hard on the table.

"It's not me that's changed," he said and lopped off another bite of pie.

~~~

Hannah struggled up from the deep well of sleep to the sound of her name and the scent of her mother. Nutmeg, she would realize years afterwards, when the scent had faded from the mother's skin. Her bedroom windows shook.

"Is it a whirlwind?" She mumbled. If it were a whirlwind her mother would take her to the cellar. "Is Daddy in the barn?"

"Just a summer storm." Her mother whispered, lifting Hannah in her arms, setting her bare feet on the linoleum floor.

Rain slashed against the windowpane.

"Let's go back to sleep, Mommy. You can get in bed with me." The child climbed back onto the bed and started to snuggle underneath the sheets. Her mother gave her a little shake, and Hannah roused a little more. Her mother was wearing her hat and coat. It wasn't morning yet, and she was already dressed. Her hat had a blue feather stuck in its band.

"I want you to get up, now, Hannah and get dressed." She said.

The sky still was dark. The birds hadn't even begun to sing.

"We're going on an adventure, Hannah. Just think, when you start first grade, you'll get to go to a school where no one knows you." Hannah's mother spoke in a sad voice that didn't match the words. "You can be whoever you want. We'll go together to the store and buy clothes to fit the new Hannah."

"Is Daddy in the car?"

"No, darling. Daddy's asleep."

"Isn't he coming?"

"No."

"Why not?"

"He can't leave the farm."

They left with just the clothes on their backs. That's the way Yarrow put it every time she told Hannah this story in the years that followed.

"Come on, Hannah." She closed the door of their North Dakota farmhouse behind them and ran through the wind and rain to the car. Wind caught Yarrow's hat, snatching it from her head and sailing it like a kite out over the fields into the dark.

"Your hat!" Hannah yelled over the sound of the storm.

"It doesn't matter. Quick. We have to leave before your father wakes up."

Her mother grasped her hand, pulling her faster than she could run.

Yarrow leaned forward into the steering wheel and squinted through the windshield that flattened to a blur after each swipe of the wipers. Hannah sat clutching her rag doll, grabbed at the last minute as Yarrow pulled her from the house like something rooted there, a tooth or a tree, so that the girl felt the twist and crack as her own heart also tore loose. The car swerved in the wind, but Yarrow held the wheel tight. Hannah reassured the rag doll.

"Don't be afraid, Raggedy Lily, it's just a storm." Her daddy had given the doll its name. "Why not call her Lily, like the flower?" he had said back when she first brought the doll home.

"I want to go home now," she told her mother, thinking of her father alone in the bedroom of the creaking farmhouse.

"No, no, dear. We're on an adventure."

"Please, let's go home." The windshield wipers swiped back and forth, back and forth.

"Don't you want to go on an adventure?"

Not with the gusts of rain slashing the car, washing the gravel down the road into the ditches on either side, making it impossible to see much farther than the silver thingamajig on the hood. "I want to go back to bed."

"That's silly. You always wanted to find the mountains of the moon." Yarrow kept her hands on the steering wheel. The skin pulled tight across her knuckles. Hannah noticed that the ring she always wore, her wedding ring, was missing, and instead of the gold band with its gleaming blue jewel Yarrow's finger was circled by a scar of white. Gusts shook the car.

"Did you lose your ring, Yarrow?" Hannah felt transfixed by the scar and wanted to reach out to hold her mother's finger just the way babies did, to hide the white sign of some deep wound.

"I left it behind." That was all she said.

Hannah clutched Raggedly Lily, distracting herself with a memory of the time Gran had handed her the rag doll a few weeks before.

"Here. You might as well have this." Gran's hand shook, making the doll jump up and down.

"Thank you, ma'am." Hannah held the doll out from her. She had blue button eyes.

"It was your grandmother's."

"The one in the circus?"

"She made it for your father, early on. I took it away."

"Why?"

"Don't be silly, child. He was a boy."

"Didn't he like it?"

"He was a boy."

"What did he play with?"

"He had chores."

"But when he was little?"

"I don't remember."

If it had been a girl doll she would have had braids of yarn. Instead she wore a cap, like a farmer. She wore overalls and a red farmer's hanky around her neck. Maybe when Hannah's father was a boy he'd named the doll William or Buddy. But now he said her name was Lily. She could be a girl doll now, even without braids and a dress. Hannah wore overalls. She wore a cap. And she was a girl.

Maybe Grandma Lily hadn't joined the circus after all. Maybe she was a farmer living on the mountains of the moon.

Mother and daughter finally pulled over to the side of the road and lay down in the back seat of the car. Yarrow cradled Hannah into the hollow curve of her body. Hannah hugged Raggedy Lily. Yarrow had stopped on the outskirts of a little Minnesota town called Red Pine. The prairie and North Dakota and the storm they'd left behind. It was safe enough to sleep. Hannah curled her hand around her mother's ring finger and closed her eyes.

She woke to the nutmeg smell of her mother and the warmth of her belly pressed against the girl's back. Yarrow must have sensed a change in her daughter while they slept, although the girl didn't move or even alter the pattern of her breathing.

"Hannah?" She murmured. "Are you awake?"

"Mmhmm."

Mother and daughter lay still. Hannah listened to a sound she had, so far in her life, never heard. It resembled the whisper of wind through the barley fields, but with a deeper more resonant shwweee. God is singing, Mommy."

"It's the pine trees, Hannah. Wind in the pines."

"Does God know where we are?"

"If he doesn't then he isn't God."

"Will God tell daddy?"

"He might."

"Will daddy come for us?"

"Daddy doesn't listen very well."

Hannah thought again of her father waking up alone in the empty farmhouse. He'd think her mother was in the kitchen fixing breakfast. He'd imagine her, arms white with flour, her apron powdery, kneading the bread for dinner. He'd wonder why he smelled no coffee. He'd call out.

"G'morning there!"

He'd notice the dent in her pillow and feel comforted as though she had just raised her head from sleep. He'd angle off the side of the bed and pull his work pants on over his briefs.

"Get on up now, Girl!"

He'd walk toward Hannah's bedroom and try to ignore the flutters beginning in the pit of his stomach.

"Does daddy know how to cook breakfast?" Her voice came out of her sounding small and she wondered if rabbits had voices other than the way they screamed at night when an owl swooped down.

"He'll manage." Yarrow tipped the visor down and checked her face. She took a tube of lipstick from her purse.

Hannah wondered when he would find Yarrow's ring. At that moment her father became in Hannah's mind a skull without eyes. He became bones fallen on themselves, dusty, in the chair by the front window of her house where he'd sit day and night awaiting her return. His tractor would rust and vines grow up around its tires while the fields reverted to wild grass whispering and moaning in the wind.

Yarrow stood Hannah up along the side of the road and washed her face with spit on a piece of Kleenex. "You probably won't understand this until you're older, Hannah, but your father has an affliction that eats away at his soul. I thought love could ease him, so I promised that I would never leave. I could have kept that promise if he'd have just talked to me, or called me by name, or even cleaned the sink after he washed his hands. It takes so little, really, to make a woman stay."

After she braided her daughter's hair she bent and brushed her own, tumbling it up and over her head, brushing and brushing until strand by strand it leapt to the brush and shone in the sun.

"What do we need, Hannah?" She smoothed her hair back and studied her face again in the car's rearview mirror.

"Breakfast?"

"That's exactly right. We need breakfast." She smiled at her reflection. "So let's see what we can do."

Yarrow started the car and pulled out onto the road past the white and black sign that announced "Red Pine. Population 536. Home of Big Red, Minnesota's second tallest Norway Pine." The road led straight north up Pine Street and there it was, an enormous pine tree, right in the center of everything. Pine Street divided and circled around it, coming together again on the other side. To the east and west lay Fir Street in what would have been a crossroads but for the tree that encouraged the citizens to create, instead, a park outlined by a traffic circle. Because of this, Red Pine possessed a spaciousness and circularity uncommon among the typical Midwest design for towns.

"We might like it here," Yarrow mused as she parked the car diagonally in front of the Pine Cone Café. "See that sign in the window?"

It was hand lettered with little yellow, blue and pink flowers on a green vine painted around the edges.

"What does it say?" Hannah asked.

" 'WAITRESS WANTED.' Now there's a job I know how to do!"

A mind gets formed to a place and takes on its contours. Hannah's mind conformed to the prairie. In Red Pine trees and buildings hid the edge of earth. If a wind built clouds at the horizon, clouds that began to swirl and rush towards the town, how would the people know to close the windows and doors and hide in the cellar? The wind was a dancer in a swirling skirt, a gypsy keening over everything ripped loose and torn from her heart.

"Wait here for a minute." Yarrow closed the car door and then turned to tap the window right where Hannah's nose touched the glass. She grinned and then she disappeared into the café.

"Don't worry," Hannah consoled Raggedy Lily. "I'll buy new clothes for you. You can let your hair grow and wear a hat with flowers. You can be whoever you want, and everyone will think that's who you were forever."

~~~

For two weeks after the mouse ran away James sat, and the grain grew and started turning gold and the grass of the yard went to seed. His phone rang and he let it. One afternoon someone banged on the front door. Sheriff Mattson, most likely. He locked himself in the bathroom in case whoever it was might break the door down, but the man left without doing anything more than hollering "James!" four times. Probably Gran sent him out, if it was the sheriff. It sounded like the sheriff's voice. James suspected the man sniffed around a good deal and figured no one died inside and a man was entitled to his privacy. Bad enough that everyone in Cold Creek probably knew by now that the wife and girl had run off. Another man had sense enough to know you didn't ram a thing like that down a person's throat by bothering him with the fact of it.

James turned into a long dark tunnel empty except for the dripping of water. He found a kind of peace in this. From time to time he cried out, but couldn't say for certain if the sound he made filled the house or just the tunnel in his mind. It was an animal cry that he heard as much as uttered. And it echoed like every cell in him bellowed inside its own dark chamber. He realized that he was, himself, the empty house, heavy with dust and stinking from the droppings of mice. He had nowhere to go from there.

One afternoon, and he didn't know how much time had passed as time became irrelevant, he woke sweating on his gray sheets. The temperature upstairs had soared to over a hundred degrees. He sat up and looked down at his body, naked on the bed, and streaked with lines of sweat through the dirt. I need a bath, a voice inside his head proclaimed, and I need clean sheets.

That day James called Ida Gunderson.
"Sure," she said. "No problem."
He started her off at three dollars a day, which he thought generous.

But the first week when she took all the furniture out to the yard to air, and when she pulled down the curtains and burned them, and when she scoured the kitchen with Lysol, and washed all the walls, that week he felt such gratitude he paid her a whopping twenty-five dollars and it was well worth every penny.

Sometimes James thought that he had something else in mind from the beginning. The mind holds secrets stashed away so deep we've no memory of putting them there. Those secrets drop out in things we end up doing without knowing why. And this is how it was with Ida.

Ida was a plain woman, quiet like himself. She'd been an orphan, brought up by a foster family on a farm outside Cold Creek where, as she laughed, they worked her good and taught her lots. She married Steve Gunderson right out of high school. An older man and a bachelor, Steve had already needed help after his parents died, and he had the farm to himself. For years folks turned the other way and said nothing when he left town for the weekend. Men had their needs, and he'd been discreet. He should have a wife, though; on this the townsfolk agreed, and it was mentioned several times at the beauty shop, and talked over at the town bar, and even mentioned casually on Sundays after the services down at the Presbyterian Church. By the time the idea reached those dimensions both Ida's family and Steve Gunderson himself had caught wind of it. So Ida ended up engaged. Some people shook their heads over the whole thing. "Poor girl, caught up in such a mess." She married him, anyway. You make your bed, you have to lie in it, the dissenting women said at first. Later, though, when she came into the grocery with bruises on her face they lowered their eyes. Who would have thought it? They'd seen it before, the men with anger simmering deep inside. Is it the prairie that does it? The men work so hard. Was it something Ida was doing wrong? Who knew her, really? At school she didn't exactly shine. She'd no extra-curriculars listed under her name in the yearbook. Some plotted ways to get her out of Steve's house, married or not. Others countered with how rescuing women like Ida isn't so easy. Steve could be one of those territorial types. Best to let things be.

James wasn't one to get involved in town gossip and had never thought about Ida's situation much until he saw her every Friday going about her work at his house, doing laundry, baking bread, scrubbing out the tub. That woman got more done in eight hours than ten women like the wife. It came to him that he never had known what the wife wanted other than what she already had. There were times she just sat, staring at the horizon, a basket of peas or beans in her lap, dreaming. The things women need to do around the house are simple really--nothing to complain about. There's the garden, the kitchen, the cooking, washing, cleaning and so forth. You can't help but appreciate a woman who keeps a clean house without constantly harping on you for messing it up. Ida simply took it as it came. Cleaned up the mess James made and then went home. Hardly a word out of her.

One Friday she showed up with such a shiner. That reminded him of the whispers he'd heard through the years around town. Up to then he'd considered such things idle gossip. She covered for Steve though. Said she fell. James admired loyalty in a woman. He'd never laid a hand on the wife, but she up and ran away. When he compared the two women, it made no sense at all.

By October Ida had started bringing baked goods and hot-dishes over in the middle of the week. "Just 'til Yarrow gets back." And she'd set them on the table for him. "You can't be eating only that stuff from cans. You've gotta keep up your strength."

The thing he kept thinking is that she didn't ask anything of him for herself.

Even the evening she came crying, right after supper, it wasn't for herself. She'd never cried before, not in his presence. She'd been beat up pretty bad.

"What am I going to do, James? How can I help him?"

It was for him she asked, not herself.

"Where is he?" He wasn't clear in his head why he asked. What did he imagine he would do? Shoot the bugger? Reason with him? Neither option felt within his capabilities. Did he say it only to resemble John Wayne or Randolph Scott? As though he, Ida, Steve, even the wife existed only as characters in a story. Maybe they did. Maybe that's all life is: a string of stories we create about ourselves, some finished, some not, some left dangling in the middle of a sentence with no more words and making no more sense than that.

"He took off..."

"But why did he..." James let his eyes take in the whole of the woman, the cut at the corner of her mouth, the swelling around her left eye, red marks on her arm, probably more that he couldn't see. "Why would any man..." The ends of those sentences stuck inside him, refused utterance.

"There's a thorn in him, James. An anger so deep. It comes loose sometimes. It's not me he's hitting, I know that. It's something so much bigger, and he just strikes out at whatever is there. It's pitiable, really."

James ran a tub of cool water for her. The air held an October chill, but she was bruised, and cool water takes down the swelling. He set up the space heater in the bathroom and told her to take all the time she needed. She looked pitiable herself, standing still fully clothed in his bathroom, her arms crossed around her in a hug of protection or self-comfort. Maybe the body makes its own demands and has its own solutions. He saw her in that moment in a way he'd never seen any person before, rather in the way he saw fields ripening or the glint of sunlight on freshly turned soil. He closed the door softly and went downstairs.

He watched the moon rising over his fields. He heard those careful noises of a body easing itself into water, the intimate sound skin makes against porcelain. Then silence. Is there never a release from the loneliness a man feels in the center of his heart? Winter would come again this year, and then again, spring. He picked up a newspaper from the pile that had accumulated alongside his chair and began to read the local news--mostly gossip from the various townships around Cold Creek--who spent last Sunday afternoon with whom, who was visiting from out of town, whose fields got caught in the early October rains still not harvested. Life's heavy for everyone, he thought.

It was at that moment she began to sing. Everything suddenly stopped. Time stopped. Maybe the moon stopped in the night sky. Maybe James stopped breathing while the fine thread of Ida's voice wound around the heaviness and lifted it. Despite her life with whatever pain she'd known, this song had survived. Her voice drifted up through the silence and, hearing it, James felt rising within him a delicate glimmer of tenderness, of hope.

~~~

In March, when the black dirt crept up through the snow and he smelled it coming to life, that dank smell it has before it breaks out green, he sharpened the blades of the plow for what looked like an early planting. As he ran the blades along the whetstone, it came to him that his wife was gone, really gone, and the girl gone with her. But as for himself, he'd stay. Each year he'd plant himself again like seed in this land that was a man's land no matter where the women might go. His land.

He got up off his haunches and walked out into that melting day. Off toward the horizon the fields stretch on and on, past his own farm to the Murdock farm and beyond that to where the St. Germaine's used to live, in the distance where the sky meets the land in a haze.

"Good luck," James shouted to the wife wherever she might be.

4

Yarrow curled her hair and piled it on top of her head. She wore a ruffled pinafore over her dress and looked like Wanda's sister. Wanda owned the Pine Cone Café, a real boon for Yarrow and Hannah since she took to them right away.

They ate breakfast at the Pine Cone that first day in Red Pine and after they washed the dishes back in Wanda's kitchen she led both of them upstairs to her apartment.

"If we don't look like sisters, girl, I don't know who does! I swear, it's like gazing in a mirror."

"I can't believe it," Wanda and Yarrow posed in front of the vanity table in the bedroom, "we could have been separated at birth. Don't you think so, Hannah? Couldn't we have been twins, even?"

Hannah didn't think so because Wanda's hair was the color of a ripe barley field, but Wanda's excitement made her bob her head up and down as if nothing could be more obvious.

"We certainly could have been." Then Wanda brushed Yarrow's hair up for the first time and fastened it with a band. "All it needs is a few curls." And that was the beginning of Yarrow's new look.

Yarrow smiled into the mirror. Wanda smiled. Hannah hugged Lily close. Some sort of agreement was being made; she could feel it.

~~~

There's more room than one might think on top of a café. The living room windows looked out over Pine Street Circle. Hannah got her education through those windows. She slept in that room, on a green sofa that opened into a bed, and often went to the window, late, to watch the goings on down at the park. Secret meetings, or so she imagined them to be. Four-eyed Jake, the town drunk, passed out on the bench. Sometimes even Yarrow and Wanda, on a summer night after the café had closed, sat together on the carved pine bench talking and laughing under the moon.

"How long will we stay with Wanda, Yarrow?" Hannah asked her mother one morning after watching them until the moon set behind the tree.

"I don't know." Yarrow was filling the salt and pepper shakers after the bacon and eggs breakfast crowd left, and business slowed down.

"Do you like her more than Daddy?"

"What a strange question." She stopped what she was doing and looked straight at Hannah.

"Do you?" A physical urgency accompanied the child's need to know, a heaviness in her chest she imagined might be her heart squeezed by a giant hand.

"Are you missing your father, Hannah?" Yarrow made her voice soft as the wind in the big pine.

Hannah had no words for what she felt. "You answer me first." She said.

"It's a hard question."

"Why?"

"I don't know."

Hannah pictured them the way they were the night before.

"Wanda makes you laugh."

"Yes."

She saw tears in Yarrow's eyes.

"Daddy made you cry." She said.

"I suppose he did." Yarrow said. She didn't move. Hannah thought she'd never seen her sit so still.

Hannah's father walked into her mind suddenly, as he often did with the murmur of wind or the buzz of insects on the summer air.

"I'm afraid Daddy disappeared just like I thought he would."

"When?" Yarrow reached over the table and took her daughter's hands in hers.

"When we left." Hannah's voice caught on her heart like a fishhook she cast into Cold Creek caught sometimes on hidden rocks.

"No, Hannah, I'm sure he's still there."

"How are you sure?"

"I'm sure."

"Will we go back to see him sometime?" How Hannah wanted her to say yes, so much that she felt her mind try to cast a spell. All of it happened in a breath of time or shorter than a breath. Hannah's mind held her mother's in a magic that would force Yarrow to say yes.

"I don't think so, Hannah." She said.

Hannah struggled to be free of the fist of her mother's words. She couldn't breathe. Her voice came out in little gasps. "Is it because of Wanda?"

"Wanda doesn't have anything to do with your daddy."

~ ~ ~

Wanda enclosed her curls in a silk net and rolled out piecrust that flaked and melted in your mouth. Hannah stood beside her on a three-legged wooden stool and practiced.

"Barely touch it," Wanda instructed as the child drizzled ice water over the crumbles of flour and lard. "Just toss it with the fork, then pick it up like a snowball only don't pack it hard. There. No, it doesn't matter if it's not even; the rolling pin and the oven will take care of that. The less you work it, the better."

They filled the crusts with blueberries picked fresh in the bog out by the Simpson place, or with a custard combined with gooseberries from the bushes that surrounded the cemetery behind Last Days Bible Church at the edge of town. June-berries tasted the best of all. Tiny and burgundy red, they popped between your teeth and flooded your mouth with summer. Oh, Wanda made the regular pies too, the apple and banana cream and sour cream raisin, but it was her wild berry pies that people drove all the way to Red Pine to sample on a Sunday afternoon.

It's been said that children can't see past the world they occupy and, knowing nothing else, they form themselves according to that mold. Hannah watched her new world from the last booth in the café, in front of the swinging Dutch doors that led to the kitchen. While Wanda and Yarrow whirled around the café balancing metal trays above their heads, the girl drew pictures of a farm in North Dakota where a man sat on his tractor and a woman and child waved goodbye. She also drew circuses, the long curling trunks of elephants and her grandmother, Lily, wearing gold bangles, riding on the creature's head.

~~~

Bonnie came up to Hannah the first day of school, at recess, while Hannah's stomach still reeled from watching Yarrow walk out of the first grade classroom leaving her trapped in a desk alongside eighteen strangers.

"Don't go!" She'd cried when Yarrow stood up from where she'd been kneeling in the aisle beside the first grade desk. All the other parents already had left.

"You have to do this, Hannah. You'll be fine."

"No!!!" She heard her voice stream out into the air like the tail on a kite. She held on to Yarrow's dress, but her mother pulled away. The child's mind ripped; her heart seemed to float out and away from her body that was trapped in a desk attached to other desks in a long row. Her mother went out the classroom door and closed it behind her. Hannah put her head down on the desktop and sobbed. What if Yarrow never came back?

"Want to jump rope?" Bonnie held out a new rope with bright red wooden handles.

"No thanks." Hannah leaned against the railing of the big concrete stairs that led from the rust colored brick school to the playground. She kept her eyes down and her head bent to keep Bonnie from seeing her face.

"I'm Bonnie, who're you?"

"Hannah."

"The girl at the Pine Cone?"

Hannah said she was because the blonde girl knew that anyway. As far as jumping rope, Bonnie had to teach her.

"What are you going to be when you grow up?" Hannah asked Bonnie whose hair hung long and straight, the color of a lemon cut open. It wasn't curled, contrary to the fashion for girls wanting to resemble Shirley Temple. Bonnie turned up her nose at Shirley

Temple. She twirled the toe of her shoe in the dust

"Well, I sure don't want to sing and tap dance."

"Why not?"

"Not for some movie, anyway."

"Where then?"

"In the woods. If I dance that's the only place I'll do it."

"The woods?"

"Like a fairy."

"Can I come with you?"

"If you know the magic words…"

"What are they?"

"They aren't for crybabies." She twirled her rope and jumped for at least five minutes with no mistakes at all.

Hannah practiced jumping rope in the storeroom behind the kitchen of the café. She practiced alone, perfecting the rope's twirl around her body, fancying herself a dancer caught in a ball of light. No one must be allowed to see if she were to catch her toe on the rope and ruin the perfect circle.

~~~

"My Grandma joined the circus."

The two girls sat in the back booth at the Pine Cone, talking while they colored in identical Cinderella coloring books.

"She did not!" Bonnie picked up the red crayon and sucked on it before she applied it to Cinderella's lips.

"Yes, she did. She left everyone. She left my dad standing right in the middle of the kitchen. He wasn't any older than we are. Younger, in fact. Three." Hannah paused. A bubble of pink spit had collected at the corner of Bonnie's mouth. "You aren't supposed to eat crayons, you know."

"It doesn't matter." Bonnie bit the tip off the crayon. "See!" She grinned. Her front teeth looked like Yarrow's when she smeared her lipstick. Hannah was stunned. It was her crayon and the box was new with sixty-four crayons of every imaginable color, and most of them still had the flat, sharp circle on the tip from having never been used. "I didn't know you had a dad," Bonnie continued as though she'd done nothing extraordinary.

"He's a farmer." The very words conjured the image of him in a swirl of sunlight and barley chaff. One image clicked into another as they do in a View-Master when your thumb depressed the lever on the side. Her father coming up the path from the barn. His clay-encrusted work boots by the kitchen door. Hands, large but still gentle, working the cow's teats. The squirting sound of milk against the corrugated metal of the pail.

"Where is he?" Bonnie put the ruined red crayon back into the gold and green crayon box and concentrated on making her next selection. She touched each crayon as though her finger had the power to discern her preference. Cerulean blue.

Hannah had stopped coloring and was staring at her friend. Bonnie pressed the blue crayon, but not too firmly, on the empty field of Cinderella's dress. "Cold Creek," Hannah said and her voice came out sounding far off, like thunder on a summer afternoon so distant on the horizon that you can barely see the clouds.

"Where's that?"

"North Dakota."

"That's a long way."

"I know." Hannah picked up the black crayon and scribbled on the prince's castle, long heavy gouges over the door.

"You're ruining it!" Bonnie reached out her hand to stop her.

"I don't care. I want it this way." The black crayon broke in half.

"Why did you leave your dad?" Bonnie said.

"There was a storm." Hannah kept her eyes on the blackened castle. She ripped what was left of the crayon's paper and drew with both hands. Clouds above the blackened castle. A whirlwind. The tail of the whirlwind created in circles of black crayon, moving toward the turrets.

"Did the house blow down?" Now Bonnie had stopped coloring, her cerulean blue crayon poised, forgotten, as she watched Hannah.

"No. But we left anyhow." Parents could break the world apart and there wasn't a thing you could do. Here, Hannah, put on your clothes. Put on your hat. Grab your doll. Let's go. And you had to leave home. Even if you held onto the doorknob, she could pry your fingers loose. She could pick you up under her arm like you were no more than a sack of grain. She could tell you that it was for the best and you were too little to understand.

"And he didn't come to get you?" What an idea! Bonnie sat on the other side of the table, her crayon poised in the air above the coloring book and Hannah stared at her. Such a possibility hadn't occurred to her before this minute. Would he do that?

"I don't think so." It was like clicking the View-Master, fast, from one picture of the farm to the next, and coming up with no picture of her father actually climbing into his truck and driving away down the road and turning on the highway past Cold Creek to search for them.

"He must not have been very nice, then." The voice held no meanness toward Hannah. The voice of Bonnie took Hannah's side, or at the very least, wanted to take Hannah's side. But Hannah, when she heard her friend refer to her father as not very nice, began a frantic search through her memories and came up with all the times he'd driven her to town to see Gran. It only took an instant to spin those short trips out to longer ones and to put her father alone in the truck. Suddenly she could, yes, definitely she could see him clearly. He drove slowly through the little towns, through Minto and Ardoch towards Grand Forks. Or maybe northeast into Minnesota, through Donaldson and Greenbush. Maybe even to Red Pine. He might have sat in his truck right outside the Pine Cone Café and not realized she was there.

"Maybe he couldn't find us." She put her black crayon back into the box.

"Maybe."

Hannah had covered the castle in the black, swirling wind. The whole page had disappeared under her crayon. You couldn't see anything. She looked up and saw that Bonnie had barely moved during their entire exchange. She still had her blue crayon poised above Cinderella's dress.

"Where's your dad?" Hannah watched Bonnie take up her blue coloring again, pressing harder now on the dress, outlining it in a thick blue line that left flakes of crayon to be blown off the page.

"With Jesus." Bonnie said. She bent her head to the side and her blonde hair fell over her shoulder.

"Dead?" Grandmas died, and baby rabbits.

"He got shot in the war."

For a reason Hannah didn't understand, her own father hadn't gone to war. "I'm glad my dad is alive."

"What good does it do if he doesn't come to get you?" Bonnie spit the words.

Hannah tried to lock her mind against those words, but they rang on and on in her head, louder than they were when Bonnie first said them. If her daddy was alive, if he had come to search for her and Yarrow, and especially if he had parked his truck outside the Pine Cone Café, then why didn't he come inside? She would have been right there. He could have seen her there. How could he miss her? And even if he didn't recognize her—she was older, after all—she'd know him right off the bat. She'd run to him and throw her arms around his waist and cry--no, she'd sing, "Daddy." But he hadn't come inside. She could find no explanation for this strange behavior on the part of a living father. She'd reached the end of the circle of images in the View-Master of her imagination. The girls colored in silence until Wanda arrived at the booth with two big bowls of strawberry ice cream.

"Bonnie and Hannah! Sweets for the Sweets."

~~~

Hannah pondered the question of fathers while keeping an eye on Yarrow and Wanda from where she sat at the upstairs window. Sometimes Yarrow bent double, laughing from deep in her belly, so hard that she must have ended up with tears in her eyes because Wanda circled her with one arm and handed her a hanky with the other. Sometimes they sang, softly, not to disturb anybody, songs like "We ain't got a barrel of money..." And on nights like this Hannah thought perhaps what her mother had done was the right thing after all. Maybe it was a mercy that Hannah's dad didn't find them, even if he was alive.

~~~

Behind Last Days Bible Church where the gooseberries grew, a path of sorts led to a stream that cut through the scrub pines. It must have emptied, eventually, into a river that carried the water up to Lake Winnipeg, but Hannah had no concept yet of the veins and arteries of this earth and how they connect, by blood or water, all the living. Her attraction to the stream was simply its movement, and that movement simply for its beauty. That the flow of its water could be purposeful, that it might lead somewhere, did not occur to her.

Bonnie took her hand. "Come on."

"Where?"

"To the Rock of Ages."

Bonnie had the advantage of having lived in Red Pine all her life not to mention belonging to Last Days, a fact giving her right of access to the path. Had it not been for the Vacation Bible School there would not have been a path at all. Years before either of the girls had been born the young members of Last Days had established the trek through the woods and its surrounding gooseberry thicket as a kind of initiation rite, a test of faith and whether or not a child really had been saved.

"Is that where the fairies dance?" Hannah hadn't been a crybaby since that first day of school. Maybe Bonnie noticed.

"No, Silly. Fairies are pagan. They're magic. The Rock of Ages is Christian, but there sill are words we have to say--prayer words," Bonnie instructed. The gooseberry leaves were little green fists, loops of knuckles, covering the thorns.

"What words?" Hannah pushed her own fists deep into the pockets of her overalls. Yarrow had braided her hair and fastened it with rubber bands. The braids, shorter now than they had been when she was little, stuck out behind her ears.

"Protection words." Bonnie's eyes flashed. She grinned. She licked her lips with her bright pink tongue.

"Okay." Hannah said.

"Repeat after me: though I walk through the shadow of death…" Droplets of sweat decorated Bonnie's hairline, dampening the fine blonde wisps against her forehead.

"Though I walk through the shadow of death." So death was actually a shadow. She hadn't known that. Yarrow ought to have told her about the shadow of death when Grandma Harris died. No wonder they hadn't opened the coffin—Grandma wasn't there. Grandma was walking in that shadow, walking and walking, and now Hannah wondered what stood big enough to cause such a shadow and if that shadow had an end. Could a person walk through the shadow of death and come out the other side into the sunshine?

"I will fear no evil." Bonnie took her two hands and squeezed them as if to say that something fearsome awaited them on the tunnel's other end.

"I will fear no evil," Hannah repeated. Good comes of good, and evil things do not befall good little girls. Gran Olson told her that a long time ago. Gran pulled her over to the oak rocker and gave her the words like a secret, whispering them in her ear. Gran's breath tickled the inside of her ear and made it damp so that afterwards she needed to stick her finger in there, deep as it could go, and twirl it around to stop the sensation like tiny gnats brushing transparent wings against her inner ear.

"There, that'll do it. Pastor Hanson teaches us to use these words against every evil, against heathens and Catholics and even the bums that pass through town."

Bonnie grinned again and motioned toward a slope where, as Hannah's eyes began to differentiate leaves and branches from grass and earth, she saw in the thicket a tunnel, worn smooth by the backsides of seven-year-olds. She followed her friend.

"Now," Bonnie said, pushing aside the branches with one hand and pointing with the other, "lie down on your back. Cover your face with your hands. Keep your arms close to your body. Feet first and slide."

Hannah plummeted, twisted once to the right, and landed on the bank of the stream. It was no wider than a ditch and would have been, a disappointment except for the way it bent into the woods. Sunlight slipped through the pine branches and reflected off stones that lay on moss under the shallow water. They seemed to waver in the greenish current.

"Want to follow it?" Bonnie landed right behind her. She stood and brushed off her overalls.

It was like a long cord leading out and back from the tunnel.

"To the Rock of Ages?" Excitement tasted like peppermint on Hannah's tongue.

"The very one." Bonnie enticed.

Hannah followed her lead, searching the stream as they walked along its banks, for something inarticulate. Hardly did she know she searched, but she was aware of seeing things underneath the current, and it seemed to her that she'd been looking for that very thing and here it was. A perfectly rounded stone the color of rust. One feathered wing of a blackbird with its spot of red. She felt a desire more powerful than safety or than home, but the object of her desire was hidden somewhere in the future, or maybe in the stream itself. Perhaps she thought to find her answer in the stream, perhaps in the act of following.

The girls kept to the stream even after all signs of a path had disappeared. Pine contested with birch and poplar for light and finally relinquished its rights to the land. The color of light softened. Some of the trees, never logged, grew trunks so large that Bonnie and Hannah together could not reach around them, and so tall the girls felt dizzied when they tried to find their tops. Here grew the large leafed beech and giant elm like gods in their chamber of judgment. Along the stream, pink and yellow lady slipper orchids danced before the jack in the pulpit. Here they could no longer jump across the water that had deepened and turned the color of Concord grapes. Just ahead three enormous granite rocks jutted up from the earth, narrowing the stream's path between them and creating a pool above and a small waterfall below.

"Nobody else comes this far." Bonnie began climbing the tallest of the rocks. "Nobody else even knows this place is here."

Again Hannah followed. "Let's pretend we're climbing a mountain," she called up to Bonnie. A spray of little stones tumbled past her down to the stream.

"Okay."

"Did you ever see a mountain?"

"Never did."

"Maybe this is one."

"Maybe."

The rock did have a small birch tree growing from a crevice, its roots curled around the granite, its trunk curved painfully upwards. At the top the girls sat on a ledge, their legs dangling over the stream. From this vantage point they took in the whole drama of the place— the stream, the pool formed by the rocks and the waterfall that sprayed off the sides of the other two rocks and continued in a new stream about thirty feet below.

"This is the rock cleft for us." Bonnie murmured.

"Cleft?" Hannah followed the crevice down from the tree to the other side of the rock where it opened wider into a small cave.

"You know, 'Rock of Ages, cleft for me/Let me hide myself in Thee.'"

~ ~ ~

"Do you like to go to church?" Hannah asked Bonnie after school started in September and they had recited the protection words and slid through the tunnel once again to the best place.

"It doesn't matter if you like it. The Bible says thou shalt keep holy the Lord's Day." Dry leaves had stuck in Bonnie's hair on the slide down. She didn't notice or didn't care. Already the leaves had turned and were falling, even though it was just past Labor Day. Dry leaves made the tunnel path more slippery

Keep holy. What could that mean? Hannah thought probably it meant the same as "be good." With a little effort, she could be good anywhere. She told Bonnie so.

"No. I think you have to go to church." Bonnie's eyes held the serious and confident look of an insider.

"And anyway, what's so important about the Lord's Day?" Hannah started off down the trail to the Rock of Ages. She scuffed her feet and the white part of her new oxfords turned grimy. Dust filled even the little white holes in the black leather part. They were getting ruined.

"Don't you know anything?" Bonnie's words struck Hannah's back like little stones. "It's cuz God made everything and then he rested, so he got that day all for himself."

Hannah stuck her hands deep into the pockets of her overalls and didn't turn around to face the other girl. "That's stupid," she mumbled. She hadn't meant to talk about God at all. What she really wanted to know was the reason why people stopped coming to the café for wild berry pie. The reason seemed to have something to do with church and local people who used to eat pie there every Sunday. Folks still came from Caribou and Haug. They drove from as far as Piney, Ontario.But the thoughts wouldn't connect in her head. She'd asked the wrong questions and now Bonnie was being a smarty-pants, and Hannah had called her and her church stupid. Stupid. Hannah wanted to reach out and grab the word before it rushed through the air and flew like a black fly into Bonnie's ear, but it was too late.

"Who says?" Bonnie caught up with her and grabbed her arm, swinging her around to face her, hands on hips, eyes like chipped glass.

"I do." Hannah's words stamped down hard like a foot.

"How come?"

But there could be no how come, and Bonnie knew it. She had a whole church-full of people on her side. She had all the years since Jesus. Hannah stood alone in defense of Wanda and the Pine Cone Café. Hannah took a deep breath and clenched her teeth to keep more bad words from slipping out.

"You'd better watch out, Hannah."

"How come?"

"I might not be able to play with you if you say God is stupid. Lots of kids can't play with you already."

"That's not true."

"It is. Susie Oaks can't play with you. Melanie Dodds can't play with you. Sally Arneson can't play with you."

"They can so. They play with me all the time at school."

"But they can't come to the café. I'm the only one who can come."

"I never called God stupid."

To Hannah her friend looked suddenly plain, even horrible. She saw a spider crawling in Bonnie's hair and Hannah allowed it to crawl. "And I didn't invite anybody to the café except for you." She lied.

"Even if you did, they couldn't come." Bonnie jeered. The spider dropped on its thread over her ear and onto her shoulder.

"You're lying."

"It's not a lie."

"Well, smarty-pants, if you know everything just tell me why they can't come." Hannah saw the white spot on the spider's back.

"Because it's bad not to have a daddy." Bonnie lifted her head and pointed her pug nose toward the sky.

Hannah laughed with relief. "I do have a daddy. You're the one that doesn't have one." Her voice came out too loud. Leaves drifted from the little birch tree and one landed on her lap.

"I know. But mine's dead." The spider dropped off Bonnie's shoulder and landed on the granite rock.

"That's what I mean." How come she was acting so stupid?

"It's okay not to have a dad if he's dead. My dad's in heaven and he's a hero. It's your way that's wrong. Your dad never went to the war. He's a yellow-bellied coward, and he doesn't take care of you like he's supposed to or you and your mom never would have come to Red Pine in the first place." The sun behind Bonnie's head made it hard for Hannah to look at her.

"It's not my fault." But maybe it was. Maybe Gran was right. Maybe she hadn't been good enough.

"It's your mom's fault."

"It's not her fault either."

"Whose, then?"

But Hannah didn't know.

Sunlight slammed onto the granite like a swarm of crazed bees diving headlong, insane with futility. What could Hannah do? She was only seven years old, an age of clarity when it came to blame. Someone must take it. Her skin stung. The poison seeped through every pore.

"Maybe your mom doesn't want you to play with me either." Her voice sounded brittle enough to shatter on the rock. Her teeth stuck to the insides of her lips. Her eyes burned.

"She doesn't care," Bonnie said. Her voice pouted. It oiled something stuck in Hannah's mind that she'd taken in but hidden in a tight crack hoping it wouldn't get loose.

"You're the one no one wants to play with!" Hannah snarled at the other girl.

Hannah's white-hot poison burned up and out. Bonnie sucked in air like someone drowning. Then she started to cry.

"You're just mean." Her sobs hiccoughed out of her and snot ran out her nose and collected on her upper lip.

"And let that be a lesson!" Hannah stamped her foot.

Her bones had turned to granite. Her anger seeped through the rock like water that had been blocked there for a thousand years. It seemed that she could hear echoes of Yarrow crying behind a thin rock wall in her mind.

"I'm sorry," she murmured, taking Bonnie's hand and trying to forgive, but she couldn't really forgive anyone—not Bonnie nor her own father and mother Mostly she couldn't forgive herself for feelings powerful and dangerous enough to make another person cry.

~~~

Hannah's father used to sit on his haunches facing the wind that bent his field of new green barley in waves that rolled in from the horizon, bordered by Murdock's, theirs all wheat, as far as the eye could see. Vast distance formed his sight. Mornings, when Hannah awoke, she used to run to him out there. He'd take her on his knee, not seeing her, but enclosing her in a wider, longer sight that was of his world. She could lose herself in her father's wideness. He didn't speak. She felt the long bone of his leg under her, the tight muscle. She felt his arm lightly around her, and his hand upon her knee as she melted into his silence and disappeared in his vision of the world.

He must have thought she could not be taken from him. She must have been to him a stalk of barley in the field of himself, or the scent of wet grass in the air he breathed.

As she struggled to forgive him for making Yarrow cry, she began to dream that he never came in from the field. He sat facing the wind while it ripped the barley from the ground and swirled it around him. He disappeared in it and there was nothing Hannah could do to bring him back.

~~~

Hannah set Raggedy Lily, on a little shelf in the bedroom Yarrow and Wanda fashioned for her in what could have been the dining room of the apartment if they'd had a kitchen. A wooden archway separated the space from the living room. Wanda painted it sky blue, installed a wooden rod from one end to the other, and hung a brocade curtain woven with roses the colors of jewels. She'd found it at the fall rummage sale held by the Christian Ladies' Society of Last Days Bible Church.

Bonnie's mom had been there, collecting money for the rummage. She sat at a card table by the basement door of the church and sorted the change into a metal box. When Wanda handed her fifty cents for the curtain and some dresses, Bonnie's mom raised an eyebrow and looked away. Wanda laid the fifty cent piece on the table and tossed her barley blonde curls as she took Hannah's hand and said "We got what we wanted, honey. Let's go home."

Yarrow painted wooden apple crates the same sky blue and across the front she hung the curtains she'd made from the Last Days ladies' old summer dresses. "Tres elegante!" Wanda kissed the tips of her fingers with a loud smack and her hand flew open like sunlight.

"Now for a real bed!" Yarrow stood with her hands on her hips and her face beaming like the true God's probably did after he finished landscaping the Garden of Eden.

"Are we staying here?" Hannah asked. She must have thought that as long as she slept on the sofa, there was a chance Yarrow would pick up one morning and go back to the farm.

"Looks like it." Yarrow pulled Hannah close, holding her between her knees.

"Forever?" Like the mountains, the real mountains that don't disappear when the clouds blow away. But even from the other side of the mountains a father might come searching if he got lonesome enough.

"Nothing's forever." Yarrow leaned forward and kissed her on the nose.

Bed or no, Hannah's sofa days were over. Wanda spread a thick Army Surplus sleeping bag in the space left for the bed and started checking the Red Pine Gazette want ads.

"Look here. They're selling off old widow Hintz's estate." She'd laid the paper out on one of the café tables and was going down the ads with a red pencil. The breakfast crowd had gone, and the lunch crowd hadn't yet come in. They called it a crowd from habit, even though not even half the tables were taken at any meal.

"Auction?" Yarrow, came around from behind the counter where she'd been taking clean glasses from a tray and setting them on a shelf.

Wanda circled the ad several times in red. "On Saturday."

"Beds?" Yarrow bent over Wanda's shoulder. Her hair brushed against Wanda's cheek and Wanda's hand rose to touch it as if it were her own.

"Three."

"A single?"

"A trundle."

"Perfect."

On Saturday afternoon Wanda hung the "CLOSED" sign on the café door. Hannah walked in the middle, Yarrow holding one of her hands and Wanda, the other. She lifted her feet from the ground, using their arms as a swing, to leap across entire squares on the sidewalk.

All Widow Hintz's belongings, including even her housedresses and several boxes of old shoes, occupied her back yard. Yellow birch leaves drifted down, alighting on dressers and overstuffed chairs.

"Doesn't she want this anymore?" Hannah asked Yarrow. Her mother continued to hold one of her hands and Wanda held the other as the three of them maneuvered through the crowd.

"Who?" Yarrow turned and looked down at her.

"The widow. Doesn't she want her things?"

Yarrow and Wanda stopped. Yarrow bent down and put her hand against the side of Hannah's face.

"I'm sorry, Hannah; I thought you understood."

"What?"

"Widow Hintz died, honey. That's what an estate sale is. When people die, the family shares what they need, and they sell the rest."

"Was she old?"

"Very old. Ninety."

"Will she mind if we buy her bed?"

"She's dead, Hannah. Don't you remember when your Grandma Harris died? We went to her funeral. Remember?"

"I remember." In her mind Hannah saw the amber light from the Presbyterian Church windows shining on a closed coffin. "But will Mrs. Hintz mind about the bed?"

Yarrow and Wanda looked at each other like they did sometimes before they told Hannah she was too little to understand.

"Nobody knows, Hannah." Yarrow took both her hands and held them tight.

"Nobody at all?"

"Nobody."

The trundle bed, a four-poster with swirled rungs painted white and trimmed in fine lines of gold, sat beside a brown-leafed oak tree along with the other bedroom furniture.

"Look here, Hannah." Wanda bent down and pulled a second bed out from underneath the four-poster. At a flick of the lever on the bed's metal frame, it popped up like a roll-a-way cot.

"You see, honey. You can keep this tucked away and just pull it out when you have a friend over."

"Bonnie?"

"Or anybody you want."

An oak leaf floated down and landed on the gray and white striped mattress. Wanda sat on the bed and bounced, then lay down.

"Feels firm enough," she motioned for Hannah to try the cot. There they were, under that brown leafed oak, lying flat out on two beds with Yarrow beaming like Mrs. Santa Claus, when Pastor Hanson's wife, in her brown rayon dress with the white collar and its matching brown felt hat, walked by on her way to inspect Widow Hintz's kitchen appliances.

She murmured something low to another woman, skinny in her blue cotton skirt and white blouse, with a wiry shock of dyed black hair that she'd tried to tame into a knot. The other woman nodded.

The auctioneer's tongue flapped like clothes drying in a high wind.

"Two dollars!" Wanda bid.

"Five!" bid the Mrs. Reverend.

"I didn't know she wanted the bed," Hannah held tight to Yarrow's hand.

"Six-fifty!" Yelled Wanda.

"Eight."

"Eight dollars and fifty cents." Wanda snorted.

"Ten dollars!"

Too much money for a second-hand trundle bed. Even Hannah knew that.

"There'll be another bed," Yarrow said as much to Wanda as to the child.

A perfect brown leaf detached from the tree and rode the light breeze down to land beside the other leaf on the mattress. Hannah watched it drift. She didn't know how much she wanted that bed until the two leaves touched.

Wanda let Yarrow lead her from the yard to the sidewalk. All the way back to the café nobody said a word.

"I'm sorry, Hannah," Wanda said as she unlocked the door to the Pine Cone Café. She stood aside so Hannah could go in first, and then she and Yarrow followed, locking the door again behind them and leaving the "CLOSED" sign up. They wouldn't open again that day.

"It's okay." Hannah lied and felt glad to be able to do it in order not to make Wanda even more sad.

"It's not okay. You should have had that bed."

Wanda and Yarrow both bent down and put their arms around her. They smelled like a combination of lilacs and bread and wild berry pie, and they each kissed her and smoothed back her hair. Tears ran down Yarrow's cheeks even though she wasn't actually crying, and Wanda reached over and wiped them with her lace-edged hanky.

"It will be all right," Wanda murmured, her eyes wet, her fire extinguished.

Wanda found a brown metal bed at the rummage sale sponsored each year by the Ladies Auxiliary of the Moose Lodge. A painted vine climbed up the center panel above Hannah's head to break the brown monotony. If Wanda hadn't looked at the child with such hope she might have cried when she saw the curved pipe construction of that headboard so different from the elegant turned wood posts of the trundle bed. Instead she touched the delicate blue flowers budding off the painted vine.

"And look at this!" Wanda pulled from a large paper sack a handmade quilt in squares of sky blue, brown and green, mixed with prints in every color nature could produce.

"Doesn't this look like somebody took a swatch of each piece of clothes they ever wore?"

And sure enough, Hannah touched squares of cotton and of wool, of velvet, satin, and gabardine. A swatch of ivory lace covered a square of satin at the center. She ran her fingers over the complex textures.

"This must be her wedding dress."

"Each square has its story." Wanda examined a diamond shaped swatch of brown tweed. "I wonder what this was."

"Whose was it?" Hannah ran her hand in a smooth sweep from one end of the coverlet to the other.

"It came with the bed." Wanda murmured as she fingered a square of purple velvet.

"With this bed?"

"And look—the blue of this star burst design just matches our decorations." Wanda continued.

"Really, Wanda? The bed and the quilt came together?"

"Right." She grasped the quilt by one side and tossed it up into the air, shaking it until it came down over the mattress like a magic carpet drifting down from the sky.

"Who would ever give this up?" Yarrow said.

"I know. It's gorgeous isn't it?" Wanda said.

"It's somebody's whole life." Hannah spread her arms wide, trying to reach from one end of the quilt to the other, trying to gather to herself all the colors and textures.

"Better than a trundle bed?" Wanda said.

"A thousand times better, Wanda!" Hannah sat up and threw her arms around Wanda, giving her a big hug right around her waist.

Often after that, on sunny afternoons or mornings when rain pelted the windows of the café and Hannah was alone upstairs, she sat on the quilt and made up stories from its swatches of cloth. Raggedy Lily listened. The doll sat where the girl had placed her, propped on the pillow against the metal headboard, and Hannah imagined her smiling and nodding her head. Sometimes she spoke, in a voice very like the child's own, but different enough for Hannah to believe it truly came from the doll's embroidered lips. Together they spun tales of mothers who ran away and children lonely for fathers who disappeared.

Nights, when Hannah climbed between the sheets and pulled the quilt up under her chin she felt enclosed in the life of someone who wasted nothing and who seemed to know that anything you live with long enough becomes beautiful and dear.

~ ~ ~

Yarrow's lips turned pale. Hannah found a dime in the bottom of her top dresser drawer and a nickel in the cracked cream pitcher sitting on the windowsill. She dug her hand into the cracks between Wanda's sofa cushions and turned up the edges of the living room rug, and when she had enough, she laid a fistful of change in the hand of Mrs. Ness down at Ness's Drug in payment for a tube of Revlon Wild Cherry lipstick.

When she gave her mother the lipstick, Yarrow started to cry. "Do I look that bad?"

"You look beautiful!" And Hannah showed her the picture of Snow White with her perfect red lips. "But your lips aren't the right color."

Yarrow put her arms around the child. "You're right, Hannah. I ought to take better care of myself."

In the other room Yarrow and Wanda made sounds like thick cream poured over cherries. To Hannah even their weeping flowed around her like satin. Night after night she heard them talking while they thought she slept. She curled into their sounds and wrapped herself in the comfort of their breathing. In dreams, when she did finally sleep, their hair grew long and swirled around her. They were mermaids and she was a fish. The three of them swam in satin water and they sang green songs to stay safe.

Whispers ran with little feet through the town, in and out of stores, down the hallways of the school. Even in the church the whispers could be heard like a scattering of roaches behind the picture of Jesus on the wall. They passed from one blade of grass to another, barely audible except in dreams when the grass catches flame and burns. You may be locked in your room in the prairie, in the woods, in the mountains, by the sea, but the whispers would continue. The whispers became a hot dry wind. In their wind fanned by locust wings, tender flesh dried. It flaked from the bones.

~~~

Christmas of 1947 came and went again. Wanda played being Mrs. Santa Claus in her soft red flannel granny gown and her white pinafore. When she put the Sparkle Plenty doll in Hannah's arms, the child's tears dripped down all over Sparkle's wavy yellow hair.

"Whatever's wrong? I thought you wanted Sparkle Plenty."

"I did, Wanda. I do. She's just exactly what I want." And then she cried harder.

"There must be something wrong." Wanda and Yarrow cooed and wrapped both Hannah and Sparkle in a firm hug.

Outside the window colored lights spiraled up the street lamps and reflected in the snow. Bonnie and her mom, in fact the whole town except for the three of them, probably were singing Christmas carols inside the Last Days Bible Church. "I don't know what's wrong." She looked up at Yarrow and Wanda who had shadows in their eyes like clouds that pass over on a summer day without bringing rain.

At school she stood in a bubble that separated her from the other children. Whispers swirled around it like mist. She looked out through her bubble all round Mrs. Anderson's fourth grade class room, at Bonnie huddled with Susie Oaks and Melanie Dodds in the reading corner under the windows. Above their heads mustard colored paint curled off the wall and hung loose like a dead worm. God must feel like this, Hannah thought, as he watches us from heaven, wherever heaven is. Heaven, maybe, is a bubble, and God, just like herself, walks everywhere, seeing but not being seen, yearning towards us and not being recognized.

This is why their invitation to the Rock of Ages came as such a surprise.

Bonnie sidled up to her and talked like brown sugar. She talked like she'd never stopped talking over a year ago. She draped her arm around Hannah's shoulders and walked with her like that all the way to the Pine Cone Café and up the stairs into Hannah's sky blue room where Lily sat looking down from the shelf at Sparkle Plenty enthroned upon the thrift store quilt.

"You got a Sparkle Plenty doll for Christmas?" Bonnie reached across the bed and touched the ends of Sparkle's long yellow hair.

"Umhum."

"I wish I had a Sparkle Plenty. Can you really comb her hair?"

"Yes, but you have to be really careful not to pull it." It occurred to Hannah that if she were polite, she would offer to let Bonnie comb Sparkle's hair, but instead she sat down on the quilt between the doll and Bonnie.

"You're lucky. You should bring her along."

"I can't."

"Why not?"

The place on Hannah's neck where Bonnie's arm had been began to tingle. "I don't know," she said. Don't be selfish, Hannah. How often had Yarrow said those words? Be a good girl, now, and share your things. Her mind whirled with indecision.

"Please bring her." Bonnie gathered the doll's yellow hair into a ponytail.

Maybe the other girls would like her better if they saw she had a Sparkle Plenty doll.

"Okay." Hannah conceded, and bundled Sparkle Plenty in a wool scarf to protect her from the cold. She put her own coat and boots on and wrapped a long knit scarf around her neck. She looked at Sparkle lying in her wool scarf on the thrift store quilt and wondered once more if taking her along was the right thing to do. Then, as though she were breaking through a store window and snatching something that belonged to someone else, she grabbed the doll, and she and Bonnie hurried down the stairs and out the front door of the Pine Cone Café.

The two girls slid down the snow-slick tunnel to the frozen stream and walked the path to the bottom of the Rock of Ages where Susie Oaks and Melanie Dodds and even Sally Arneson waited. They looked with barbed eyes straight at Hannah. The bubble around her broke under their gaze, and left her standing in front of them with no protection at all.

"Sparkle Plenty!" Melanie Dodds grabbed the doll from Hannah's arms. "Wow! I wish I'd gotten a Sparkle Plenty doll. My mom and dad said we're too poor."

Susie laughed. "Probably Hannah's mom makes lots of money at the cafe." She raised her arms and motioned to Melanie. "Throw her to me."

"No!" Hannah yelled and reached for her doll, but missed, as Sparkle Plenty hurtled through the air. Susie caught her and threw her over Hannah's head back to Melanie who tossed Sparkle up again, up towards the snow-laden branches of cedar where her yellow hair caught and held.

Hannah jumped for her but Susie, who was taller, caught hold of one leg and pulled. A chunk of hair stayed on the branch.

"Bonnie!" Hannah yelled, hoping she'd make them stop.

"Bonnie ignored her and joined the desperate game. And when Susie tossed Sparkle by that one leg to Bonnie, Hannah sat down in the snow and started to cry.

"Cry baby, cry baby," the girls chanted as they tossed Sparkle Plenty back and forth between them, tearing her dress, scratching her face, pulling out chunks of her yellow hair until she was bald.

"May as well give the cry baby her doll," Melanie sighed. "She's no good anyhow without her hair."

"She's a mess." Bonnie tossed the broken corpse onto Hannah's lap.

They climbed the hill and left Hannah at the Rock of Ages with her ruined doll. She sat for a long time in the snow, looking at Sparkle Plenty sprawled under the tree. She listened to the winter wind in the cedars. A tiny bird, a bunting, hopped on top of a snowdrift, leaving delicate, four-pronged tracks. Snow fine as dust blew over the doll's broken body.

Hannah buried Sparkle Plenty in the cleft of rock in a grave of cedar boughs, and covered her with fresh snow, for she was surely dead. Then she went home to her sky blue room above the Pine Cone Café where Raggedy Lily looked down at the empty spot on the thrift store quilt and saw that she was alone again. And Hannah wished Raggedy Lily could talk because she would like to ask her how a girl could get so strange that nobody in the whole town liked her. And she would ask Raggedy Lily if she knew of any way to change her back into the girl she used to be, if she still remembered who that girl was.

~~~

Snow fell the night of the fire. Wind drove it swirling around the corners of the café with a sound Hannah ever afterwards associated with the world's end. Years later she would read the poem by Robert Frost, slam the cover down with an eerie sense of the prophetic, and after that even his name would be enough to scare the bejeebers out of her.

Snow pelted the windows on the second floor where Yarrow and Wanda had already tucked her into bed and sung her to sleep with "Goodnight sweetheart..." She lay listening to their creamed cherry sounds mixed with wind, and then fell asleep.

Who can know what God wants? Maybe nothing at all. Maybe none of it matters—not lost fathers or ruined dolls dead and buried in the cleft of the rock. Maybe all of it is an experiment and God watches, standing by a chemistry table, to see how it will turn out. A little wind, a little fire and "Aha! So that's the way the world works!"

Yarrow screamed. "Hannah!"

She woke to a gush of flame and Yarrow and Wanda leaping through it towards her, wrapping themselves in it, burning, burning.

"The window, Hannah! We have to jump!"

"Hannah first!" Wanda yelled.

Cold smashed against her body, ice and fire. Yarrow and Wanda pushed her out. She became a bird, then a stone and then the air inside her body exploded out her mouth in a cry as she hit the snow bank. Yarrow split the night with flame as she soared from the window and landed on ice. She moaned. Hannah covered her with snow to dowse the flames.

Where was Wanda? Had she gone back for something? How could she go back, already cocooned in fire? Lily. Maybe she went back for Lily. Hannah screamed her name. "Wanda!" Later Hannah would dream of her and wonder what had happened inside that burning room. It would haunt her that perhaps Wanda died because she made them jump first. Maybe by the time she reached the window the fire had claimed so much of her that she simply gave up the rest. But Wanda wasn't like that. Not beautiful Wanda who tossed her curls, who made Yarrow laugh.

Maybe for some of life there is no reason.

This is what Hannah saw: Wanda finally appeared again in the window like she was fastened there, and she burned. The sky burned. She screamed; she was silent. Her hair flamed. Her head became a torch. She lifted her arms. She danced on her death. She spread wings like a firefly, like a moth, a moon-moth drawn to flame and into the candle's fire. She stuck to the candlewick and burned.

Hannah watched as she shriveled, a tinder, a dry pine on a hill. She watched as nothing of her was left for earth, yet she burned. She watched as Wanda ceased to be the one who sang lullabies on warm October nights while dark leaves fell.

5

The phone woke him. It rang down in the kitchen and James opened his eyes to the predawn dark, a thick darkness such that if you didn't know you'd think the world had ended while you slept. It'll stop, he thought, referring to the phone. It would stop and he would go back to sleep. It must have rung twenty-five times before it stopped. James had just settled his brain when it started up again. Damn. Must be an emergency.

All of it moved in slow motion, how he swung his feet from the bed and thought the furnace must have gone out during the night. Bone numbing cold. Burns the feet. Then the thought came that he needed slippers, wool slippers such as Ida knit. The thought to ask her. The thought to offer her fifty cents for a pair. The thought of thick yarn, midnight blue. The thought of Ida's fingers plying it. The thought of Ida in his living room on a Friday afternoon, her hair transformed by the sharp winter sunlight angling in upon it. Three winters now that she'd been coming there each Friday and he had watched the sunlight on her hair.

"Mr. James Olson?" asked the woman's voice at the other end of the line.

"Yes." He felt a mild impatience as Ida's image slipped underneath the professional-sounding voice and disappeared.

He lifted his bare feet, one at a time, off the icy linoleum, shivered and wished he'd grabbed his jacket from the back of the chair by the bed.

"Do you know a Yarrow Olson and her daughter, Hannah?" Said the voice.

"Who is this?" A snake of fear curled up from the pit of his stomach.

"This is Mrs. Talbot. I'm calling long distance from Doctor Gibsen's office in Roseau, Minnesota. Do you know Yarrow Olson?"

Good God! It was the middle of the night!

"My wife," he said. Roseau. He'd searched in Roseau. A doctor's office. God! "Is there a problem?"

"I'm sorry, Mr. Olson," she said.

"Why? What happened?" So damned cold in the house his teeth had begun to chatter. Nothing fit together. A dream of Ida and the phone rang, or was it the other way around? And Yarrow? What of Yarrow? Yarrow had been gone for years. His legs felt numb as though something cold had been thrust up his body from beneath, through his legs directly into his guts. Thoughts shot into his mind as though originating elsewhere—so this is how it will be. Then his mind stalled, like an old tractor, just went blank, silent on the topic of his wife.

Mrs. Talbot said what she had to say and James heard himself saying yes, and that he understood, and that yes, the pilot at the landing strip there in Roseau should definitely fly both the wife and girl to the hospital in Grand Forks where they had a burn unit. Yes, there was insurance and even if there wasn't, of course he would pay. He heard her as someone at a distance hears. He heard as a witness to someone else's life, someone he had ceased to be four years before that night.

Afterwards he wrapped himself in Gran's afghan and sat in the chair by the window until the sky turned pearl over the winter fields.

~~~

James wondered how it was that when you let a thing go, only then does it come back, but in a way so twisted from the original you'd swear it had turned into something else altogether. But you know it. You know. What kind of joke was it that when he finally got to where he might have called her by her name, she wasn't Yarrow anymore?

Before he brought Yarrow home, he asked Ida to fix both rooms, just in case. After her work was done, Ida lay in his arms as she had now for at least the past year. This, though, was the last time his house would be empty enough to hold them. He made love to her on the living room sofa, not wanting to soil the beds, trying to leave as little trace of them as possible. He saw and treasured, maybe for the last time, the way her hair curved over the pure line of her jaw, the soft contours of shoulders and arms, the lift of breasts, translucent with little blue veins that might be roads to paradise. He had never thought of what they did as wrong. Each of them had been lonely and then found themselves together. That's all it was.

She cried the whole time. Sobbed when he entered her. "Oh James, James…" she bleated like a wounded lamb and he felt himself break apart inside.

"She's my wife, Ida. There's nothing else to be done." He traced the contours of her face with the tip of his finger. She shivered under his touch.

"I know. It's as it should be." Her lips trembled.

"We'll find a way." He said, but he had no inkling what that way might be.

"Oh James, I don't know." She cried again, more quietly now, tears running down her cheeks but without sobs. The quiet of it was odd to witness, the contradiction it implied.

"We will. It was a terrible mistake, you with Steve and me with her, but there's nothing can be done. We have a duty to them." Then a different thought came to his mind, a vague thought, still unformed. "Still and all, there might be something we can save out from it for ourselves."

"I've come to need you, James."

He had kissed her again, and breathed her breath into his own lungs. He had been breathing her so long he wondered if he would be able to survive on regular air.

"I didn't know love could be like this," he whispered into her ear as his passion rose again, but he entered her tentatively, carefully, almost as though she were God and her body a cave where he might hide from all he felt coming toward him, all that threatened to take his life, turn it upside-down, and never set it right again, never in this world.

~~~

When Hannah saw her father walk up the corridor towards the waiting room at the Grand Forks hospital just two days after the fire, she turned around and ran in the opposite direction. The nurse told her that her father had arrived. Here comes your father, she said to

Hannah. But the father in her mind and the man coming towards her didn't look the same. How can you trust the magic that brings your father out of nowhere when you can't remember his face? And how can you trust God to let him stay?

Nothing stays.

Even your clothes don't stay. She was wearing Melanie Arneson's old Levi's and Bonnie's red sweater, both collected by Mrs. Pastor Hanson's good will drive, and brought to the hospital the same day just before her father arrived. It made Hannah come close to throwing up! The very girls who killed Sparkle Plenty. Raggedy Lily and Sparkle Plenty, both of them dead—Lily lost in the fire. But what can you do? You can't go naked. Her father sat with them in the visitor's lounge listening to them talk for quite a while that day. Lies probably. Hannah left them and went to stand by Yarrow's bed, not touching her because all her skin hurt. But standing there singing softly about the wind in our hearts.

~~~

James carried Yarrow through the front door of their house in Cold Creek. Hannah stood alone for a minute on the threshold watching the prairie drift off to the horizon, then she disappeared up the stairs to the room that used to be her own.

"There, that'll do it then." James deposited Yarrow in the old chair by the guest room window where she could watch the snow drift over the severed barley stalks.

If she wanted to watch. Who could know what she wanted now, or didn't want? It wasn't that she couldn't talk. Her voice was scratchy with smoke, but she could talk. Maybe she decided it was useless since all the world's words put together didn't have the power to bring back who she used to be. She looked awful. Her hair was just beginning to grow in, seared as it was from the fire but not burned deep into her scalp. He remembered that she always loved her hair, and he felt relief that she would be left at least with this small pleasure in herself. She kept her body covered, but he could see some puckering of her skin.

"Hannah will tend to me," she said.

He wasn't sure it was right to make the girl do so. "She's so young."

"She's old enough. She's seen worse. She saw Wanda, you know."

No one thought that she would walk again. She couldn't run away from him, not now, not ever. He came in from the fields, day after day, seeing her from far, sitting by that window, watching. He never knew if she was watching him or something beyond him in a world only she could see.

~~~

Yarrow lost her skin in patches, where the fire ate through the drape and stuck to her. But that wasn't the worst of it. Not being able to move was the worst of it. Legs that hung like Raggedy Lily's cloth legs used to hang, that was the worst of it. Having to be wherever James put her—that was the worst of it.

Mid-morning each day, James carried Yarrow into the living room and set her on the big leather chair. Hannah covered her mother's legs with Gran's knit afghan and followed her gaze through the living room window, past the frozen fields, as far as she could towards the world's curve, but she never could see far enough. When springtime thawed the field, Hannah tried to run that distance, but when she turned she still could see Yarrow's silhouette in the window, or see the window itself as a mirror reflecting the horizon toward which she ran. Whether she turned toward Yarrow or away, the sun mocked and blinded her.

"Sing to me, Yarrow." Hannah sat on the arm of her mother's chair and smoothed her cheeks with the palms of her hands. Yarrow's eyes had thickened like milk that sits too long in a hot room.

"I can't sing anymore, Hannah." She said.

"You can sing the 'wind in our hearts' song." Hannah told her and kissed the smoothed place on her cheek.

"I don't remember that one." And she took Hannah's hands into her own, setting them on her lap, away from her face, like objects not connected to either one of them.

"You must remember." Hannah began to sing Yarrow's lullaby. She sang it directly into her mother's eyes, certain she would remember because how could a mother forget her favorite lullaby?

"Be quiet, Hannah." She said.

The song stuck in Hannah's throat. Yarrow looked away from her and out the window again, but Hannah knew she didn't see a thing.

At night James lifted Yarrow from the chair by the window and carried her down the hall into her bedroom.

"Come along now," he said to her as if she had a choice. His voice was soft and thick as the yolk of a soft boiled egg taken whole into your mouth and broken on your tongue. Hannah wanted to yell at him, "No. She doesn't want to go to bed. Take her where the stars can kiss the top of her head. Lean her up against the cottonwood tree beside the creek; she wants to listen to the sounds that water makes in the dark as it slips over rocks." But Hannah didn't know for sure that Yarrow wanted stars and the language of water any more than she wanted her daughter's hands on her face or than she remembered how to sing. The girl saw her mother's head fall and rest on her father's shoulder as he stepped through the bedroom doorway.

~~~

The cat came just after Easter when snow lay in gray patches on dead and matted grass. She stepped lightly, disturbing nothing, leaving no track, as though she were a spirit cat, only visiting in this world where touch can leave bruises. Hannah saw her suddenly, as one might see a ghost, not as mist, but as a body standing where before was nothing but a shadow stretched across the grass. The cat appeared, the color of a cloud or as cream that rises to the top, with gray tips on her ears and tail, and rubbed her body up against Hannah's leg.

Hannah sat on the porch steps. The cat circled her twice and then climbed onto her lap, kneaded the tops of her legs like dough, curled into the hollow beneath her stomach and went to sleep.

"You know your father won't abide a cat." Yarrow spoke the words as though absent from them. "Not even in the barn will he abide a cat, despite the field mice in there. I've never understood that. House cats, now that I can understand, but in the barn—you'd think he'd be grateful for a cat's help. But no. A cat is something James just can't abide."

"Why?" Hannah asked.

"Who knows?" Yarrow stared out the window and Hannah wished she'd look at her as she spoke. She wished something would bring back into her eyes that softness that they used to hold when she would pat her lap and smile and tell Hannah to come over to her there because she had a story she was bursting to tell. But now Yarrow just stared out at nothing.

Maybe if they had never run away, and maybe if they knew nothing of the Pine Cone Café and Wanda and trundle beds and Sparkle Plenty dolls, then Yarrow would take her into her arms and let Hannah breathe the nutmeg smell of her. She would say that she could handle James, and Hannah could keep the cat. On the porch, dear, she would say. And then she would let Hannah help her bake a cake to surprise James when he came in from the fields, and he'd end up so absorbed in eating that even if the cat walked right across his shoes, he wouldn't notice her.

Ghost, the obvious name, took to living under the front porch. Hot spring afternoons she'd leap into Hannah's lap whenever she sat on the old rocker staring into the haze where field and sky met. Ghost settled in and purred, her body heavy against Hannah's chest, a pressure on her belly. The weight of another creature resting on you, trusting you enough to sleep, fills a hollow space you don't know you have until it disappears.

That spring after the fire Yarrow had watched from the window each day as the gray snow melted and the tender grass poked through the wet black earth. The martins stole the bluebird house James had nailed to a log pole pine.

"I'd thought we might have bluebirds." Yarrow sighed when she saw the white throat and the blue-black head of the martin poking out through the round hole of the bluebird house.

The bluebirds followed the martins that very week. The soft brownish blue female fluttered in front of the house as if she couldn't believe her bad luck. Her startling blue and burnt orange mate attempted to pacify her with suggestions of this or that nook in the ancient gnarled oak tree by the porch.

"Look Yarrow," Hannah pointed out the window to the birds making forays in and out of the branches. She had just brought her mother's oatmeal and coffee on a tray and set it on her ruined legs. "Your bluebirds."

"Are you giving them to me?" Yarrow smiled at her. Hannah's heart rose right up into her throat. Her hand felt an impulse to reach out for the smile, to hold on. If only a smile could be captured and kept in a box to be taken out to soothe her during those lonely times when the lines carved Yarrow's face into an image of sadness. Or better yet, if she could invest her mother's one smile to make it multiply into millions of smiles, she'd give her all the bluebirds. The moment spread out like spilled water and then evaporated. Yarrow picked up her spoon and dipped it into the oatmeal.

"They are already yours." Hannah said, but Yarrow was no longer paying attention.

"That cat's pregnant!" Yarrow pointed her finger at Ghost's belly. "Go pick her up! See! See how heavy and hard that belly is?" As springtime rounded into summer, Yarrow spent every afternoon on the porch, just watching, as though each leaf of the oak tree slowly shaping its lobes from the curl of buds were a classic theatrical production well worth her time. She watched James disk harrow the fields and plant the barley.

"Pregnant?" Hannah bent down and cupped her hand around the cat's belly where she felt the hardness and underneath it an unmistakable flutter. Kittens!

"She certainly is. You know, Hannah, your father may have overlooked the cat so far, but he can't miss a litter of kittens. You'll have to figure out a way to get rid of them."

"I'll give them away."

"Nobody needs more cats! And besides, cats and birds don't mix. If those bluebirds lay their eggs there in the oak, that cat will hunt them down, you mark my words."

Ghost lay curled on Hannah's lap, heavy with sleep and pregnancy. If she gave the cat enough food, Ghost wouldn't need to hunt. Hannah rested her hand on the cat's round belly where she now could see the movements of her kittens, and she wondered just how many there would be.

Ghost wandered up and down the yard, from the space behind the latticework where the ferns and lilies of the valley had begun to grow, to the hollow in the trunk of the old oak. She lay for a while behind the old rocker, and checked the space between three lilac bushes that Great-grandma Adeline planted way too close to the dining room windows so that every time storms riled up the wind they scratched and banged like a creature returned from the dead.

Hannah opened the door to the pantry and reached for the light cord, a brown string with a hard Bakelite knob on the end. She felt the slight resistance as she pulled and heard the click of the switch turning on the bare bulb high above her head. Jars of preserved vegetables and fruits lined the shelves that extended from floor to ceiling. Her father had somehow managed to put them up even though her mother had been gone. He also had begun to purchase canned goods at the grocery in town, easy to fix foods like Campbell soups. Hannah was looking for the cardboard box he'd brought home just last week. He had put it on a shelf without emptying it, and she set each can on the floor before she slid the box off the shelf. Then she arranged the store-bought goods in proper places on the shelves.

She took the box to the kitchen table and with the sharpest knife in the drawer she fashioned it into a cave, cutting diagonally into the cardboard on each side and then straight across about two-thirds of the way up. She brought the flaps over the top and taped them, forming a roof. Finally she dug through the trash bins in the shed to retrieve an old mattress pad Yarrow had told her to throw out the week before. Somehow she knew Ghost would prefer a softness that felt old, like rags, something that smelled a bit like sweat and breath and the skin of earth. She set the box on the porch beside the swing.

Two mornings later Ghost birthed four kittens as Hannah watched. The sun had just come up when she went out on the porch in her pajamas to peek into the cardboard cave. The first kitten must have just been born and the white mattress pad was smeared with blood. Ghost licked herself clean and then looked at Hannah who was sitting beside her cave and meowed as if to say it's about time you showed up. She lifted her head like she was stretching herself in the sun, and birthed the second kitten, and the third and forth, until they all were born. She ate the slimy red after-birth, licked the kittens clean and curled around them so they could blindly find their way to nurse.

For a week Hannah watched. She lifted the kittens from the nest, one by one, and held them in her hand, kissed each of them on its furry head and set it back with its mother. Ghost barely left her cardboard cave. Hannah borrowed a small white dish from Yarrow's kitchen and kept it filled with food, and the cat ate lying down, eating and nursing both at the same time. She drank water from the girl's hand. Hannah had never felt so large. She could feel the thing that Bonnie used to say the Last Days Christians felt when they were saved from hellfire and damnation; she felt full of God.

The bluebirds did build their nest in the big oak, high, where two branches formed a nook and a third branch had broken off years before to make a crevice in the wood. They carried bits of straw and tufts of moss. In the afternoon sun, the male bird shimmered. Hannah watched from the porch bench. Yarrow sat in the rocker, her legs covered with a granny square afghan, more to hide them than to keep them warm. The rockers squeaked as Yarrow mindlessly propelled the movement with the pressure of her feet against the porch floor. For the first time since the café burned down, Hannah felt a rightness and continuity about the world. Safety, she thought, could be restored even after you thought you'd lost it for good.

Just as thoughts of security were reaching down into her like tendrils reach to take root, the mother cat darted up the trunk of the big oak.

"No!" she yelled. "Ghost! Get down from there!"

"I told you," Yarrow said, her voice dulled by the exhaustion of one who has already lost so much that the additional loss of a bluebird can subtract nothing from the emptiness. "Cats and birds don't mix. That cat will get those bluebirds yet."

"She won't."

"It's her nature, Hannah. She has to teach those kittens how to hunt."

Hannah conceded this, but held to the illusion that Ghost would hunt mice, not birds. She ought to have prepared herself, but instead she argued for a benevolent universe in which what is loved is not taken away after all. She argued this despite the imprint of fire behind her eyes and the human pyre Wanda made. She wanted to work magic on the past and turn history back upon itself so that the things in her memory, real things, would never have happened at all. She was young enough, yet, to believe she had such power.

Consequently she was not prepared. From the window Hannah saw Ghost on the path that led to the field. Something looked odd.

She went to the kitchen door and opened the screen. She sensed the need to sneak up on the cat. She walked on tiptoe. Closer and closer. Stop. The thing in Ghost's mouth dragged on the ground. The cat didn't scamper off even now that Hannah stood so near. She sat on her haunches at the edge of the field and applied herself to her kill. Wings splayed from the headless catch. Brown wings spreading from that dusty blue back. She ate quickly but deliberately with a detachment that raised in Hannah a kind of horror at the ease with which a living creature could become another creature's food. But she didn't think of the bluebird as food, but as another mother, snatched from the nest, where even now her babies cried for her. The cat tore at the bird's body and Hannah heard the crunch of tiny bones as she chewed, and then the softer crunch of feathers. She watched it all, too stunned to wonder at the sort of world she occupied. In a moment the bird had been consumed and the cat lay, satiated, in the warm afternoon sun. Suddenly Hannah hated each moment she'd spent feeling the cat's soft fur against her hand, the cat's head burrowed up under her chin. She hated that she had let the cat stay, that she had fostered four monster kittens, that very moment sleeping under the lilac bush. Hannah hated nature or God or whatever thought up the horrific laws that place life and death so close to one another they could not be separated, and then somehow made her feel responsible for an outcome that was inevitable.

For the remainder of that day Hannah's mind crouched before the memory of Ghost eating the bluebird and waited for the image to yield up some reasonable explanation. That everything is food for every other thing, she would not accept. That a mother will do whatever is necessary to make herself strong enough to nurse her young was also unacceptable because, in this case, such a law would pit one mother against another. She held off the suspicion she could feel gathering force in her mind that life is random, and reasons for the terrors it serves up do not exist. She opened store bought soup for supper and sulked when her father asked her if that's all they were going to eat.

~~~

Yarrow and James were listening to Lux Radio Theater when

Hannah slammed the screen door just to find out if anyone would say, "Come back," and walked slowly in the silence to the cottonwood by the creek. She waited to be found. She leaned against the hard bark of the tree and looked up at the stars that didn't really kiss the head of anyone. If only she could hold Raggedy Lily in her arms again, but the doll was burned up just like everything else. Just like the blue quilt that made a map of someone's entire life. Just like Wanda. Just like Yarrow. She started to imagine dying in the Pine Cone Café. If she'd stayed with Wanda instead of jumping with Yarrow, then someone else would make Yarrow's breakfast and someone else would listen to her dull voice that no longer sang about the wind.

The constellations moved across the sky and no one called her name. In the living room and then upstairs in the Olson farmhouse the lights went out and she rocked herself back and forth to the sounds of her own humming, "Song of our lives forever free," until she fell asleep.

~~~

A red-winged blackbird rocked on a cattail at the creek's edge and announced the morning. Something that wasn't Hannah opened her eyes and slipped out of her, leaving her asleep under the cottonwood tree. She became a shadow on the grass that no one else could see. Something else ran toward her father's house and it had her legs and her breath, and her heart pounded in its chest.

Something slammed the kitchen door and sat down at the table. It watched Hannah's father carry Yarrow from the guest room and put her in the chair by the window.

"Hannah, fix some oatmeal for your mother." He said.

"I'm not Hannah." Though it was good to hear him call her something, finally, other than just Girl.

"I don't have time for games. Just fix the oatmeal." He picked up the coffee pot. "Didn't you make coffee yet?" But he didn't wait for her to answer. Instead he began to spoon coffee grounds into the pot.

Something measured half a cup of thick flakes and added a cup and a half of cold water. Hannah's mother liked it cooked that way, creamy, with the oats substantial on her tongue. Something cooked it less than half the time indicated on the box and poured it into her blue bowl, sprinkled brown sugar over the top and slathered it with thick cream. Hannah's father drank a cup of his coffee poured from the big blue enameled pot and went to the fields without another word.

"Who are you, then?" Yarrow spoke softly when Something set the tray with oatmeal and a cup of coffee on the lap her ruined legs still made.

"Something." Maybe she was the blackbird perched over the shadow of Hannah. The girl laid the green and white checked napkin next to the tray.

"What happened to Hannah?" Yarrow lifted her coffee cup to her mouth and sipped. She examined her daughter above the rim, and then set it down again on the tray. From outside the window came the grumble of James's tractor.

"She won't wake up."

"Is she in bed?"

"No."

"Where then?" Yarrow began to reach out to her daughter, but something stopped her, an invisible but tangible veil of unreality that seemed to have fallen between them.

"By the creek, under the cottonwood." The girl acted like this was the most normal conversation in the world. Yarrow shivered.

"Alone?" she said.

"No." The girl went back to the stove for the blue coffee pot. She filled her mother's cup. "There's a red-winged blackbird watching her," she said, just as calm as she could be.

"I guess it's as good a place as any, then." Yarrow murmured, picking up her spoon. "But who might you be?"

"I'm Redwing," and only as she said the name did she know it was the truth. Redwing had been her name for a long time, ever since she'd perched on the windowsill of the Pine Cone Café. Ever since Wanda and her mother pushed her and she cried out as she flew.

The one who was not Hannah paid no more attention to Ghost or her kittens, and one day when she lifted the branches of the lilac bush and looked underneath, all of them were gone. She didn't care one way or the other. Hannah had been foolish to feel the way she did about a stupid cat. Hannah's heart had been way too soft.

Hannah couldn't do the things that Redwing had to do. She had tried. She just couldn't. She couldn't wash clothes. She couldn't cook meals. She especially couldn't put the bedpan under Yarrow when she did her job. Hannah couldn't empty what came out of Yarrow. The smell of it made her cry. Redwing put the doctor's salve on Yarrow's new skin, the patches on her shoulder, on her breasts where it pulled and puckered.

"You shouldn't have to do this, Hannah." Yarrow said.

"It's okay." Yarrow kept forgetting Hannah was asleep. She should have known Hannah was too much of a baby to keep doing these things even if she shouldn't have to. Redwing could do it. If Hannah couldn't be good enough to keep the cat from eating the bluebird; how could anyone expect her to be good enough to care for Yarrow? You had to be good and do everything just right no matter how you felt. Terrible things happen when a child isn't good.

Hannah's father continued to work outside or at the big roll-top desk where he subtracted the cost of seed from the selling price of ripe grain. He kept the radio tuned to WCCO and charted the ups and downs at the grain exchange. He ate whatever Redwing put on his plate, whether it was pork chops or macaroni, and soaked up every speck of food and gravy with a piece of bread. Redwing could have put his plate right back into the cupboard without washing it if she were still a child and not the only responsible woman of the house. Sometimes he said "Good meal, Girl," and gave her a little pat on the top of her head.

~ ~ ~

James watched the girl make her mother's oatmeal. She stood on the little yellow stool by the stove and wore an apron way too big for her. He watched her lug the sheets to the washing machine and saw how she protected her eyes like a frog, with a membrane nearly invisible. He watched her empty her mother's bedpan. He watched her draw a basin of warm water and carry it into her mother's room, closing the door behind her.

"The girl needs help," he told the wife.

It was a Sunday in August with heat that crawls down your back like chiggers from a cut field. He had just carried her downstairs and set her in the chair by the window. Her hair had grown out more and wisped around her face reminding him of how she looked when they were in grade school.

"I think so, too," she said.

He had expected an argument, some reticence on her part, some reluctance to be seen, to be touched by somebody other than family.

"I could get Ida Gunderson." A surge of energy accompanied the name. He looked up at the wife wondering if she had noticed.

"Ida Gunderson? Isn't she related to you somehow?" Probably her eyelashes never would grow back. Her eyes, questioning him, seemed vulnerable. Naked. "Oh, I remember. It's her husband, isn't it? That lost uncle of yours, that Ste. Germaine boy the Gunderson's adopted—Steve." He'd been relieved that Yarrow remembered the connection which by linking him with Ida might also cast her in a family role—objective and at the same time duty-bound. "Does she do that sort of thing?" Yarrow asked.

"I had her Fridays, those years you were gone." With enough concentration he could keep his voice smooth and detached. The effort annoyed him, like having to pick up and finish a task that rightly belongs to someone else.

"Well, then…" She looked away from him and back out into the fields.

"I'll call her later, then." He still was testing her, examining her for the slightest suspicion about his actual involvement with Ida. Wary with words anyway, he could hardly believe how few of them it took to construct a lie.

She merely nodded.

The next Friday, Ida sat on the sofa, the wife in her chair and James in his. Yarrow stared straight out at Ida who kept her eyes lowered. Her cheeks flushed pink.

"There's the house, but James tells me you know the house." Yarrow spoke in a business-like tone.

"Yes." Ida glanced up but didn't smile.

"You can handle that, then?"

"I used to do it once a week."

"There'll be more now, I'm afraid. Hannah's off to school in a few weeks, and James can help me up to a point. But there are things…"

"Of course…"

"Things a woman prefers her husband not be burdened with."

"I understand."

"Hannah's been very good, as much as a girl can."

"I'm sure."

"But there are other things, things she shouldn't have to..."

"I understand, Yarrow. I'll help however I can."

James was left out of it. He watched them stitch themselves together into one piece.

Mornings, after the school bus picked up the girl, he drove off to fetch Ida, bringing her home with him straight away. Whatever the wife needed, Ida did. All the washings and the salves. The bowel movements and the blood times. She fussed with her, making her pretty, keeping her clean. One morning about ten o'clock he heard her singing through the closed bedroom door. Later that afternoon, on their way back to her place, he asked about it.

"Oh," she said, "it was nothing. Just a little lullaby while I washed her back. It distracts her from what she knows I'm seeing there."

James smothered whatever qualms he retained about his love of Ida, even though the wife had returned. Over the months the two women in his house became one wife and he learned to give himself to each facet of that wife differently.

Before the snow fell he and Ida found places outdoors. Almost every afternoon, driving her back to her house, he stopped somewhere. One day it might be the little shelter of trees by the creek, another, the hayloft in the barn. Once she picked an autumn flower blooming where she lay. "I watched this flower the whole time you were inside me and I'm going to save it to remember."

Oh, the sun on her hair!

Her breasts in a mist of rain.

If she'd never come to him, he could have lived without her; but as it was he needed her, every single day.

Later he would wonder why he hadn't considered her husband in all of this, but he hadn't. And she never spoke of him at all.

Later he would ask himself why he hadn't been noticing the girl, but she'd become so quiet he barely knew she was home. And when he did say anything to her she frowned and turned away. Girls must go through something growing up that fathers can't fathom.

As October gave way to November even the hayloft was too cold. There was almost no discussion. Ida closed the door on the wife's room after putting her in bed for a nap. She took his hand, and they went together upstairs into the big bedroom and took off their clothes.

Surely the wife heard. If nothing else there was the grinding of the bedsprings. Once he groaned so deep and loud that he startled even himself and Ida placed her hand over his mouth. But the wife said nothing and he took this for assent. He took it for understanding, a kind of sympathy on her part for his situation, even a form of gratitude that Ida would be willing to assist her to this extent.

When Ida's strong hands caressed his back, and when she rubbed his body with warm oil, he imagined her doing the same for the wife in the other bedroom downstairs behind that other closed door. And he fancied himself a generous lord of that house, prodigal with his most precious possessions.

We love as we can, James consoled himself. We seek love where it might be found. There could be no other explanation.

Yarrow gave up her body's secrets to Ida during those sessions in the guest bedroom when Ida bathed and oiled her body, and later when Ida's fingers massaged her scars and her paralyzed legs. The first time the other woman touched her, the pain shot straight up and lodged behind her eyes. Yarrow gasped, then she cried out for her to stop.

"Get your hands off me!" Her body jerked on the bed the way it does when you fall out of a dream.

Ida's hands lifted immediately.

"I'm sorry, Yarrow," she said. "I didn't know it would hurt."

"Everything hurts."

Yarrow couldn't bring herself to tell Ida at first that the nerves, all crazy, shooting this way and that, burning, accounted for the least of the pain. The touch brought back Wanda, the loss of Wanda.

After that, for weeks, Ida always asked. "May I touch your shoulder, Yarrow? Just with this warm water, just lightly?" And Yarrow could steel herself, prepared for whatever might come. But it was months before she relaxed, before she closed her eyes and allowed herself to feel the touch of Ida, and through that touch to feel the memory of Wanda and everything the two of them had been and all they had lost.

She knew Ida left her and went to James. She heard their sounds. At first she felt glad Ida had taken up that burden, and that she need not feel responsible anymore for such wifely duties. But as time passed and she memorized the sounds coming from the upstairs room, she began to feel a longing for a James she hadn't previously known, a James whom Ida was able to summon in the act of love. Then she turned to the memory of Wanda. She cupped her scarred breasts in her hands, as she listened to Ida's moans, and imagined Wanda's kisses and soft tongue on her puckered skin. She cried with the memories and whispered to Wanda's ghost, "I'm sorry; I'm sorry. I killed you, Wanda, and I'm sorry."

Once when Ida bathed her and then lingered over the oiling of her body, being gentle with the scars that laced the skin on her breasts, smoothing that skin, a sob welled up so large that Yarrow thought it might split her apart.

"I killed her, Ida. I killed her." She moaned and felt the muscles under her skin tighten.

"Who? Who could you have killed?" Ida continued to touch her, not breaking contact, and Yarrow felt the warmth of those hands drawing her deeper and deeper into memory.

"Wanda. I killed Wanda."

"How could you have killed her? She died in the fire."

She knew that Ida meant to gentle her, murmuring the words as one would murmur to a child waking up from a nightmare.

"I caused the fire." Yarrow blurted it out.

"How could you have done that?" she said, so calm.

"By leaving here. By leaving and going to her. If I hadn't been there, no one would have known about her—what she was. Both of us. What we were." Yarrow's voice felt out of control, rising in pitch, close to panic.

"No, no, no," Ida murmured, "No. Dearest Yarrow, no. You loved her." Her hands stroked from the center of Yarrow's back, coaxing her muscles to relax their tight hold and encouraged Yarrow to lie flat on her chest. She stroked and stroked from the center of her back out to her fingers and then she shook her hands as if to cast away some dark spirit that she'd found clinging to Yarrow's skin.

~~~

Until she met Wanda, Yarrow knew nothing about women loving women. It just never occurred to her. When she married James and when Hannah was conceived, she loved him. She never forgot the feel of him inside her and she would always swear she knew the moment their cells united and created Hannah. Nothing could make her forget the longing her body held for him. Neither could she forget the longing of her mind. She wanted his words, but not just any words. She wanted words as a container for his soul. Maybe, at the time she left him, he didn't know he had a soul.

With Wanda souls came first.

About a week after she and Hannah arrived at Red Pine, Wanda and Yarrow were sitting together in the cafe. She'd turned the little sign in the window to announce that she was closed. They sat in one of the booths and Yarrow told her about James, trying to explain why she had left him.

"He always looked away when I talked to him." She remembered saying. She looked Wanda straight in the eyes and the other woman didn't flinch.

"Men do that. It's the intimacy. Makes them nervous." Wanda said.

"Do you think all men?" Yarrow felt the intensity of Wanda's eyes that contained gold flecks and a burst of deep amber dissolving into green.

"Maybe not all." Wanda reached out across the table and took Yarrow's hand in hers. "All I've ever known do, though. Only time they really look at you is when they're trying to get you into bed, and then it's that arrogant, I've-got-something-you'll-really-like sort of look."

Yarrow laughed. She knew Wanda wasn't completely serious, but just talking released something pent up that she'd been holding onto for a long time.

"Women now," Wanda smiled and her eyes gleamed with mischief, "women are different."

"Women are easy to talk to." Yarrow remembered how she thought this was Wanda's meaning.

"More than that…" Wanda's hand moved lightly across

Yarrow's.

Yarrow's mind drained itself of words. She looked at Wanda whose eyes locked with her own in a way that went beyond the flecks of gold and the bursts of amber and green. She felt a spring of clear water begin to ooze out of dark ground. For just an instant she thought of looking away, but such avoidance was the very method James had used on her, so she didn't look away. She let Wanda see into her eyes, into herself. A silence, nothing at all like the silence of James, claimed both women and bound them. It became a binding so firm that they understood they would never be separate again.

Whoever it was burned down her café, that person just didn't understand that love is love and the imagination people have for expressing love is boundless. Wanda kissed Yarrow first on a moonless night under the big pine in the park at the center of town. And that kiss released every desire Yarrow ever felt for James and more. Desire welled up in her like Cold Creek in April when it swells over its banks and floods the Olson fields with rich black Dakota earth. She didn't even try to stop her tears, and while she cried she thought of ancient women in some other world where such love could be lived in the full light of day. But in the world she and Wanda inhabited, not even a moonless night could be dark enough to hide what Yarrow had begun to realize about Wanda and herself.

"Oh Wanda, what are we going to do?" she had whispered.

"What we need to do."

The two women had walked for a long time up and down the dark streets. It must have been three in the morning when they climbed the stairs of the café to her bedroom. Yarrow remembered how she could hear Hannah's even breathing where she still slept on the couch under the window. Wanda lit a candle and undressed slowly. She unpinned her pale curls and her hair fell over her breasts. Yarrow thought of a poem she once read that had embarrassed her, something about seeing my lady naked in her hair.

Wanda moved like smoke curling around Yarrow's body. She learned from her to be a gentle wind. She learned to be rain. And all the while Wanda's eyes sought hers in the candlelight. It was an intercourse of eyes. A mingling of souls. And when their bodies shuddered as their fingers drew out the wet thread of pleasure, Wanda's eyes closed and she whispered, "I waited a long time for you, Yarrow. A long, long time."

~~~

Ida listened to Yarrow's story, bits of it here, tears and sighs there, as she touched her body, smoothing out the pain. "No love is wrong," Ida told her softly. "No love is complete. And every love is dangerous."

6

In September Hannah's cattails puffed into ragged cotton balls that hung like stuffing from an old sofa and tore apart in the wind. When Redwing walked past her shadow on the grass she sighed. Cottonwood leaves whirled and settled on the creek. Redwing sat down a ways from where Hannah fell asleep and counted the ones that drowned in the current. Not everything survives. Some things shouldn't.

The first two weeks after she fell asleep under the cottonwood, Redwing came almost every day to talk to her. "Hannah," she would say, "Yarrow smiled this afternoon." Or "James and Yarrow made up, Hannah. He said he's sorry about the black scum in the sink. He said he'd scour all the sinks himself from now on." None of it was true. It wasn't that Redwing forgot about her or ever could forget about her. But under her shadow on the grass she fell deeper and deeper into a sleep Redwing couldn't penetrate with words. Instead she watched the leaves that rode the current to where the creek turned east and disappeared from sight.

The red-winged blackbirds left their cattail perch and the Canada geese followed them in the long V moving south. At night the girl stood far from the creek in the stubble of James's wheat field and watched the Northern Lights curtain the stars. Snow fell after that and covered Hannah, because by then the girl had begun to think of that shadow on the grass as a grave with Hannah buried so deep that even if she were to cry her name in the blackbird's startling call, Hannah wouldn't hear a thing.

In thick dreams Hannah and Wanda rose together from an earth molten with fire. They curled around the girl's head, keening. Redwing wanted to lean against their song, but it was made of smoke and she always passed through it, breathless, falling, a bird with fiery wings. She fell with fear of the ground beneath her, of its sheen like glass. But it opened like water. It received her like a hand that opens and then closes.

Each morning she woke to reconstruct herself from wisps of things remembered, a thorn from the bush with red berries, the summer wind in the cottonwood.

Whenever Redwing touched Yarrow she moaned. Hannah would have cried to hear it. Hannah had a pit in her belly full of tears and snot that swirled and rose up her body like vomit. She would have run to the toilet with a gagging sound that might have been a word stuck in her throat. It might have been her hopes turned sour, turned to damnation in her chest.

To save her mother, Redwing could close her ears to pain.

"Please, Hannah. Just because I can't get myself out of this chair, it doesn't mean I've stopped being your mother. I didn't lose my mind, either, when I lost everything else except for you. And sometimes I wonder about you."

"I'm not Hannah." The girl reminded her as calmly as she could.

"Well, that's the truth!" Yarrow sighed and turned her face away.

It was just like jumping out that window all over again. The girl felt the breath knocked right out of her. Yarrow had agreed. She said it's true, you really are not Hannah anymore. The girl stared at her mother. Wasn't it her own right to say who she was—Hannah or some other? Yarrow had no rights in this. The girl herself should be the one to say "I'm not Hannah." Yarrow, as her mother, was supposed to argue for her existence.

Yarrow huffed her breath out in a little burst and didn't look back at her daughter.

I am, I am Hannah. Her bones cried it out. Her skull rang with it. I am Hannah. But from her mouth there came no sound. Redwing clamped her jaw down tight and squinted her eyelashes over black dots of eyes.

I hate you! She heard the words inside her head and breathed through clenched teeth. Such words must never be spoken. I wish you were dead, the voice clattered all over the inside of her head like hail. Whom did she hate? Who should be dead? *Ku nam wi cu.*

Yarrow stared out the window at James who was plowing, and the girl wondered if one person could know what another kept behind her teeth, inside the darkness of her own skull.

The only one who took the girl seriously and remembered to call her Redwing was Hannah's Gran. She hadn't changed a titch since Yarrow ran away to Red Pine, still sitting in her oak rocker and plucking at her old afghan, still smelling of urine and stale ashes. James would drop Hannah off and go down to the vacant lot beside Murphy's Grocery to play horseshoes. He didn't care how long she took. "It's good of you to do this," he told her each time she climbed down from the truck in front of the Pioneer Home.

"Here, girl." Gran's voice rasped like grating a turnip. "Let me look at you."

She let her great grandmother turn her around.

"You've grown up." The old woman held her by the shoulders and gave her a little shake that the girl took to mean "good for you!"

"Yes ma'am. I was ten last summer; I just finished fifth grade."

Gran pulled at the girl's sleeve where it was caught under the strap of her overalls. "Girls ought to wear dresses," she said. "Still and all, your mother and father must be proud of you."

"I hope so, ma'am."

"They should tell you. They don't tell you? I always said I should have told my Joseph more often what a good boy he was. James and Yarrow—they ought to tell you, Hannah."

"I'm not Hannah." With eyes beady as a hawk's, or so she imagined, she dared the old woman to disagree.

Gran cackled. "So that's it, is it?"

"What?" The unexpected response threw the girl off her game and deposited her into Gran's well-honed control.

"Who is it standing here, then, if it's not my Hannah?" She gave the girl's cheek a little pat with her dry hand.

"Redwing." She whispered it so that it sounded, unintentionally, like an apology.

"Aha. Redwing is it? That's a bird's name. Doesn't seem to suit you." Gran stared her straight in the eye.

"I don't know about that, ma'am." She put her hands behind her back and looked at her feet.

"And I'm not ma'am," she said. "If you can't bring yourself to call me Gran the way my Hannah used to, then the name Addie would suit me just fine." She put her bony hand under the girl's chin and lifted her face so that the child could see the kindness there.

After that it seemed to the girl that she shared a secret with her great grandmother, and Addie turned out to be her best friend.

"You know," Addie said to her one Sunday, "Yarrow and James are pretty young to be suffering this affliction."

"They're thirty-seven!" An age that seemed prehistoric.

"Thirty-seven's young. And all that sorrow. It's no wonder Hannah didn't want to stay." Addie sighed and shook her head.

"It made her cry."

Addie bent her head and looked hard at her from under wiry eyebrows.

"You're the stronger part, aren't you?"

"But I can't take care of everyone." She suddenly realized it was true.

"Of course not." Addie agreed.

"Hannah couldn't even take care of herself."

"She needed a mother." Addie shook her head and began nibbling at the inside of her cheek as though she were pondering how to solve this need.

"I can't do it because I have to be Yarrow's mother." The girl reminded the old woman.

"Hannah needs a mother of her own." Addie said.

"Yarrow couldn't be her mother anymore, and Wanda died." The explanation knotted something inside the girl's head.

"In the fire?" Addie asked, frowning.

"Yes." The word exploded in a burst of wind.

"Hannah saw that?" Addie put her cool hand on the girl's cheek and whispered.

"Hannah saw her burning." The girl also whispered and felt herself looking back at the fire through the eyes of someone else. Despite this distance, it seemed she felt the heat on her face and the ice under her back.

"Poor child." Addie motioned for her to come closer, to sit on her bony knees, and she hugged the girl just in case Hannah might be close enough to feel the safety of her arms.

~~~

Christmas came. James took the girl out to cut a tree and Ida helped with the decorations while the wife sat in her chair unwrapping glass balls and handing them, one by one, to be hung on the branches. My women, James thought. Even of the girl he thought that. Afterwards they sang carols and Ida made Tom and Jerry's. It would have been easy to forget she lived anywhere else but at the Olson farm.

But on Christmas day she didn't come over. Steve needed her at home, she said.

And she didn't come the next day either or any day until the girl returned to school in January.

"It was nothing," she murmured when James picked her up, but he could see she had been crying.

The wife smiled at Ida when James brought her into the house. The three of them took the tree down, Ida and James doing the climbing and the removal of ornaments, and the wife wrapping them one by one. He fit them all into the big box and carried them out to the garage while Ida tidied the room and fixed sandwiches for lunch.

"I'd like to stay here in the Christmas room for today." The wife gazed out the window at the pearl sky of January. "You two go ahead with your day."

That this didn't feel strange to him is a measure of how far he thought they had come together.

When he and Ida climbed the stairs, they could hear the wife humming that old lullaby she used to sing.

He undressed her carefully for she had been bruised. He kissed each bruise and wept for the beauty of her. He knew himself to be a man not good with words, but how he wanted to be able to tell them, these women, what being caught between them had done to him. His heart felt large, like seeds expanding under soil. His hands felt tender and warm with a heat that flowed into them from somewhere so deep in him that he couldn't follow it to its source.

"I don't want to hurt you." James looked into Ida's eyes and they were deeper than the night sky.

"You never do."

"The bruises…"

"It will be all right."

He reached into her as into a holy being. Once she had seemed to him as the earth itself. And now it felt to him as though earth had become, because of her, a goddess.

They made love, or more precisely, they created it. He entered her reverently, slowly, moving in and out of her. He heard her gasp, and he felt a constant shimmer of pleasure that spun through both their bodies. A pulsing began at the base of his spine and flowed, spreading out, up his body and out the top of his head. He cried out.

They lay exhausted on the bed. James listened to Ida's breath against his ear, and from downstairs the sound of the wife, still singing.

The morning Ida came out to the barn to tell James about the baby it was February, a Sunday, close to Valentine's Day. She rarely came at all on Sundays because the girl was home. On that day both the girl and the wife had been sitting at the kitchen table pasting paper doilies and red construction paper hearts on a shoebox when he went out to do some chores. A blade of sunlight angled through the barn door onto some bales and she stood in it saying James.

"James?"

He looked up and thought she seemed an apparition such as Catholics claim to have of an angel or saint.

"It might be his. At least he'll think it's his," he told her afterwards, his arm around her, her head leaning on his chest like a child's might.

"I hope."

"He will."

James seldom thought of it, of Steve and Ida together, and it shook him to have to bring it up at such a time. Even with the evidence of him in her bruises, James had kept himself from the thought of that bastard as her husband. Family connection there might be, but the Olson's disowned him a long time ago and were the better for it. Steve Gunderson seemed a force against her innocence. To James she seemed innocence itself, the primal innocence of nature, simply existing like the fields.

He kissed her, a tender kiss salty with her tears.

As the months wore on and she swelled like fruit with their child. Ida arrived each weekday morning as she had done before. She and the wife whispered and laughed like sisters now. One noon James came in from the fields and saw the wife leaning out from her new wheelchair, her arms around Ida's waist and her head against Ida's round belly, listening. If it could be like this, he thought, the three of them and the girl and the baby. He wanted to go up to them and kiss them both. He wondered if the wife would allow that.

"Oh, James," Ida turned to him, "you're here already."

She brought sandwiches to the table and he ate his quietly while the women jabbered on of babies and other close-in things.

It was summer so the girl ate with them that noon, keeping herself as quiet as he did.

The child came early, in September, 1949, a girl, born in Grand Forks. They'd put her in an incubator at the big hospital there. Ida called him as soon as possible after the birth.

"She looks for all the world like you, James."

"Still it could be his," he tried to relieve the fear he heard in her voice. "Same Ste. Germaine blood."

What did he think would happen? He went about his chores. Maybe he thought she would bring the baby to the farm, and all of them would live happily ever after. Maybe he didn't think at all. Harvest time was on him. The wife could get about pretty well on her own by then and the girl helped after school. A week passed. Two weeks. Then the call came.

"Mr. Olson?"

"Yes."

"This is Mrs. Enge at the hospital in Grand Forks. Your baby is ready to go home, Mr. Olson."

"My baby?"

"Yes, she's ready for you to take her home."

"There must be some mistake."

"I don't think so. It's your name listed as next of kin. Mr. Gunderson's nephew, I believe."

"What about Ida?" He felt panic starting up.

"The mother? I don't understand, Mr. Olson. The mother is deceased."

"What?" Implosion. He collapsed like a barn falling in on itself. Like a sinkhole in the field.

"I'm sorry. How could you not have known? She began hemorrhaging not long after the birth. She'd seemed fine. She was back in her room and had bled out too severely before we got to her. Mr. Gunderson gave up rights to the child. You are next of kin; his nephew, I understand This must be terrible news, Mr. Olson. Someone ought to have contacted you immediately. "

He looked up from the phone at the wife who sat in her wheelchair, her eyes full of questions.

"Dead." He groaned. "Ida's dead."

The wife motioned to him and he went to her, his knees buckling, all the life in him seeming to run out, sobs rising up, his voice moaning, "Ida, Ida," like a child's voice. And his wife holding his head on her lap, stroking his hair, murmuring. "You go ahead and cry, James. Just cry. We loved her. We loved Ida so much."

That afternoon James laid the infant on his wife's ruined legs.

"We'll call her Emily," she said. He would have called her Ida but for the hurt that name might cause. His wife would have called her Wanda, he supposed, but didn't for much the same reason.

"Emily." He touched the infant's downy head. "Come here, girl, and meet your sister."

Hannah stood back. There'd been too much; she hadn't grown into it yet.

Too much for all of them.

We don't know what it will require, he thought as he looked down into the tiny face. We can't foresee all we'll have to take in. All the stretching and the marks left on us, just to make us large enough. He could see that Emily's face mirrored his own with just faint shadows of Ida, mostly in expression. Her smile. Little lines between her eyebrows when she stared intently into your face. It came to him that each glimpse of Emily would forever be like Ida's shadow passing over him, eclipsing his heart.

"We've all had our losses," his wife murmured as if to the baby, and James reached down and squeezed her hand.

~~~

Winter passed into spring and rain fell on the fields steady and soft. Yarrow watched Hannah who stood in the green barley, its heads just forming, its tips feathering. Between Yarrow and Hannah, the window. Between them the infinite distance from Red Pine.

So young. Her daughter's body stretched tall with the quick growth of a twelve-year-old, but not yet curving into the form of a woman. If only Yarrow could reach her. She woke from a dream of fire to find her lost. Losing herself, she lost Hannah too. She remembered now the way Hannah came to her, those little hands on her wounds. She remembered her tears, her whispers. "Yarrow, sing the forever free song." But Yarrow couldn't sing. Instead, Hannah sang to her, her voice the voice of a bird or of summer wind through the Red Pine. Hannah fed her oatmeal and hummed Yarrow's lullaby. Then one day she stopped singing and she was lost.

"What were you doing out in the rain?" Yarrow asked her in a voice more harsh than she had intended. The girl was dripping wet. Drops clung to her eyelashes and she didn't wipe them away.

"Nothing." She responded in that infuriatingly adolescent way.

"Surely you had some reason..." Yarrow said, trying to make her voice gentle.

"No."

In the next room the baby cried.

"Get Emily for me, would you, Hannah?"

She turned and left without a word.

The doctors insisted there was no physical reason for Yarrow not to walk. Her bones had healed, though her burns would always lace across her body in their spider way. Perhaps she simply didn't want to walk. But if that were so, she didn't know it. Her mind said walk. Just stand up, Yarrow, said her mind. Just do it! Ida used to say to let it be. She said Yarrow would walk when she was good and ready.

If only she could walk to Wanda...

But that was a thought leading nowhere but into the dark night.

Hannah brought Emily and laid her on Yarrow's lap.

"I changed her." The baby cooed and waved her arms and legs. Outside, the sounds of rain against the windowpanes, running from the eaves and into tiny rivulets toward Cold Creek.

"Good, Hannah. You're becoming quite the little mother." She said as she lifted the baby to her shoulder to feel the soft fuzz of baby hair against her neck.

"Redwing." Hannah said.

"Yes. I forgot."

Her daughter lowered her eyes.

Emily kicked her little legs with more determination. Yarrow gave the baby her finger and she held on. "Look Hannah!"

"I gotta go."

"Yes, dear. You go have fun."

"Here's the bottle. She'll fall asleep after."

"Thank you, Hannah. You have a good time. Take an umbrella."

Mother and daughter spoke in code. Hannah's eyes would not meet her own. Yarrow felt her pull against the cord that held them inseparable.

Wanda and Ida, both dead and Hannah lost. Well, Yarrow was lost too, wasn't she? What was left of her? A ruined woman sitting by the window staring at the fields. Remembering. Where are they? She asked the green barley. She asked the bluebirds. She asked the rain. In a place unknown. Heaven, some say. Others might say both Wanda and Ida burn forever for their sins. Heaven. Hell. Insanity. Yarrow had thought about that, don't think she hadn't, thought both she and Hannah came up from the fire insane, their minds melted. Sometimes she remembered the fairy tales she read to Hannah when she was small. She remembered magic curses that changed people into birds, and the work required to knit garments to throw over their wings. Sometimes Yarrow spent all afternoon knitting in her mind. From memories of Wanda she spun a strand of yarn. She spun of Ida another strand. And of herself she spun a third. They wound around each other, three-ply yarn, and from this Yarrow imagined she would knit new life. Perhaps she thought that if she could construct a garment strong enough, she could throw it over Hannah like a spell to bring her back, release her from what had begun to seem her destined flight.

Perhaps she called their spirits back into her life, or perhaps she only opened herself to a presence that never left her. She began hearing their voices on the day old Sarah arrived at the door with a wild berry pie.

Yarrow had seen her off at the edges of the woods ever since she was a child. She had heard the woman sing, just as Hannah used to hear her sing and asked about her—who she was, where she came from. Yarrow had asked the same questions as a child and was told that the woman lived on an old piece of Murdock land, a useless bit of woods filled with gooseberry brambles and stinging nettle. Yarrow's grandmother told her the woman was a squatter. Uncle Ancil said she was a witch. Actually, she'd bought the land and built her little cottage with her own hands.

That day she came to the door Yarrow could smell the wild berry pie. Hannah had run off somewhere as was common then. James must have been in the fields or barn, and Emily, down for her nap. Yarrow smelled the wild berries, warm as they were when Wanda used to take them from the oven, warm and thick with sugar. You could smell the sugar mixed with tart purple juice. Yarrow smelled the berries as she heard Sarah knock at the kitchen door of the farmhouse.

"You'll have to just come on in," she yelled out towards the kitchen from the living room where her chair was placed as usual by the window. "Door's open."

She never would forget the sight of her, standing in the doorway between the kitchen and living room, red shot through with gray hair flying. The woman was wearing Yarrow's hat with the blue feather, the one she had lost that night she took Hannah and ran away to Red Pine.

"I brought your hat," Sarah told her. "And a pie. I hope you like wild berry pie. This one's quite a combination. Blueberries, gooseberries, those tiny wild raspberries you find growing in the grass, and some juice from the chokecherries out along the creek."

How could Yarrow say what wild berry pie meant to her? She couldn't. She would need words not yet thought up, sounds never yet made by a human voice.

"How kind of you," she said.

She went on about picking the berries and knowing as they fell into the basket that she'd be making them into a pie for Yarrow Olson. She didn't apologize for not visiting in all the time since Yarrow had been home—several years by then. Most people would have bent over backwards with excuses for not having done the expected thing.

"How about if I make some coffee and cut a piece of pie for the both of us?" Sarah said just as if she'd been Yarrow's best friend and knew her kitchen like the back of her hand. Such familiarity startled Yarrow enough to draw her right into it and she said, "Fine, Sarah. That would be really nice."

"Good enough," Sarah said to her, and then took the hat off her head and laid it in Yarrow's lap. "I expect you're happy to see this again. I knew the time would come when I'd bring it back."

"This is amazing. I thought it was gone for good." Yarrow said as she rubbed her finger along the blue feather.

"Hardly anything's ever gone for good." Sarah laughed and then disappeared into the kitchen to slice the wild berry pie.

"I've heard you singing." Yarrow slid her fork under the flaky crust and then deposited the first bite of pie on her tongue. Oh, the sweetness of it. Oh, summer!

"You hear me? I suppose you do. Do you hear me howl, too?"

"Howl?"

Sarah laughed again. "I call it howling. It's as the dogs hear it, I imagine, because they answer me. Ancil Murdock's hunting hounds? I sing. They howl." Her black eyes twinkled. "I expect you've heard it, Yarrow, and didn't know I was part of the chorus!"

"I don't have much to do with Ancil." Yarrow took the last bite of her pie. "That was delicious, Sarah. I don't know how to thank you."

"No thanks required." Sarah took her plate and washed it along with her own. "I'll leave the whole tin so Hannah and James can have some." She rummaged in the long drawer by the sink and pulled out a dishtowel. "I'll just set it here on the counter and cover it to keep out the flies. They're really thick this year, don't you think?"

The two women spoke a while of careful things—the crops, the way the creek was high. Then, when Sarah got up to leave, Yarrow picked up the blue hat. "I don't expect I'll be needing this, Sarah. You found it; why don't you keep it?"

"I did always like that hat." She took it from her hands and gave the blue feather a little flick with her finger before putting it back on her head. "I do thank you, Yarrow. You're very generous."

Yarrow watched through the window as Sarah walked up the road between the Olson and the Murdock farms. She watched the blue feather until every trace of the hat disappeared into the woods.

It must have been the taste of wild berry pie that brought Wanda's spirit. She must have drifted on the taste and scent of wild berry pie right into the house, for that night in bed as Yarrow lay thinking about Hannah and how she kept on flying off, Wanda came.
Shhhh.
Yarrow heard her say.
Shhhh, Yarrow.
I did this, Wanda. It's my fault.
The words were made of breath and heartbeats.
It is the fault of wild berry pie and summer days.
Yarrow heard her laughter, clear.
It is the fault of fire.
Fire. Yes.
Yarrow felt the quickening of Wanda's heart within her own.
We can never be the same.
Because now we are the same.
But we're losing Hannah.
Wanda sighed, ragged, like a final breath.

Who could Yarrow reveal this to but a crazy old woman who came to her house often after that. She listened. The things Yarrow didn't say, or couldn't, Sarah found laid out clearly in the fortunes she told, in the patterns of the bones she scattered.

~~~

After James installed railings here and there around the house, Yarrow managed to drag her body from the chair. Thus she could more easily care for herself. Her arms grew strong making the care of Emily easier too. As evening darkened into night, she and he sat, listening to "Lux Radio Theater" or "Fibber McGee and Molly." James whittled; Yarrow knit. He made animals of balsa wood, little mice and birds, intricate in detail.

"I'd no idea you could do that, James." She turned a perfect little mouse round and round in her hands.

"Me neither." He flushed with the embarrassment of her praise.

"It's just natural then? A natural talent?"

"I never thought to try it until Ida died."

Hands want for something to relieve the sorrow, something words can't give. Yarrow looped the yarn over the needle. The gentle repetitive rhythm governed her breath and steadied her heart. James formed the delicate paws of a mouse holding a bean.

"If I didn't know better, I'd think that one was alive."

He looked up at her and smiled.

In the quiet of such handiwork her mind drifted off to that secret place where Wanda waited.

Wanda, you would have loved this blue yarn.

Yes.

It could have been a sweater or a shawl. You could have worn it winters to protect you from that draft. Remember how snow came right through the wall upstairs and we woke with snowflakes in our hair?

I remember.

I remember too.

Before long Ida joined the conversations, and that was the moment they became the three ply yarn. Their spirits visited her in dreams and previous to dreams. They listened constantly and just as constantly she spoke to them.

"I'd better go to bed." The moment the nightly news was finished, Yarrow released the brake on her chair and began to wheel herself toward her downstairs room.

"You go ahead then." James strained toward her but didn't stand. When lives become unwound the acts that once made sense no longer work. Maybe hearts stay frayed until people can spin new life from the collected wisps remaining of the old.

"Put Emily in with Hannah?" she said.

"In a while," he said.

As Yarrow swung the chair around to close the door she noticed he had risen, taken the baby from her day-crib, and was standing by the window with his back to her, holding Emily up so she could see the moon.

In bed she felt again the presence of Wanda and Ida. They spun. Their arms wrapped her in music. During her first moment in bed, she lay on her back, inviting them, opening her heart to them. Then like two shimmers of light they came. Every night without fail they enticed her soul from her body and the three spirits rose together, spinning, dancing onto the path the moon makes through the dark.

What can I do for Hannah? Yarrow asked them.

In their spinning her true questions surfaced and shot out from her like sparks.

There is nothing you can do.

Wanda never tired of this discussion.

You can sing. You can call her to you. You can tell the stories of your life.

Ida washed over her like rain.

Fire claimed her. If the fire releases her she will be changed. There is nothing you can do. Wanda murmured.

You can feed her honey from your heart.

You are already being everything that can be done.

Sometimes Emily cried upstairs. Yarrow heard Hannah's bed creak and then her feet across the squeaking floorboards. Finally, the song. Hannah's voice, so seldom heard then in that house, singing.

"Blow, blow, the grasses blow
Wind in our hearts, child, singing low,
Song of our lives forever free
Will bring us home, far though we be."

~~~

Back when Yarrow was four years old she would climb into her grandmother Murdock's wardrobe to hide. Clothes hung like tatters of ghosts around her and smelled of onions and sweat. As an adult she barely remembered this and sometimes when she did, she wondered if it could have been a dream. But it was not a dream. She sat cross-legged in the corner among the shoes and sometimes she amused herself by slipping her small feet into them. Other times she simply sat there humming a disjointed melody that wound on without a theme and proceeded toward no satisfying end.

Thin cracks around the door and where the floor was warped permitted light to enter, something it did by stealth as though it were alien to that place. She examined her hands in it, every detail, like they were someone else's hands, or like they were the only part of her, inside the wardrobe, that continued to exist.

If a family fight threatened to break out, her grandmother always locked the wardrobe. Yarrow had always thought her grandmother knew by some magic only gnarled old women possess that she was behind the clothes, and that Marcia Murdock locked the wardrobe door to keep her safe.

The family came to her grandmother's bedroom as if it were an arena, or a temple for conducting rituals of hate. From inside the wardrobe Yarrow could hear Marcia Murdock's footsteps across the wooden floor and then the small key turning in the lock, then the footsteps once again and finally the squeaking of her rocker.

They all lived in the same house: Uncle Ancil, her mother and dad, and Grandmother Murdock. Their meetings sounded civil at first. Who deserved more, always seemed the question. More of this or that. Money. Gifts. Property. No one mentioned love. Then the accusations began. You got what was mine. Finally the fray. Words that mustn't be spoken filled the room and seeped in through the wardrobe cracks.

Uncle Ancil will kill Mama! There was nothing Yarrow could do. She was too small. And besides, she had been locked inside.

Always after the shouting stopped, and after her father said "Hush, Agnes, hush now," and after her mother's sobs and gasps softened into deep breaths and everyone left the room, Grandmother unlocked the door of the wardrobe. Yarrow didn't know then that she kept her money there, not trusting banks since the Great War. You could never know when a collapse might come. You can't trust a soul except for yourself. So she banked it her own way, in rolls of gold coins, in land deeds, and in jewelry bought but never worn. She kept these riches in the metal strongbox stowed in the corner opposite from the shoes. But Yarrow knew nothing about money in a box.

One day her grandmother left the room with the others. Yarrow waited like a fawn. The supper bell rang. They called her name.

"I'm here." But her voice trembled and thinned with her tears.

"Yarrow, Yarrow, where are you? Come to supper."

"I'm locked in."

Their voices faded. She heard doors banging and the silence of the house while they searched the fields and the woods behind the fields.

Yarrow banged on the wardrobe door but there was no one in the house. Eventually she curled up on the wardrobe floor and fell asleep.

"Good heavens! Yarrow!" Grandmother stood in her nightgown, her gray braid hung down over her shoulder. The sound of the key in the wardrobe lock had wakened Yarrow and she parted the ghosts of her grandmother's clothes.

"You locked me in!" And then she began to sob.

"What in heaven's name are you doing in there?" She scolded, with what Yarrow later realized was relief, as she took the child's hand and pulled her out and through the hallway to the room where her mother and father slept, if they slept that night, terrified as they must have been.

~~~

Sometimes those nights after Hannah was lost to her, Yarrow wished she could wheel herself into her daughter's room and watch her face for clues, any hint she might give off in sleep as to where she was hiding. And then she wished she could get up from her chair and climb the stairs. If she could have done that, she would have taken Hannah in her arms and sung to her. Even if Hannah sobbed and blamed her. Even if Hannah looked into her eyes with a child's sorrow and accused her, saying as Yarrow once had said to her grandmother, "You locked me in." If Yarrow could have done these things, she believed that she could have found her daughter. If she could have sung to her as she used to sing when Hannah was small, Yarrow believed she might have stumbled upon the place where Hannah was hiding, and called her back into the world. But as time went on Yarrow concluded that the key to that secret place in her daughter was a key she did not possess. If such a key even existed, Hannah needed to turn it herself.

~~~

Except for Emily, Redwing would have had no question at all. She would know what she had to do. She drifted on Emily's soft smell and steady breathing into a different land. Emily's heart beat in rhythm with her own as though the infant had returned to the girl something lost but necessary. James had set Emily's cradle right beside her bed as if he knew. At night, sometimes, she had lifted the baby from her tiny bed to lie with her on her own, the moonlight washing all over both of them. The girl let the baby suck on her, and Emily's little mouth gave back to her what had been lost. Emily's sounds, like sounds of the woods on a spring day or of the creek around its stones, took the girl back almost where Hannah lay. "We're drinking the moonlight," she had whispered into Emily's feather hair, because even though the baby could bring up no milk from the girl's small nipples, she didn't cry. Redwing imagined that the baby drew from her a kind of life and feeling she thought she had lost for good. At those rare moments Emily's eyes, looking into those of the girl, seemed the eyes of Hannah risen from her grave.

When her breasts began to grow she thought at first Emily had caused it in order to feel the soft fullness with her little hand. The baby was almost a year old by then and slept with Redwing. "Mumu, Mama," she whimpered, and reached for her.

"No more mumu, Emmy." Because who knew when she would talk of such things with Yarrow and how could it be explained? The girl's body yearned for her even though her mind rejected that yearning. It was the yearning of trees to send roots to the bedrock. The yearning of Cold Creek to join the big river running north to Lake Winnipeg.

At school the girls began to talk their talk of boys and meeting in the alley behind the movie theater. They talked of kisses and whether or not to lick their lips to make them slick, of touches and how to stuff their bras with cotton underneath their small breasts. Redwing felt ancient as a woman of the Chippewa who lived on this land long before any of her family arrived, older than the cottonwood beside the creek. She felt she must know everything of men and women, having already nursed a child, a secret Redwing whispered beneath the blazing sun to Hannah lying virginal under grass and listening to the water rush over stones.

It probably didn't matter, though, not really, not even on the day she would die. It was just bodies and that's all it was. Bodies that crumble like leaves in hot late summer. Bodies that become candles and turn to fire, burning until the wick crumbles and the melted wax is all used up.

PART TWO

7

The year 1905 broke down the middle, in July, just before harvest when a scythe of God sheered through the almost ripe wheat. A swath cut by the divine hand curved across these three farms in Cold Creek, North Dakota—the Olson's, the Murdock's, and the St. Germaine's. Lily St. Germaine, eight years old that day, stood in the open kitchen door, her arms reaching toward her father, her small body leaning into the wind, her cries and long black hair blown backwards into the house. Papa! Papa! She saw the hail, large as walnuts, striking him, and imagined it breaking his head open, spilling his brains like thick ropey seeds of an over-ripe melon onto the ground. Papa! He made no sign of hearing her, but knelt on the ruined grain, leaning forward, his head lowered to the soil of the field, calling out through the din to the God of his ancestors. *Kyrie eleison* to a God seeming suddenly without power over the world he had made. "Lord, have mercy. What have we done wrong?"

Upstairs in the farmhouse her mother cried out, shrill and high, the scream of a chicken hawk. Lileeeeeeeeeeee. Ghastly and long, the scream wove in and out of the wind and pulsed with the hail like the heart of a martyr pulses to see her executioner lift his first stone.

Lily looked at her shoes. Laced up to her ankles, the once sturdy shoes now were worn and too short. Her big toes made scuffed lumps in the brown leather. The toes ached.

Liiiiileeeeeeeee!

Maybe she couldn't hear her mother. Later when Papa asked why she hadn't gone upstairs immediately when her mother called her, she would make her eyes wide. Maybe the sound of wind and hail drowned her mother's voice. Maybe she wasn't even in the house when Mama called her. Or maybe she was in the cellar, except her father never would believe she would enter the cellar, even if a tornado blew outside. He knew that last year her Mama forced her into the cellar to fetch canned goods for supper. At the top of the steps Lily had cried,

"Come with me, Mama!" She'd held her mama's apron in her fist, but Aimee St. Germaine pried the little fingers loose.

"Get on down there. Get me a jar of beets."

"Come with me." Lily pleaded, grabbing hold again.

"You get on down there alone. I'll not have people saying I raised a crybaby and a scaredy cat." And her mother gave her a little shove.

Lily imagined it a hole dug for the dead. The field rock walls stood thick against the rich valley soil. Dim light filtered through grimy glass in the small windows at ground level above her head. A spider the size of a quarter hung against the windowpane over the shelves that held her mother's canning. Lily grabbed a jar of beets and ran back up the stairs.

"It's about time," her mother grumbled and snatched the jar away from her.

Liiiiiiiiilllllllleeeeeeeeeeeeee! Now her mother's scream became impossible to ignore. Once more she looked toward her father kneeling in the field. The hail had let up, but now the rain itself blinded her even to an outline of Philippe St. Germaine. At the bottom of the stairs she paused for a moment, and her mother screamed again. She sat on the bottom stair to remove her shoes, and carrying them in her hand, she tiptoed toward her mother's voice.

Lily called her "Mama" in the French fashion with the accent at the end. Mamá, her first word, the root of every word, the embryo of language. Her mama pinned lilies of the valley in her hair, white and green against the black. It was like seeing past and future, to look at the two of them, the girl and her mother. It was the same black hair, the same skin, French skin, her father said. Translucent skin. Skin like the lilies that grew on the north side of the house under ferns taller than Lily's own head so that she felt herself standing in green filtered sunlight, a true lily, a towering white flower, not the tiny bells on their green stem. The only different thing was the color of their eyes— Lily's so dark you couldn't find the way into them, and Aimee's a perfect sea-foam blue.

Her mama bent down to her and said "My sweet Lily" and kissed her nose. Lily looked up, plunged into her mama's eyes, and swam in them like a fish. Unpredictable as shallow lakes, those eyes of Aimee St. Germaine, one moment calm and shining in the sun; the next a roil of currents, quicksilver, catching the child and tossing her onto sharp stones that seemed to guard the shore of her mother's love.

"Mama?" Lily peeked in the door of her mother's bedroom. Her mama was too old to wet her pants, but there she was, standing in a puddle of water, peering at Lily, holding her ample belly that contained a new little brother or sister.

"Lily," said her mama in a voice that no longer screamed but trembled. "go get your Papa. Tell him my water broke."

"Your water?"

"Just tell him, Lily."

"He's in the field. There was hail."

"Go!"

She brought a son into the world that day of hail and named him Stephen to honor Christ's first martyr, whose bones cracked and broke, releasing his spirit to rise upward through the hail of a thousand stones.

~~~

Lily watched her mama's breasts seep blood that stained her dress.

"Oh!" Aimee was leaning over the dinner table with a plate of roast beef when she noticed the dull stain, wet.

"What's that?" Philippe reached out as if to touch his wife and then pulled back his hand.

"I don't know." Aimee left all the rest of the food on the stove so that Philippe had to dish it up and bring it to the table himself. He had to spoon crushed peas into little Stephen's mouth. When she came back she wore a different dress and she smiled at Lily.

"Maybe you should see Doc Martell," said her husband.

"I'm sure it's nothing. Likely it's the nursing that caused it." She lifted her hand and brushed away his words from the air around her.

"But maybe you should, just to be sure." Lily's papa said again.

"It's nothing, Philippe. A little blood in with the milk. I'm sure it's normal."

Papa had been in the fields, and Mama in her room. The farmhouse became a cave and Lily, a wraith of bones walking here and there searching for a door. She could hear her mama whimpering, a rabbit in a trap.

"Mama?" A whisper through her mama's door.

"Go away!" Mama snapped.

The Mama's locked door. The child's knock. Lily's knuckles barely touched the wood.

"Mama?" How uncontrolled is the human voice. The trembling of a rabbit under the plow.

"I said go away!" Mama's voice—split light on a sharp edge of glass.

"Please, Mama." Lily's words melted into water drops.

A crash of something against the inside of the door and the sound of china falling to the floor.

Lily stepped back. Her heart paused, waiting. Then the lock clicked and the door banged against the inside wall as Mama flung it open, and with her right arm she brushed her daughter aside like a cobweb, like something worth nothing. Her blue chenille bathrobe hung crooked on her body. Her face—a wild mess of hair and tears.

She stumbled down the stairs to the cellar, drunk with something Lily yearned to taste so she could understand.

Now Mama screamed. The baby, who had been sleeping, started to cry. Lily huddled in the corner where she had been tossed. "God! God!" She heard her mama scream. Lily crept to the top of the stairs.

"Mama?" Her voice piped, reedy, almost not there at all.

Silence. Was Mama dead?

"Mama?" Lily's voice, pitched high, seemed to come out through the crown of her head.

Nothing.

This time Lily went down the stairs against her mother's bidding. Aimee St. Germaine's bathrobe lay on the dirt floor. It was the bathrobe that the child noticed first, the way it had soaked up the water that puddled, bubbling up like vomit when storms soaked the prairie earth. Bubbled first and then ran downward through the French drain.

Mama knelt by the storage shelves, naked but for her cotton panties. She'd rested her forehead on the edge of an empty shelf and clasped her hands above her head against the rock wall. Was it a curse or was it prayer when she cried "God?" Her breasts hung down and dripped blood.

"Mama, come upstairs." Lily begged. Instinct commanded her to turn around. If she saw what was in front of her, she would see it all her life. If she saw it clearly as something actually taking place. As it was, Lily saw her mother in the same way she saw her nightmares, too vivid to be something real, too stark, with edges like the sharp blade of a knife that gleamed.

Mama didn't answer her. Maybe Lily wasn't really there.

"Mama, stop crying now and come up to bed." A large spider hung in the dim light of the cellar window. Lily shivered.

The girl had only seen her mother's breasts when she was nursing the baby. That was different. Then she took them carefully out, one by one, and kept their fullness covered a bit by the baby's blanket. Her breasts looked to Lily like great pearls, then, with flowers on the tips. She wished that she could suck the sweetness as her brother did, and wished she could remember herself as a baby when Mama had let her touch those breasts that way and let her drink the milk.

Mama finally looked at her.

"Do you see what you've done? You and your brother?"

What did she mean?

Aimee St. Germaine took her breasts in her hands, holding them out to her daughter, and Lily watched her mother's fingers get sticky with the awful mixture that oozed from them.

"If it hadn't been for you this never would have happened."

What? She couldn't speak. She felt stuck in place like a weed growing out of the dirt floor.

"I wouldn't be here bleeding like this; don't you understand? I'd be in Paris or New York. I wouldn't be canning beets and washing clothes and nursing babies. I'd be painting. I'd be famous. I'd be showing my work in all the best galleries. You took that away."

How?

"You were a mistake. Stephen was a mistake. Getting married and moving to this godforsaken place was my biggest mistake."

Mama, Mama. Her mama was weeping now. The sobs freed Lily from the place she stood, and she went to her. She wet a cloth and washed the blood from her mama's hands and from her beautiful breasts. She pushed her mama's words away so she'd never have to hear them again, not in her head, not anywhere. She told herself that her mother had gone crazy with pain, because there must be pain. There always is pain when there is blood. She kissed her mother's face and told her she was beautiful. She smoothed back her hair and said she would do anything for her, would give up anything, go to the cellar any time. She would cook the meals and take care of baby Stephen. She would wash the clothes. Anything. Mama could draw and paint if she wanted. Lily would be the mother. It would be all right. Mama would get well.

"Go upstairs, now," Aimee said to her daughter, and Lily went. She took her mother's granny-square afghan off the sofa and brought it back down to her. She draped it over the shoulders of her mother's body that now seemed the body of someone who had lain in the grave for years. She put her small arm around her mother's waist and Aimee let her daughter raise her from her knees. Together they went up the cellar stairs.

~~~

Yellow leaves of the cottonwood detached, spun to the surface of Cold Creek and floated north toward Canada. Aimee St. Germaine wrapped Stephen in Adeline's crocheted blanket and carried him to the creek-side where she laid him on the bank under the tree. She couldn't nurse him anymore, not from her sick breasts. Philippe had arranged for a wet-nurse, a Mrs. Gunderson from town, someone Aimee hardly knew. "I'll die first," she said when he told her of the arrangements, and immediately she caught herself on the words because, one way or the other, that's exactly what would happen.

The bleeding had not been normal. Inside the mammary glands

hid deadly tumors. Most of the time bleeding like hers was something simple--an infection. Not this time. Not hers.

She began to sing to the baby, a lullaby, a song in French her mother used to sing. The words were gibberish to her as the meaning and most likely even the correct pronunciation were things her mind lost over the years. But the melody brought a comfort rather like being wrapped in a soft quilt left from childhood. If only her own mama could have been there to tell her what to do. People speak of a mother's instinct about children as if such a thing existed. But does it exist? Wouldn't she know what to do about letting Stephen go if such an instinct were in her?

She hadn't wanted to be a mother, nor a wife, either, if the truth be told. She wished, though, that she hadn't told Lily. The expression on the girl's face when the words escaped her mouth made her want to take back every bit of it. True or not, seeing Lily so stricken, she wanted to deny it. But once out there, words can't be withdrawn. You can wear a mountain down but a word, once lodged in somebody's memory, is there to stay.

Too late now. Too late for everything. She reached over and picked up Stephen. "You'll be better off with somebody else," she murmured into his deep brown eyes. "Maybe I could have loved you, little one, but I don't know." She stood and started back to the house. "You'll be better off, you'll see," she said again.

~~~

Within a month, Aimee St. Germaine was dead, Stephen was living full time at the Gunderson's who cared for him like their own, and Philippe St. Germaine sent Lily to the nuns in Crookston, Minnesota. She cried at night, lying in the white draped bed alongside similar beds occupied by high school girls. She was ten. Some of the older girls cried too, but only at the beginning of the school year. Sister Irene's rosary clicked as she approached the bed. She drew back the curtains and sat down. Her hand on Lily's head, smoothing back her hair, felt dry and soft as flour on a breadboard. "I miss Mama," Lily sobbed.

"Of course you do, sweet Lily," Sister crooned. Young. Clear faced as a plaster saint.

"Why did she die?"

"Hush, child. These are mysteries only the love of God can answer."

With her thumb, Sister Irene traced a tiny cross on Lily's forehead, and then she bent down and kissed the place. Maybe she did this to let her lips love the girl and bless her Lord both at once. Maybe she wanted to protect herself with the sign of the cross. Lily never knew, and neither, perhaps, did Sister Irene.

"Pray to your angel, Lily. Your angel is with you always. The angel who now hides your dear mother in her wings, remains close to you every moment, in every cool breeze and warm breath."

Together they whispered. "Angel of God, my guardian dear, to whom God's love commits me here. Ever this night be at my side, to light and guard, to rule and guide. Amen."

"Go to sleep now, Lily." Sister smoothed the white spread over the girl's small body. The wing of her veil swished against the curtain as she left.

Lily walked the hallways of the academy for girls and listened to the voices of the nuns singing Gregorian chant behind the closed chapel doors. Windows framed the first ash of snow. Under her shoes the wooden floorboards creaked, and the nuns' voices rose and floated behind the door, seeping under it, escaping through the cracks and entering into Lily like a silk thread cast from a golden spider. The chant rose and fell and spiraled in her ear. It rose and webbed the whorls of her brain. It fell and her heart ate it like transparent sugar boiled to a wisp of thread that cracks in the chill water. Lily walked the hallways with the voices of nuns in her body like bees, and the chant collected in the bowl of her mind like honey-flavored divinity.

Gaudeámus omnes in Dómino, diem festum celebrántes sub honóre Sanctórum ómnium chanted the nuns because it was the feast of All Saints and Lily's mother certainly must be in heaven by now. Outside the window, snow drifted onto the already frozen earth, onto the gray-with-death grass, onto the empty trees. And the nuns sang "Rejoice" because the saints had left the cold gray and gone to heaven.

Lily wondered if in spring the lilies of the valley would grow under the ferns on the north side of her house since her mother was not there to tend them, and she walked the hallways of the academy for girls. First the top floor where the chapel was and all the dorms and the wooden lockers that gave the hallway the quality of dreams with doors that closed secrets inside, away from your sight. She reached the wide staircase and went down to the classroom floor where the sound of chant grew more faint. In the assembly room beneath the chapel the ceiling muffled the nun's voices as though she heard them through a pillow at night, the way she used to hear her mama whimper in the next room, and she remembered how she clasped the ends of her feather pillow to pull it up around her ears and thus shut out the sounds of pain. Now she traced the ivy vine that branched up from its pot and attached itself to the wainscoting, marveling at its age and length and the number of its leaves. Someday she would count them.

By the time she reached the main floor of the academy she couldn't hear the voices of the nuns at all.

The truth about her mama came slowly to Lily's mind. She learned it from the nuns' eyes, eyes that demanded nothing of her that she couldn't give. The nuns wanted only simple tasks. Keep your things in order. Make your bed. Do your little chore. Clean your plate. Study diligently. Say your prayers. Go to mass. Tell the truth. Be kind. The eyes of the nuns held no contradictions.

"What a good girl you are." Sister Irene turned to her after she checked the perfect order of her clothes locker. "I wish I could say as much about some of your older companions!" She looked down the row of lockers at the nineteen teenage girls who shared Lily's dorm and stood ready for inspection. Lily beamed. Still a child, and better than the others. In school she worked hard, got straight "A"s, and waited for the nun's love. "What an intelligent, hard-working girl. Your father will be so proud."

"Do you think my mama would be proud? Do you think she loved me?" Lily asked Sister Irene one night before she went to sleep.

"Of course she'd be proud. Whatever do you mean? She was your mother! I'm sure she loved you."

"How can I know for sure?"

"These are questions not to be asked, Lily. Some things simply must be believed. Your mother loved you and that's an end of it."

Early every morning, at mass, the rhythm of Latin hypnotized

Lily into her mama's presence and she gazed into the blue depths of her eyes. Mama's eyes, so different from Sister Irene's. And it wasn't just their sea-foam color. Mama's eyes wanted something that Lily hadn't given her. Lily's heart ached like a tooth.

Her mind brought back memories like dreams.

She hummed with them a lullaby. Was it a song Mama used to sing? She didn't think it was. Mama, Mama, she heard herself cry inside her head as the priest lifted the gold chalice past the light of altar candles and toward the angels painted in the dome above him. He lifted it like sun over the roof of the barn at home and tipped back his head adoring the gold that shone and dissolved into her mama's face. The little bell rang while the nuns bowed their heads and the priest fell to his knees, suddenly weak. No one heard Lily cry. Did God hear? Did Mama? From inside her mind it sounded loud.

The priest knelt before the gold chalice every morning Lily spent at the academy for girls, and at the same time his knee hit the sanctuary floor, her inner cry peeled, "Mama!" like a bell. And as the years passed, she heard her mama's voice respond to her again and again in a tiny cave of her mind. Finally she could not deny the truth. Her mama needed from her something she could never give. She had been too small.

~~~

Light from two walls of windows in Sister Irene's corner classroom shone on the brilliant colors of Jesus' cloak in the half finished painting on her easel. The place smelled earthy, layered with clay, linseed oil and turpentine. Lily breathed slowly and held the odor deep in her lungs like one might hold a mother's old clothes to her face and close her eyes, imagining the softness of breasts and belly. She seldom mentioned Mama anymore, although her heart still ached. Sister Irene painted slowly, applying the oils with smooth strokes, sometimes using a brush no wider than an eyelash to create fine hairs on the savior's head. Lily watched the nun's arm, its grace, like a dancer's arm. She stared at the nun's face, a lost face, a face given over to something deeper even than prayer.

If the nun would notice her, still as she was, still as candle flame on the altar, then she would know she hadn't disappeared when Mama died. Eyes confirm your presence. Some eyes. Other eyes look straight through you as though you are thin as smoke or not there at all. Lily sat in the corner of Sister Irene's classroom. She sat on the long table, the one scattered with the nun's tools, large jars of paint, scraps of wood, sometimes a clay figurine draped with a damp gray cloth. She sat cross-legged, her elbows on her knees, her chin cupped in her hands, and she watched. Sister Irene never said a word. She didn't hum as she worked the way Mama had from time to time, or blurt out bad words when her brush went wrong. She had the workings of a well-balanced clock inside her mind. Steady. Sure. When the bell rang for her communal prayer, she put her brushes in a pot of turpentine, removed her big checkered apron and the matching coverings for her long black sleeves, unpinned her veil so it floated down around her face, and left the room. Lily waited for her to say, "Come, Lily." But Sister closed the door and Lily heard the latch click in place. She sat on the table and stared at the way wind had blown fine hair across the face of Sister Irene's Jesus.

"Will you be my mama?" Lily asked her finally after a year of watching. She watched her walking up and down the center aisle of the dorm as she prayed aloud to keep the girls quiet as they slipped into their white nightgowns and settled into bed. She watched her go to each girl, one by one, and bless her with the little cross traced on her forehead. She wondered if the nun kissed the others on that cross as she sometimes kissed her. She watched her bow low towards the altar during prayer, and watched her chant the hymns and sequences of the mass that promised to bring God down to touch hearts and forgive sins. She watched her laugh. It was a laugh that wouldn't stop, that enslaved her and shook her until tears fell slick down her cheeks.

"I can't, you know," she said.

Lily supposed she meant she was a nun and couldn't adopt her. Lily knew that. Adoption wasn't what she wanted, but whatever it was she actually did want seemed to have no words, as if it hadn't yet been tried.

"I don't mean you should marry my dad or anything like that!" Lily argued.

Sister Irene laughed in that way that wouldn't stop until she was breathless. After she pulled out her big white cotton hanky and wiped away her tears, she put her hand under Lily's chin, and raised her face in order to look her straight in the eyes.

"I can be a sister to you, just like I am to all the other girls," she said.

Lily felt different words on her tongue. She would have said she needed to be special. She needed even more than that, but if she said too much or said it wrong, Sister Irene might turn away, taking with her everything she'd already given.

"Will you teach me to paint?" Lily asked instead.

"Hummm." She considered it. "Well, you're too young for the freshman art class. But, I'll tell you what. If you'll work an hour a week for me, sorting and cleaning in my supply closet and picking up things around my classroom, I'll give an equal amount of time to you. An hour a week. Your private painting lesson."

"Really?"

"Really."

They spoke from then on through the medium of art. Lily loved Sister Irene with paint on canvas. She pleased her in the motion of the brush, in the combination of color, in design and in form. But always the nun remained distant, as if Lily had to reach through something thick and resistant to get to her, and she never could. She remained on the other side of the nun's reserve, feeling as scattered, as torn, as lost and stripped bare as earth under her papa's plow. It was in the bones of that feeling that Lily painted one afternoon in February, on an afternoon she least expected any response from the nun. Sister Irene took her hand, the hand that held the brush, and curved their arms together in a motion unrepeatable without her. "Do it now," she whispered. "Do it just like that." And Lily tried it herself, in a motion like an act of God, a motion that a human might attempt, but without the wing of grace it would fall short. Always. She gasped. It might have been only a slight intake of breath. It might have been nothing at all. She looked at the nun who might have noticed or might not have felt a thing for the girl, as though Lily were but an odor in her room like that of the linseed oil or turpentine, just something connected with her art but not her art itself. An instrument of form, a tool, a thing replaceable.

Lily painted anyway, despite her crippled form. She painted veils and a woman bowing under them as Sister Irene bowed when Lily watched the nuns from behind a large stone pillar in the choir loft early in the mornings before the other girls got out of bed. Lily wrapped words around the woman's head in calligraphic swirls of paint. "I am the mother of fair love, of fear and of holy hope." She painted the nun's veils like violet clouds around the sun, and her body, barely visible, a candle flame bending to the air. She painted the woman with pearl breasts dripping clean milk that swirled like galaxies and flung out white stars across the universe. Blue and white, gold and silver, this painting poured from Lily's fingers without a touch of red anywhere.

"You are doing well." Sister Irene smiled. She lifted up the paintings, helping Lily frame them. "We'll have a showing, don't you think? Would you like to invite your father?"

Until that moment Lily hadn't thought of her painting as meant for any eyes but those of Sister Irene and her own. She thought of the paintings as codes, as hieroglyphs. She imagined that the nun knew the meaning of her work, even though she herself remained like someone unable to read, a child who wonders at the markings on the page and how those markings might transfer themselves into the mind of the reader silently, without passing through the ear to trip that tiny hammer and vibrate the delicate drum that releases sound.

"I don't know." Papa appeared in her imagination. He stood in front of the painting and frowned. Did he see or not? He turned from the painting and his eyes were dark with recognition, seeing a secret of which she remained unaware, something that came through her fingers to expose to him a reality still concealed from her own eyes. Lily's mind wound itself like an intricate fence around some secret, a fragile growing thing beginning only now to poke itself up from the dark ground.

Sister Irene picked up the woman with pearl breasts and held it out from her. She set it in the sunlight's winter angle where it slanted through her studio window. "This is just elegant." She didn't look at Lily when she spoke. She looked at the painting as if she were seeing herself for the first time and it all had nothing to do with the girl. Or maybe she didn't see herself at all, maybe she saw only the paint, the strokes of the brush, the colors, the texture, something outside both of them and having a being of its own. Lily would never know.

~~~

Sister Irene stood beside the white curtain that surrounded Lily's bed in St. Helen's dorm. She stood stopped in time, seeming to have appeared magically and without sound. "Your father has arrived, Lily. You'll meet him in the parlor."

He actually came. He actually wanted to see her paintings. Lily thought this as she ran down the stairs, skipping steps, flying. She thought this until she pushed open the door of the parlor and saw him sitting on the tall wing-backed chair, until she saw his face and could read what lay behind the lines. Is this my papa? Lily thought when she saw him as though her own growing up had changed not her but him. The lines of her father's face, the rigid planes of his cheek bones, the unyielding set of his lips, the gray streaks appearing in his brown hair, startled her, for it was as if she'd never seen him before. Not like this. Not with an artist's eye.

"Papa!" The picture in her mind was of running to him and throwing her arms around his neck, but her body held back, stopping her forward motion just at the threshold. He stood, not so tall as she remembered. He reached his hand out toward her.

"Lily. All grown up."

"Fourteen."

"So like your mama."

Paintings hung on each side of the long wide hall on the main floor of the academy for girls. Under each painting Sister Irene had affixed a white card bearing the title of the piece and the name of the artist in perfect flourishes of her calligraphy. Her own paintings were there, alongside Lily's and several works by older students. At the end of the hall three senior girls stood behind a linen-clad table, smiling and pouring coffee from a silver pot into small china cups that they offered with sugar and fresh cream to the guests. Nuns from a different Order came from Grand Forks and drifted up and down the hall like giant birds with crests. They floated up to Sister Irene, their veils falling like feather plumbs down from their crests all the way past their waists, murmuring and gesturing toward the paintings on the wall. Women in white gloves, men in dark suits and vests laughed and smiled and shook the nun's hand. The women held her hand in both of theirs as though they held a fledgling bird too soon taken from its nest and unable yet to fly.

"Your mama would have liked this," Philippe St. Germaine commented as he moved alongside his daughter from painting to painting. "She liked to paint pictures, you know."

"I remember. She told me." Lily's heart beat so hard she could hear it in her ears and feel it at the top of her head.

"It's good for women to have a hobby," he said. "It gives them something to do when the children are grown. Too bad your mama never had a chance…"

Whenever someone stopped in front of one of her paintings her impulse was to run from the hall, up the flights of stairs to the dormitory and hide behind the white curtains of her narrow bed. How could she have allowed this showing? Each of her paintings seemed different on that day from what she had seen in them before. Each seemed to reveal more than she had intended or even than she had known she contained. She felt shame keen as though God were speaking to her from a cloud above the Garden of Eden, saying, "What have you done?"

They stood right beneath the painting of the woman with swirling stars pouring from her breasts. "What is this supposed to be?" her father said, his body tensing, drawing up to his full height. "What the hell is this?"

"I need her now," he told the nun later that afternoon by way of explanation. "She's fourteen."

"I want to stay here." Lily's voice emerged from her throat with a sound of a bird trapped in a thicket. "I've only just finished eighth grade."

"She's really very talented." Sister Irene offered.

"We have to be realistic. Lily's a farm girl. Talent or not, it's wrong to fill her head with painting and other impossible things." He put his hand on Lily's shoulder and it was warm and big. The voice he used to break her heart was tender enough to fool her into acceptance. But despite that she found herself saying, "I want to stay here and be a nun." What a surprise! Such a thought hadn't occurred to her until that moment.

"Go pack your suitcase." He gave her shoulder a reassuring squeeze and then pushed her just the slightest bit toward the door.

"My paintings…" she couldn't imagine them hanging there in the hall separate from her own presence.

"Best that you leave them here," he said. "There isn't any room for things like that at home."

~~~

When Lily walked through the door of the farmhouse, she learned at a glance how a man whose wife has been taken from him can narrow his life. It wasn't so much that he'd let the house get dirty, though it did smell of being closed. Had he opened one window the whole time she'd been gone? She took the whole thing in. The kitchen curtains, limp and beginning to disintegrate from hanging there not touched, not shaken, not washed. Boxes, packed, closed, and pushed against the far wall of the living room. Piled one atop the other. Her mother's things? Probably. It wasn't so much the dinginess as that her father had removed all the dainties that women place here and there in a room to give it a lived-in feel. Doilies. Pillows. Throws for the sofa. Pictures on the wall. He'd packed all of these things away, and the chairs and sofa that remained gave a feel of more emptiness than had they not been there at all. Over everything, the silence, and within that silence she felt, more than heard, their hollow footsteps on the wood floor.

He seemed to know what she was thinking. "I had to make it simple," he said.

"Of course," Lily said but wondered silently how anyone could live that way, stripped, reduced to less than what the nuns in their poverty permitted themselves by way of beauty. I'll make it right, she thought, and as she let her eyes roam over the stark room again she promised herself that never would she allow such barrenness into her own life. "It's so quiet. When will you be bringing Stephen home?"

He would be five years old. Already he was old enough to help her father with some of the chores in the barn. And Lily could care for him, get him off to school next year. She could sing her mother's lullabies to him; he should know those songs—it wasn't right that he had no memory of his own mother's voice.

"I won't be. He'll be staying with the Gunderson's."

"What?"

"It's all he knows, Lily. He calls them Mom and Dad."

"But he belongs to us!"

"Human beings don't belong to anybody but themselves, Lily. Didn't you learn that when your mama died?"

Sometimes, later, downtown in Cold Creek, she watched

Stephen play with groups of other little boys. She called him over to her one day and told him she was his sister. His dark eyes, so like her own, regarded her solemnly and then flashed defiance. "I ain't got no sister!" It was a bad place her father had put him, she concluded. What kind of people would cut you off from others of your own blood?

Lily washed clothes and cooked and became, except for sex, her father's wife. He never bothered her that way and she was too innocent then to imagine any father might. She went to church and tried to keep from her mind the image of Sister Irene's soft veil as she turned and bowed before the golden chalice. Whatever the secret Lily's painting had sought to reveal to her now became locked in the boredom of repetitive tasks.

For two years she lived as though asleep, with no dream of herself as real. She learned to knit. She spent evenings making socks and sweaters while she listened to the sounds of crickets in the fields. She spoke softly and never disagreed. She felt nothing, yearned for nothing. When she opened her eyes in the morning and shuffled out to the kitchen to put the coffee on, she didn't think there could have been another way. So just before New Year's Eve in 1913, the year that she turned eighteen, she barely understood her father's words when he asked if she wanted to go to the big celebration in Grand Forks.

"What?" Lily said.

"Some big dance band is coming up from the Twin Cities. We could get a room at the hotel there."

"If you want." She said, because by then the question of her own wants had little meaning.

She took her Sunday dress, not a dress for dancing, but it would do. Light brown with tiny blue forget-me-nots, and a skirt that didn't swirl. And it was in that dress she found herself between Joseph Olson and Ancil Murdock. Though she'd lived between the two of them, on land that bordered their two farms, she'd always before that night blended them in with the barley and the wheat, the sound of the threshing machine and the dust of the harvest. But that night they came, walking together up to her, light and dark, clear and riled like Red Lake River mud. They each stood out in vivid relief from her entire world, in stark contrast to each other, and already they wanted her to choose. The one like sunshine on the chalice in the Academy chapel. The other like paint mixed on a palette that you want to apply with your hands and smear upon your skin everywhere until you're wet with it, smelling like ground flax, like linseed broken open.

First one and then the other, Lily danced with Joseph and with Ancil, the one held her like thin glass and danced slow, his body touching hers in a shiver of recognition. The other made her body do what, without his firmness, it never could. She glided on his will for her. It was as if the floor had been transformed into air and the couple drifted on it, swirling like companion hawks above the fields. At midnight Joseph kissed her first while the Minneapolis band played "Auld Lang Syne." He kissed her beside the fireplace at the long end of the ballroom, and the firelight alternately lit and shadowed his face. He kissed her sweet and soft and whispered "Happy New Year," and the breath of his words was wet when it touched the inside of her ear. After that kiss Ancil grabbed her hand. He pulled her outside into the snow and kissed her under the stars. He reached one hand down low on her back until it came to rest on the flair of her buttocks. His tongue pressed against her lips and teeth until she opened her mouth to his insistence and his hot tongue tasting of bourbon.

Lily dreamed those kisses and awoke wanting both of them at once, but in one kiss. Both men, but in one man. Some nights, knowing that what she fantasized was impossible, she imagined them on either side of her in the bed. Like subtlety and madness play with the mind, she imagined them touching her body each in his way. Joseph breathed life into her and she opened to him fully. Ancil drew her out of herself into him and she turned to liquid that flowed thick like molasses liqueur.

In reality neither of them did more than kiss her for almost half a year. They came to her as if by some pre-agreement, Joseph on the first and third Saturday and Ancil on the second and forth of every month. What led her to choose Joseph, finally, over Ancil she never could be sure. Safety? Maybe it was safety. Ancil raised in her a passion something like the cry of wolves that makes you want to run to them although you know how they will surround you, teeth bared. You know you will be brought to your knees, and they will tear at you and you will feel the warm blood as it seeps from your breasts down your skin like red ochre oils and covers you making you delicious to them, making you irresistible. She feared for her sanity, wanting something so obviously painful, and wondered in quick stabs of insight what it might be in human nature that could turn it towards such obvious self destruction

"You won't be rid of me." Ancil held her arm tight, squeezing it just above her elbow, leaving small red fingerprints in her skin.

~~~

Lily married Joseph Olson in Crookston at the parish of Ste. Anne where the old priest still spoke French, and that exotic fact pleased her father for some reason she never grasped, since he and his family lost the language two generations before. These exotic circumstances only added to the discomfort of her new mother-in-law, Adeline, whose family was not only Lutheran but Norwegian as well. She sat alone on the groom's side and wore a little straw hat with blue flowers that tilted precariously on the thick blond braid that circled her head.

Joseph's father, like Lily's mother, had died young, but he of an accident in the fields. Joseph remained tightlipped about the whole thing, telling her only that his mother didn't want it talked about. It had been Marcia Murdock who found him and came running up out of the fields screaming. That's about all Lily discovered about it, that and Joseph's quitting school one year early to take over the farm and take care of his mother who clenched her teeth and went about her chores like before it happened.

For Lily, Adeline Olson became Mother #3 and took up where her own mama left off with things such as sending her to the cellar to ferret among the spiders for potatoes and carrots almost rotted and stinking from the long winter storage. But she knew nothing about this dank future on her wedding day and wondered only why the Murdock family didn't show up to join in the celebration. Until a week before the wedding she simply assumed Ancil would be Best Man, and when she said as much to Joseph he just looked at her, his eyes widening slightly. He didn't smile. He didn't explain.

"I thought the two of you were friends," she ventured by way of explanation, because she could tell by the little twinge inside her chest when she saw the almost imperceptible lift of Joseph's right eyebrow that about their friendship she had been mistaken.

"No." And that was all he said and all he would say.

It's not quite true that the Murdock's were Lily's only wonder. They were the only wonder she dared admit. It took her years after she left Cold Creek to remember how she had searched the pews for the veiled head of Sister Irene. Nuns don't go to weddings, she told herself by way of comfort as she made her long trip up the aisle to where Joseph stood. They aren't permitted. They have their rules. She'd sent an invitation, drawing the curve of a wing inside, telling her of Joseph's tenderness, his soft sky blue eyes, his deep respect for her virginity. She wrote of her love for the nun and her gratitude for the motherly role Sister Irene had played on her behalf.

Maybe she received it; maybe not. Lily never was to know.

From time to time, after she grew old, she found herself pondering this: the way that Sister Irene disappeared, leaving nothing behind, no trace, not even bones.

~~~

It never became Lily's house. Adeline Olson owned it, ran it, filled every corner of it. Even the bedroom she assigned to Lily and her son remained open to her scrutiny. "Joseph?" she called and tapped on the door any time of day or night that the newlyweds might have retreated there in hopes of a moment alone even just to look into each other's eyes. They woke often in the middle of the night, listened to be sure she slept, and then made love furtively, in silence. Joseph didn't look at her, reaching for her in the dark, coming into her up underneath her white gown. But she could feel the pounding when his large chest crushed against her breasts and she took that as a sign of love.

"Call me Mother," Adeline Olson told her over dishes the first week after the wedding. She poured boiling water over the crockery to rinse the soap. Lily waited a minute before touching the plates that would have steamed themselves dry if Adeline hadn't insisted on each one being shined and polished as if it were fine china.

"Yes, Mother," she said while looking out the window at Joseph who was coming from the barn, but she could still see, out of the corner of her eye, that Adeline nodded her head with a jerky little motion Lily interpreted as pleasure.

"You'll be in charge of the hens," Adeline said. "I'll teach you how to feed them, gather the eggs, clean the hen house. It's a simple task. And you can keep the egg money. God knows you'll need a bit of cash for yourself as every woman does." The concession Adeline made was not small, because she used to keep the egg money for herself. Lily thanked her, but had only scant awareness of the trust placed in her.

Sometimes she and Joseph felt ten years old, just waiting for a lapse in Mother Olson's attention enough to permit a bit of mischief. Instead of growing into their marriage, they seemed, under Adeline Olson's eyes, to grow away from it into something different. Nights under the blankets Lily began to shrink from him as though what they did was wrong, even unnatural. She wanted to take his hand and run into the woods alongside the creek. She wanted to hunt with him, to work beside him in the barn, to dress in overalls—pretend she was a man.

At harvest time, when they drove to town for supplies she bought powders and lipstick, rouge and a fine brush and tiny tub of kohl to enhance her eyes. Then she sat for hours in the bedroom while Mother Olson clenched her teeth and cleaned the house. Lily couldn't see her and that was a blessing. Despite that, Lily felt the ache of those clenched teeth in her own jaw's hinge.

"You look like a whore." Adeline flashed a mean eye. "Go wash that off."

"I'm not ten years old, Mother, to be ordered when to wash my face."

"I'd prefer to think you were than to think my son made a drastic error in judgment."

Lily painted her face and put on her brown dress with blue flowers, and then she left the house to walk the road toward Murdock's farm.

"You come back here, girl! Don't you be going off to the Murdock's, you hear me?" Lily heard her mother-in-law yell from the kitchen door, but she kept walking.

Would she wonder all her life what it was in her that always wanted opposites? Always what she couldn't have. Always the impossible.

Ancil Murdock met her by the fence. She supposed she knew he would.

"Just don't touch me," She told Ancil, though it seemed his eyes had already taken off every stitch of clothes she wore and that his hands had traveled every inch of her skin.

"Never." He promised but those eyes of his said different.

"I'm married," she told him. Her voice came out a whisper, as though she had said something else, something tender, enticing.

"I know that." His eyes burned.

"Really." How many ways can a word be said? Perhaps her inflection encouraged him. For years she would be condemned to revisit this scene as if to find there the key to what happened. Right here. Right here. And from here she would forever mark the changing of her course toward becoming the woman she never intended to become.

He laughed. He opened the gate and she went through.

A woman needs a friend, she told herself. Ancil's mind had been polished by knowledge, the words from his many books flowing like molten glass over it. She told herself he might keep her sane by talking to her, something Joseph rarely did.

It was October. They sat side by side on a little rise out of sight of his mother's house, and the fields rested under the afternoon sun, their gold stubble shining.

"Is Joseph good to you?" he asked.

"He's gentle." she replied. She twirled a piece of long grass between her fingers.

"Does he make you happy?"

"How do you mean?"

She knew what he meant. She wanted him to say the words, wanted him to substitute telling for touching, since actual touching was forbidden. It was because they would never touched that she had convinced herself that the afternoon together was innocent, necessary even. His time with her preserved her marriage by giving her what Joseph never could. A wider scope. A vision reaching to the edges of the world.

"Does he satisfy you?" he said.

"Satisfy?" How could this conversation continue?

"The darkness in you." Ancil looked off over the cut fields.

Finally he finished his thought, his voice husky. "The wild part."

"Wild part?" She thought of the dark cellar and how she had clung to Mama's apron "I'm not wild," she said to him. "I've never in my life been wild."

She sat with her hands pressed against the grass and could feel the way his flesh would slide against her own. Maybe words, regardless of how beautiful, were not enough to open up the new worlds for which she yearned. She could feel his hand moving over to touch hers, even though he didn't flinch. His presence beside her was quicksand. It was a bog. It was gravity and she was falling into it. She reached out her hand to him, thinking to steady herself.

~~~

"Where were you all afternoon?" Mother Olson didn't look her in the eye and Lily took that to mean she didn't really want to know.

"Walking," she told her

"Where? Don't you be going to the Murdock farm." She said, still not looking at her, but rolling piecrust out on a floured towel. The rolling pin slapped the wooden board under the towel, and Lily concentrated on the sound.

"I just walk," she lied. "I listen to the meadow larks and watch the dragonflies."

"I could use some help here." Adeline said, still not looking at her.

"I have to get away from time to time." Lily said.

Adeline sighed as if to say a girl her age didn't know the half of it. How could Lily know what women had to have and where they need to go? "What you have to do," she muttered, "is wipe that black goo off your eyes and peel the potatoes for supper."

The potatoes skins dropped from the paring knife into the slop bucket.

"Ancil Murdock's no good, Lily." Adeline's voice melded with the kitchen sounds, the plit of the peelings on water, the clunk of the rolling pin. "None of the Murdock's are. Wheeler-dealers, that's what they are and always have been. Dealers and drunkards. Marcia Murdock bought up land when folks were down and out, and that Justin of hers—he took to drink and ended up stone dead one morning in a ditch just outside of town." She paused, folded the piecrust and lifted it towards the crockery pan. "She's not to be trusted. Never has been--not from the beginning. I could tell you things..." She unfolded the dough and formed it into the pie pan.

In the beginning, before Adeline Olson had become the mother of anyone, Marcia Murdock arrived by train from Minneapolis and stepped out onto the platform in Cold Creek decked out like some princess. Who'd she think she was, anyhow? That's what Adeline always wanted to know. She'd been there, at the depot. She'd seen her with her waist all cinched in and that odd colored hair of hers, like garnet on its way to brown, waved like she thought she was the Queen of Sheba. And silk. Wearing silk the color of the prairie grass in May. Good Lord! Adeline would bet a dime to a dollar that Marcia Murdock never would wear silk again. Didn't the woman know she'd be living in that shack in the woods out by the creek until her Justin got the big house built? Any woman with a brain in her head would have been grateful for a wood house, however small. Didn't anybody tell her about sod, how she could have been living in the ground like a possum or a prairie dog? Always the dirt, the dust, the darkness and the being alone while your man went out to break the prairie.

Adeline had endured her stint. Lived those first years of her life underground just like the rest. Still, by the time Marcia Murdock arrived in 1891, Adeline had married Henry and moved into the brand new Olson place which stood white and tall against the big sky.

Adeline had watched Marcia from her kitchen window after she'd been brought down a peg or two. It wasn't long after the woman arrived at Cold Creek, and along she came, walking through prairie grass tall as her waist, her apron flapping in the wind, her strange dark hair loose from its knot.

"Here she comes," Adeline said aloud to no one in her house. "Here she comes and I'm in for an afternoon of it." Again it would be how the dirt was like to make her crazy, and how her Justin paid her scant attention, and how he couldn't seem to get her in a family way no matter how he rutted on her, sweaty, every night.

Well, Adeline could do without that information. Marriage secrets should be kept that way. And if Mrs. Murdock didn't want the rutting, she should have kept her eyes off Adeline's Henry, flirt as she was. To this day, Adeline's sympathies lay with Justin. And she couldn't help but wonder what other men Marcia Murdock lured with her downright sinful ways, preening and strutting to turn their eyes and who knows what else towards her. Adeline hoped for a baby in her own house, and it seemed best to keep her husband's eyes trained on herself.

She'd seen how Marcia looked at him, seen how she sidled up to him when he came in from the fields. She saw, too, how he preened himself for her; don't think she didn't. Men can't help it, given such flirtation in a woman. It's their nature. Marcia Murdock went past her bounds, no doubt about it.

Then she'd turn, after he was gone, and be so sweet and tell Adeline how blessed she was to have found such a man. And she'd take Adeline's hands in hers and say "You're my best friend, Adeline. Why, I don't know what I'd do out here without you to talk to. I'd die of loneliness. I would. I'd just die of boredom and of dirt."

One day the two women sat in Adeline's parlor. Summer had laid itself on them full force, muggy, barely fit for breathing. They fanned themselves with recent editions of *Goddards*, and Marcia shook her head back and forth in an irritating sort of way. "That man holds me back," she said.

"Justin?" Adeline said, thinking who could know for sure what man the hussy might have in mind?

"Yes. Over a year I've been with him and no proper house yet. But it's more than that."

"More?" Adeline told herself she didn't want to pry, but something must be said in response.

"I'm a passionate woman, Adeline. I'm intelligent, industrious, and I'm wasting my life out here with a man who can only think of plowing and eating and rutting. It's like living with an animal."

"But he's your husband."

"And more's the pity," Marcia had said.

Adeline had hesitated to complicate the issue but could hardly help herself.

"Whatever were you thinking, then, to marry the man?"

Marcia stared at the other woman as though she were a simpleton.

"What choice did I have?"

Well, Justin Murdock was quite a looker. At least some would think so. Broad-shouldered and ruddy, with those dark blue eyes. Could be she thought him a winner. Turned out he was the best that she could get. A woman like that, with a barbed tongue, well, once a man felt the sting of her he'd likely brush her off his life. Likely many a man did just that. Maybe she figured, when it came to Justin, she didn't have a choice other than to be a spinster. And who wants that kind of life? Regardless, Adeline reflected, you live with what you've got. You make do.

That September Adeline had seen her through the window coming across the cut fields, and she waited for the knock on her door, but it never came. She'd been baking apple pies then, too, paring the apples, cutting them in fine triangles, sprinkling them with sugar and cinnamon. She rolled out the top crust, pleasantly aware of being the woman who made the most flaky pie crust in the county, slathered it with fresh cream and more cinnamon and sugar, and slipped it into the oven before she went outside to see what had happened to Marcia. The other woman was nowhere to be seen, simply evaporated. Adeline heard a meadowlark sing, and saw a V of ducks passing overhead.

"Henry?" she called.

No answer. Nothing but the meadowlark.

She walked to the barn and entered into the dim light. There stood Marcia, her dress unbuttoned at the neck and a bit of her hair fallen from its knot. And there stood Adeline's Henry, staring at her, just reaching out his hand.

"Henry!" Adeline warned. As he pulled back, she walked up to Marcia and slapped the other woman's face. "You, you hussy!" She snarled. "Walking right past my kitchen window! Going straight into my barn! Straight up to my Henry." She felt herself turn to ice. "Button your dress, woman, and get off my land. Keep away from my husband. And never, never set foot in my house again."

Marcia had laughed.

Adeline took Henry's hand and pulled. He looked back at Marcia once, then yielded to his wife, leaving the other woman standing in the barn.

Adeline kept her council when it came to Marcia Murdock forever after that day. She kept track of her, too, the way you are required by common sense to know always where the snake is coiled. She kept her in her sights. She monitored the other woman's pregnancy with Ancil, counting the months, hoping that child had nothing to do with her or hers. She'd found herself in a family way with Joseph soon after the incident in the barn. And a few years after he was born, Marcia's Agnes came on the scene. And, right about the same time, just after the St. Germaine's arrived in Cold Creek, came Aimee's girl, Lily.

All the children would grow up together, as they must when going to the same school, and that's why she raised Joseph with a warning to keep his distance from the Murdock's, every last one of them.

If you find a viper den in the room, you leave and close the door.

Adeline's attention returned to her pie and to Lily, still peeling the potatoes. What had she been saying? Her minded tended to stray off into the past more and more these days. Oh yes, Justin's death. She looked up again at Lily and resumed their conversation. "Widowhood, which softens some, just made Marcia meaner. By hook or crook she finally owned all the land east of us, four entire farms of a thousand acres each. That was when her daughter Agnes appeared one winter afternoon at my door."

"Agnes?" Ancil's younger sister. A plain girl, Agnes. A girl with mousy hair and a flat nose.

"The cold that day was such that you had to bite it off and chew it up before you could breathe the air." Adeline pushed ahead with her story as she fluted the pie and put it into the oven. "Wind formed the snow into drifts like waves breaking on an ocean, curled over at the top with little sprays of white whirling there like devils. Inside the only warm spot was the kitchen. You know, Lily, how I tend to bake on cold days as the house is full of drafts and a person could catch her death. I bake by smell. It's the only way that's sure. Each thing, whether pie or cake or bread has its own peculiar smell the moment it's done, and once you know what that smell is, you never fail to take baked goods out on time. It's why the cookbooks always say: Bake 'til done. You never read one saying: Bake for thirty-five minutes, because you never know for sure just how hot the oven might be or how heat might be affected by the cold outside. And so I smelled the bread's yeast just as the knock came at the door.

"'Agnes Murdock?' I said when I answered the door and saw her standing there all bundled. Naturally, I knew it was Agnes Murdock.

Everybody knows everybody. But I'd never spoken to the girl even so much as to pay her the time of day.

"'May I come in, Mrs. Olson?' she says to me, sounding all forlorn and shivering something terrible.

"I'm a Christian woman, Lily, church or none, and couldn't very well say no, the weather being what it was and this girl nearly freezing to death.

"'You'd best do that, girl,' I says to her, and since she seemed near to collapsing right there on the icy stoop, I put my arm around her and pulled her in, saying as I did it, 'Hurry on, now. You're letting in the cold.'

"Those dark blue Murdock eyes of hers were red and swollen with crying and the scarf around her neck and mouth was frozen with the moisture of her breath and tears. I got her into the kitchen and set her in the rocking chair by the stove, removing her outer clothes and boots before I did so. She just kept shivering something awful.

"'I can't feel my feet.' She reached down to them.

"'Of course not,' I told her. 'It's past twenty below out there. Did you walk here all the way from your farm?'

"She just nodded, giving no real explanation. Not right then.

"I drew some water in a basin and added hot water from the kettle to make it lukewarm so as not to encourage chilblains. The girl stuck her feet in slowly but her face showed she felt the burning that results from frostbite. I went to the closet for blankets and tucked them around her.

"'You just sit there and get warm,' I told her and went off to make her a cup of tea.

"That was when I remembered the bread and pulled the loaves from the oven, overdone and fit for nothing but toast or bread pudding."

Adeline put a cover on the skillet, and poured two cups of coffee from the big enamel pot. She brought the cups to the table and motioned to Lily to stop peeling potatoes and sit with her while she finished her story.

"I guess the girl was about fourteen at the time. It was a while ago. Just after you got back from that convent school. Anyhow, she talked in fits and starts that day, words and sobs all mashed together. Myself, I was still dumbstruck that I had a Murdock in my kitchen.

"'I didn't know who else to tell,' she got that much out. 'And you, well, you are closest and most far away.'

"I suppose she meant to say her mother despised me but I was a neighbor and, for both reasons, safe and reliable. I knew enough of Marcia Murdock to suspect she treated that girl as a slave, kept out of school from eighth grade on in order to work the farm. Agnes worked while Marcia's boy, that Ancil, made a name for himself on the school football team and graduated at the top of his class of seventeen young people. Seventeen is not the world, but you could never tell him that. You just ask Joseph. Joseph knows the colors of that scallywag.

"'I need your help,' Agnes said to me that day.

"Well, wasn't that a turn I hadn't expected? Marcia's own daughter, giving me an opportunity to even the score between us. But that's another story, and not one I speak of now my Henry's dead and gone. I simply said, 'Then you'll need to tell me what the problem is.'

"'There's going to be a baby.'" Adeline's voice mimicked Agnes's, a whine, a sniffle, a tone so ridiculous that it made Lily cringe.

"I tell you, Lily, the girl said it like it had nothing to do with her, like it was some otherworldly thing that afflicted her like the cold she'd just breathed in hard and cutting as any steel blade.

"'You're in a family way?' I felt sympathetic despite the Murdock connection because, well, I don't have to tell you what such an unfortunate condition can mean to a young girl, now do I, Lily? Poor thing gagged on sobs as if she might vomit and she says to me, 'Yes ma'am.'

"'You're sure?' I asked, because she was so young and the young can imagine all sorts of things when there's no information but what they get from watching animals in the barn. But she told me she was sure.

"'You've been to a doctor?' I asked her then, because still I couldn't be sure the girl knew what she was talking about.

"'No ma'am,' she said, getting all teary-eyed again. 'I couldn't. I mean, there's only one in town and he'd tell my mother and she'd kill me. I mean, Mrs. Olson, she really would do that. Or she'd throw me out like she's said she would all these years except for the work I do.' That's what she told me, Lily, I swear it. Not that I was surprised. But I still pressed on.

"'Then how are you sure?' I wanted her to say the words.

"'It's three months. All the signs are there.' She looked downward as she spoke, but it was true. I could see it myself.

"'And what is it you think I can do to help?' By this time, you can imagine, Lily, I was feeling more than just a little sympathetic for the child.

"'The baby's cursed,' she said. `A curse in me. I can't let it be born, Mrs. Olson.'"

"'And you want...' I knew what she wanted, of course.

"'I need you to help me get rid of it.'

"'Abortion?' I could hardly say the word.

"'It has to come out.' She held her arms crossed over the front of her, tight, as though to try to stop the trembling.

"'I'm against abortion,' I said more as a pondering of the situation than as a conclusion or a decision. If ever there was sin, killing innocent children must be at the top of the list. That's how it always seemed to me. Add to that all my prayers for children of my own. I'd wanted a dozen is what I always said. Well, I had Joseph and that was the end of it. No more, the doctor said. No more.

"'Please...,' the girl whined. I despise whining for the way it turns a human being into something crawling on the earth, some creature of mud and slime, something weak and not worthy to live. A whiner brings out a part of me I just can't tolerate, a part that wants to step on the weaker one and grind their sniveling body into the dirt as though they actually were nothing but a worm.

"'I'm sorry, girl, but you'll have to find someone else.' I couldn't even look at her as I said it.

"'There is no one else, ma'am, and this baby can't be born.' Agnes Murdock said in the strongest voice I'd heard her use yet. Then she told me the story of it. She told me the story, Lily, and it's a story you should heed. She told me about being a child in her bed in darkness and her brother coming into her room, asking her to play, saying he just wanted to play with her. Her brother rubbing his body against hers. Her brother exploring her, every part of her.

"'I told him it hurt me.' I wish you could have heard her voice, Lily, and you'd never speak to Ancil Murdock again. `But he wouldn't stop,' she said over and over. He wouldn't stop. He wouldn't. I asked her how old she was and she said six at first. Six only. And that little bastard was nine. Nine years old!

"'And it never stopped?' I asked and she said 'Never.' And so I said, 'Even now?' and she told me 'Yes ma'am.'

"'So this baby you're carrying?' I tell you, Lily, I felt horrified to hear the answer.

"'It's because of him,' she said. 'My brother Ancil is the one who put me in a family way, and the baby is a curse.'

"She closed her eyes against her shame and tears squeezed out from the edges of her eyelids.

"'I suppose it is.' I told her. And who was I to know? That day I learned a truth about myself, I'm not God. I don't always know what's right or who's good or how is best to feel. I didn't make the world and I don't know what having a mother like Marcia Murdock can do to a girl or to a boy for that matter. I blame her. I blame Marcia for her daughter's predicament. But even though the sin is on her, that boy of hers is dangerous.

"Henry and I had just bought our first truck back then, and we drove the girl to Grand Forks the next week, on a Tuesday, after the cold snap. She made some excuse for being gone—I don't know what and it's none of my business. We left her off at a big white house where such things are taken care of, and we waited for her in a café while she had it done. Afterwards she was pretty sick and in a lot of pain, but I took care of her like my own and not the child of Marcia Murdock who didn't deserve children if she could let it come to this.

"Such things as this are never finished, Lily. I dream about that baby Agnes killed. Even after all this time, that baby comes to me. That baby haunts me. And it never grows up, that baby doesn't. Sometimes it is lying on the seat of the truck in the exact spot Agnes rode when we went to Grand Forks. Sometimes I'm putting it in a gunnysack like I do the kittens when they overrun the barn and I intend to drown them in Cold Creek. Sometimes it's just crying in the other room and I'm singing it a song, a lullaby, and thinking to myself—it will be all right, someday it will be all right.

"She must have had some sort of premonition. A baby such as that should not be born. I've not lived on a farm all these years without learning what such offspring bring with them into the world. Cats with six toes and no ears. I've seen them. Not a curse, certainly, but not right either. Not the way God intends if God could have his way, which it seems he can't where it comes to human beings and what we set in motion by the choices that we make. Poor Agnes."

Adeline picked up her teaspoon and stirred it around in what remained of her coffee.

"I blame her mother. And I blame that brother of hers as well. No doubt about it; Ancil Murdock is a snake and I hope I've convinced you of that fact. He's no friend of this family, Lily Olson, and I'll thank the good Lord when he is dead and gone."

Adeline drained her coffee cup, and stood up to check on her pie. During all this recitation, Lily had barely said a word. Now she sat, her cup of coffee still full to the brim. A worm of fear began slithering up her back and curled into a knot in her belly just beneath her heart.

"I've given you fair warning." Adeline said from over by the stove, her voice confident and clear.

~~~

Lily climbed the ladder into the attic. Hot in summer, freezing cold in winter, the attic held mostly boxes of clothes and memorabilia Adeline had collected through the years. At the east and west ends two rather small windows, dusty and filled with cobwebs, let in morning light. Joseph never came up there, and Adeline had become a bit unbalanced with age and no longer trusted ladders. Lily stood in the sunlight and took a deep breath. "Perfect," she whispered.

In town the next day she bought three large tubes of oil paint in the primary colors plus black and white, brushes, linseed oil, turpentine, and canvases. She'd been saving egg money since the day Ancil met her in the field. Something must be done with this ache she now felt, and she knew no way to keep it from consuming her except to paint it. She bought all the supplies she could afford and determined to add to them as more money became available. She would paint it all. If she couldn't buy canvas, she'd use wooden boards; she'd paint the walls if she had to, but she'd get it out of herself. The sea foam blue of Mama's eyes. The agonized boy that was her brother Stephen; she'd paint him with those defiant eyes, so dark you couldn't find the pupil. She'd paint the turbulence of Joseph and Ancil. Adeline as a sharp kitchen knife. The prairie grass flattened by her body, Cold Creek, the path to Murdock's farm. Blood, milk and stars.

She set the first canvas on an old table, leaning it against a weight-bearing four-by-four. On a base of textured gray, a scribble of black prairie grass, and through it all, crashing like a spirit of sudden awareness, a streak of red.

~~~

Winter came in a storm on November 1st, the Feast of All Saints. Lily and Joseph woke to it, the wind hard against the house, battering. He held her in the slant light. They would be snowbound. Later he'd dig his way to the barn. Later Mother Olson would call to them.

"Up now children. Coffee's on."

At that moment of wind and dawn she turned to Joseph and said please. She said, "Please, Joseph. Please kiss me."

His eyes so full of innocence, so blue. She drank them in like water.

"You're different today," he said.

"Am I?" She took her husband's hand and placed it on her breast. A pearl, she thought. I am a pearl. I am neither dark nor wild.

"Look at me," she whispered as she lifted her gown and it was as if she could see herself through Joseph's eyes for the first time. She heard him gasp. All this time of being married and he had never seen her body, never loved her slowly, never taken for himself the pleasure she could give.

That morning Lily forgot she had begun to think of Joseph as her brother, and she remembered who he really was.

Afterwards Joseph held tight to her. His right hand grasped her wrist like a hand of bone that would not unlock.

"Promise me, Lily," he said. "Promise you'll never leave."

"I'll never leave," she murmured, certain that it was the truth.

"Promise that you are mine and no one else's."

"I am yours."

It was April and Lily was heavy with James before she saw Ancil again.

"Is that...?" Ancil's eye's focused on her belly.

"No. No, it's Joseph's." She felt embarrassed to say what should never have needed to be said.

"You're sure?" Behind him on the trees the new leaves, small, perfectly formed, and pussy-willows with soft buds she felt drawn to touch, to paint.

She couldn't be sure, really now, could she? But by the calm of the child and by her own irrational melding with the life she contained, she clung to what she had said as truth itself. Joseph was her husband. What other answer could there be?

Ancil reached his hand toward her. His face hinted at that flash of something she once had seen and tried to nurture, but now she turned away from him. She moved toward the trees, the new leaves, the soft buds, enclosing their delicate gray fur in her hand and running her hand up the branch.

"I'm leaving, Lily." His voice came from behind her so he didn't see the jolt his words caused, the way the blood drained from her face.

"Leaving?" One tiny soft bud at a time, her fingers touched them, lightly, each bud the only bud. How could she turn around to face him?

"The war. I'm going to enlist."

She knew he waited for her to turn around. But if she had, what would have happened then? She watched the fields behind the willows blur.

"Perhaps it's just as well," she finally said.

The baby must be her gravity now, and whatever wildness Ancil had discovered in her must be tamed, held down, grounded in her child. Still she didn't turn to him. Still she stood by the willows until she heard him walk away.

~~~

James entered the world with summer into the hands of Adeline Olson. "He's dark." She held him up, smeared as he was with goo and blood, and Lily saw him as a palette on which all the colors of her life had been combined. "But it looks to me like he'll have Joseph's blue eyes."

"I'm the one who is dark," she told the older woman. "Just look at him. He's beautiful."

Then she was a flood evaporating in the light of her son,

absorbed into him and out of the distant Ancil as if Ancil had been only a depression in the land where rain collects. What Joseph could accomplish only sporadically, her son wrought simply by being. The cry of James in the night wakened every cell in her and she knew nothing but that sound. She rose and fell upon its vibrations as if she had become the air itself moving with the cry's passage through her. James, James, James. Milk came to her breasts and soaked her nightgown as she hurried to him and picked him up, and the milk flowed thick and warm from her nipples. He took her breast and gazed into her eyes so that although her mind told her he was just a baby like any other, her heart insisted he was the most ancient of beings. If she could sink deep enough into his eyes she would find there the hidden secret that gave rise to everything.

~~~

The seasons turned and James grew. All the common things, the talking, walking, waking, sleeping, everything simple and ordinary, appeared to Lily as miracles. Even spending herself for him, the exhaustion of walking him up and down for hours in the middle of the night to quiet him so Joseph and Mother Olson could sleep, even that gave her a substance never hers before.

Sometimes when she held James, when she babbled to him in those nonsense syllables and he regarded her seriously as if finally she had understood the great secret he came to share, she felt within her something she had lost when her mama died. She felt it first one morning while eating toast and spooning porridge into James's mouth. He was maybe ten months old. She took a bite and chewed and he reached toward her mouth with his fingers and laughed. Then she filled the spoon with his cereal and made a great show of its passage through the air and toward him and his open mouth. She took another bite of toast and suddenly she felt as if her own mama were inside her, chewing the toast. "This is how toast felt in Mama's mouth," she said aloud.

Who then, she continued her mental explorations, is eating this toast? It occurred to her that such thoughts might be crazy, but the feelings they engendered widened her perception of the world and filled her with such calm that if crazy was what she'd become, she preferred craziness to a normal state of mind. She sat at the table feeding James and eating toast and everything and everyone felt present and absent at the same time, and Lily, too—she turned into everything and nothing. She looked into the eyes of James and it was her own voice that said "You are my James." Then she kissed his nose. But another voice inside her head was saying "You are my Lily," and she could see in her son's eyes a touch of seafoam blue she had thought she'd lost forever.

"I was wrong about you, Lily," Mother Olson told her one afternoon just after James's first birthday when the two women were canning green beans. James sat in his playpen in the middle of the kitchen and chewed on one of them still fresh and warm with sunshine.

"Oh?"

"Yes. And I don't mind saying when I've been wrong."

Lily broke the tips from each side of a bean and snapped it between her fingers, dropping the halves into the colander.

"I had you pegged for something I see now that you aren't. We're mothers, both of us. We protect our sons." Adeline said.

Lily shook the beans under running water.

"I feared you'd been taken in by that no good Ancil Murdock." Adeline said.

Lily turned and reached into the playpen to pick up James. It was time for his nap and her foray into the attic.

"I was wrong."

Lily looked out the window to watch Joseph check the ripening barley. It would be a good crop this year. It would be ready early for the harvest.

~~~

Ancil Murdock turned and looked at Lily when he passed her on Main Street in Cold Creek. He'd come back from Belleau Woods where he'd fought with the Fifth Marine Corp, and he had that new girlfriend of his hanging on his arm looking like she'd won the Irish Sweepstakes. Goes to show what they say is true, the old cliché about love being blind. Or maybe it's lust. Maybe it's sex that's blind. Lily had three-year-old James in tow, uptown to buy shoes, and she bent down to tie the old ones rather than meet Ancil's eyes. Though she didn't feel a thing from his look. Nothing. She swore it; nothing at all.

Lily had bound herself to Joseph and even to Adeline through her James and nothing, she determined, not even God could untie that knot. She saw Ancil on the street and the sight of him moved her not at all. Not a whit. She stood up, took James by the hand, and went on her way into Kelly's Shoe Store.

The closest she had come to Ancil Murdock in the year since his return was the path leading into the woods to Sarah's cabin. Sometimes she caught a glimpse of him across the field. The path skirted Murdock's property and entered the woods by the big elm whose branches stretched upwards like the arms of someone waking early in the morning. It wound through the woods west to the fork in Cold Creek.

It had been by that creek, the spring that Lily's father brought her home from the academy for girls, that she'd first seen the fortune teller kneeling on a rock in mid-stream, her wild hair flung over her head into the icy water.

"Hello!" She hadn't wanted to frighten the woman, and someone coming quietly, as she had, out of the woods might have frightened anyone.

"Oh!" The young woman turned her head and looked at Lily who saw in her demeanor a large cat, a tiger, sinuous and sleek.

"I'm Lily Ste. Germaine, from the farm up creek a ways. Aren't you freezing in that water? It's only just melted."

"It's cleanest this time of year." Her hair fell in wet ropes down her back. She stepped off the flat rock and waded to shore.

There would be times in the future that the woman would appear to Lily as old, her hair a tangle of mosses, spiders weaving there as though she were a tree, an oak, with arms that hold the sky. Other times Lily would remember her as a child, mythical, a fairy or water sprite who could disappear in a sudden beam of light. Sometimes, from the distance Lily would travel, she would become certain that the woman didn't exist at all but was a part of herself, as though a person could divide in two and cast the part she wants to understand out before her in a human form. She would imagine that she actually had walked into the other woman's body and taken up life in the cage of her bones, lost herself there, finally becoming everything that's wild and marauding on sheer rock cliffs thrust up at the margins of the world.

"Where did you come from before you lived here?" They sat that day at the crude wooden table in the cabin in the woods. Gooseberry brambles and stinging nettle protected this woman named Sarah on the field side of her cabin, and the creek made a boundary on the other.

She poured Lily a cup of sweet smelling tea.

"What is this?" Lily asked, holding the cup close to her nose and inhaling the tea's perfume.

"Linden tea," she said.

"Linden? From the tree with those spreading branches and the fragrant air around them?"

"The flowers, those big clumps in the spring. I collect them and dry them."

"Ummm. Makes me feel dreamy." Lily leaned back against the chair. "Who are you, really?" she said, returning to her original question.

Sarah's nose crinkled when she laughed.

"I was a runaway from Minneapolis."

"Did you build this place?" Lily looked around, seeing it was a sturdy.

"I did. I was young enough back then to think I could do anything that I could think up." Sarah laughed again.

~ ~ ~

Lily returned to Sarah whenever she could, before and after her marriage to Joseph, until James was born, and afterwards, carrying him in her arms, and finally with him tagging after her asking the name of this and the use of that. The two women knit themselves together, coming to know of one another everything there was in them to know.

James would be turning four soon. Lily woke one morning, her mind crowded and noisy as a field of crickets. Rush off to Sarah's cabin to finish the toys they were making. A carved wooden truck with wheels that turned. A sling shot. A flute Sarah hollowed from a kind of reed that grew along the creek bed. She had several of her own, different sizes and tones, she'd play while James clapped his hands and sang his funny little made-up songs.

Afterwards Lily wondered why she hadn't waded the creek all the way? Why had she taken the path past Murdock's? But she always took the path. The heat crawled down her neck under her hair, dampening her back. Lily gloried in it. She opened her lungs to it, filled as it was with the scent of earth and of growing. The linden blossoms drooped heavy from the trees. Gooseberries along the path looked ready for a pie. The high bush chokecherries had turned. In another week they'd make jelly. Mother Olson and she would do it together, listening afterwards for the popping of lids as they drank her thin coffee and talked of sons. That very night she would lie next to Joseph and they would whisper of the birthday surprises and how their James would laugh.

Ancil Murdock strode towards her through the field.

"Lily." Standing right in her path the way he was, he appeared giant. She smelled him, the heat of him, the earth.

"Ancil." She nodded her head, saying the word as calmly as she could and making a move to go around him on her way. He reached out his arm to block her passage. She turned to pass him on the other side. He blocked again and laughed. "Excuse me, please." Her voice shook.

"Excuse you, is it? Excuse you?"

"What is it you want, Ancil?" Whatever made her think politeness could smooth the raw edges of the tear between them?

"For starters, maybe you could let me see my son."

Despite the heat a chill seeped through Lily's bones.

"I don't know what you mean."

He laughed. "Like hell you don't!"

Lily had ripped it from her mind or else she had buried it so deep it came back to her only in dreams from which she woke moaning and terrified. Over the years she had told herself that everything with Ancil must have been a dream and nothing of it real.

"James isn't yours," she declared, defiant.

"Like hell he isn't," he snarled.

"There's nothing of you in him," she insisted.

"He's dark," Ancil said.

"I'm dark."

"You're dark all right." He grabbed her arm.

"No."

"You can't hide it. I can smell you, the wild in you, the animal. You're dark. Dark and juicy and wanting a good fuck."

"Let me go!" But he wouldn't let her go

She felt the stubble of fields on her back. She felt his tongue thrust into her mouth and she gagged. How could a tongue become hard and pointed that way? She felt his hands tear at her clothes, his teeth on the soft flesh of her breast, the sticky blood. The smell of him thickened, like that of rotten fish. She heard the ripping of her clothes. She wanted to scream, but swallowed the sound. She opened her mouth and all that came out of it was gagging. She floated from herself like a sparrow over fields. She still could feel him though, pounding her into the ground with his hard body, ramming himself up into her, grunting the word, whore, over and over.

"Joseph was the wrong choice." He sneered as he looked at her afterwards, lying there, all bloody and bruised. She closed her eyes and gritted her teeth. He would not see her cry.

Sarah washed her in the creek. Sarah poured water from a bowl over Lily's head and told her it would wash her clean. Lily sobbed. She let Sarah wash her hair as she once had witnessed the gypsy washing her own. She let her put salve like holy oils on her wounds. She let her sing to her, lullabies, as though she were an uncommon mother, the mother of the world.

"I should have done something to stop him." Lily sobbed.

"There was nothing you could do." Sarah soothed.

"I should have come another way." Lily argued.

"You couldn't know."

"I should have followed Mother Olson's advice to begin with. I should never have gone near the Murdock farm."

"Then we never would have met."

They cried together after that because there really was no way they could change a thing.

~~~

Joseph and Lily lay in bed. He saw the bites, the bruising. "Ancil," she told him, and she gagged on the word.

He said nothing. She waited. The silence made a rope that pulled tight between them as he seemed to move farther and farther away.

She waited. The fear began like a germ in her, almost imperceptible. She felt it wiggle, though. She felt it grow and move from the pit of her stomach up her body. It filled her. She felt that she would vomit it.

"Joseph?" she whispered.

He lay still. Inhumanly still.

~~~

The next days she felt invisible. Joseph left for the fields without looking at her, without saying goodbye. He'd speak to his mother, but never to her. The germ in the dark pit of her being grew. He just has to get accustomed to it, she told herself. Men probably think they should have been able to protect their wives from such things. He must feel guilty, ashamed. He just needs time. It stunned her--his ability to look right through her as though she wasn't there.

She went to the attic and squirted paint onto her palette. She painted the field, a red swath of blood, and a red-winged blackbird flying overhead.

She applied ointment to her wounds, the bruises, the tears in her most tender flesh.

She went the long way to Sarah's, and when she left the house no one said, "Where are you off to?" or "Will you be home for supper?" Adeline played with James as though he belonged to her alone.

~~~

Joseph continued to lie with her in the same bed, never touching, always turned away. She reached out to lay her hand on his back. He flinched.

"Joseph? Please say something."

He inhaled deeply and the breath came out of him in a gush. Then his voice in the dark.

"What did you do to make this happen?" His voice came down on her like a wall falling, like the side of the barn, like rocks tumbling and burying her so she couldn't breathe.

"I did nothing!" How could he say such a thing? How could he blame her? Why didn't he blame Ancil?

"I don't want to believe it, Lily, but you had to have done something." He measured his words.

"No." She thought she might begin to cry, but she couldn't cry. Only the smallest sounds could escape her, useless words.

"You went there." He said.

"To Sarah's."

"You went where he could see you. So foolish! So thoughtless. You know him. You know what he is."

She wouldn't say, I'm sorry. Couldn't. She had to hold to something.

Again he was silent for a long time.

"I can't touch you now, you know. Not ever." He finally said in a voice so wooden it seemed a coffin in which all her dreams would be locked from that day on.

"But…"

"This isn't just to yourself this is done. You've done this to me, to my family, to James." He sounded strangled. "Didn't you even think of your own son before you went over there?"

It was no use talking. She turned away from him.

~~~

He'll soften to me, she thought as she pinned the wet clothes on the line. She saw him, a mark upon the distance, dust and chaff whirling, a brass sun. He will have to soften to me. A week, two weeks, by James's birthday. But he never did.

"Mama has to go now," Lily told James the morning of his birthday. He stood there in the center of the room, his little fists clenched as if he knew she never would come back.

~~~

As she walked the creek to Sarah's cabin she felt again her own mama's presence in her, stronger this time than before, and again her mama cried and bled from her breasts, and for the first time Lily understood her mama's need to be rid of flesh and reduced to bone. She understood that sometimes women leave their lives behind because their lives are taken from them anyway. Lily saw herself

154

before her life was formed, before her illusion of being someone who could stand alone and tall ever had been wrought. Her mama must have felt the same. For Aimee St. Germaine, as now for Lily, this illusion evaporated. It isn't what we do, she thought. It's what we are. Every mirror into which she'd ever gazed to find her own image shattered at the moment Joseph rejected her. Sometimes all that's left to do in life is leave what you thought would be your home, or slowly over the years, watch all your dreams crumble, mix with the earth, and be lost.

8

After that storm in 1945, Sarah saw the blue hat stuck on a thorn bush and knew the whole thing was starting up again. That's Yarrow Olson's hat, she said to herself, and I'll bet my bones she's off and run away from James. Poor man should have seen it coming. Probably wouldn't, or couldn't afford to, not with his history. Funny thing, how people can't put together their own stories, can't pick out the hints stuck into them like Yarrow stuck those bluebird feathers into her hat. Soon as Sarah saw those feathers, months before, while the hat still sat on top of Yarrow's head, she'd told herself the woman had some kind of ache in her.

Sarah saw the hints. She knew the stories. Some stories can't be told from the inside out. It takes an outsider, somebody like her, with the time and inclination to keep an eye out and listen. All these years she'd lived on the boundary line between the three families—the Olson's, the Murdock's and the Ste. Germaine's. And sooner or later every one of them had showed up at her door, carrying a story that couldn't be held onto for even one more day or it would stop the heart. She cast the bones for them and revealed most of what she saw in the patterns that fell from her hands.

Her mother warned her long ago that if her spirit matched her hair the world was in for trouble. When she turned twelve, Sarah told her mother to stop cutting it short. She didn't like the tight little tangles all over her head. Let it grow. Let it do what it wants.

"Well, it's your hair." And so it was. And so was Sarah's life—her own. And her voice, whether she would sing on stage, which she would not. "Well, Sarah, just throw that away along with everything

156

else," Mother said. And so she did. But hadn't she sung every day for all her life? She'd sung and played the flute she made from willow that grows along Cold Creek. Spent one whole day hollowing the still green wood and forming eight holes to fit her fingers exactly. She played it when she wanted a voice more familiar with the wind than her own could be, a voice drifting like milkweed seed on the North Dakota air. A voice not unlike the voice of God.

She told Ancil Murdock as much when he came to her with his swagger and his cash. You think you can buy the world with your filthy money, she told him right into his teeth. Well you can't buy me. I'm God.

You're god all right, he scoffed with his hand holding her head back by the grip he had on her hair. She still could smell him as he was back then, the smell of his guns, of the gun powder, the petroleum in the bluing, the oiled wood of the stock. His dark hair hung down his forehead to his pointed nose, and his eyes gleamed purple they were such a deep blue. She kneed him in the balls and while he was doubled over groaning she poured boiling water over peppermint leaves for tea to soothe his manhood both of body and of mind. A lot of good it did! Born under a curse, that man. It was all there in the bones, and no matter how often she cast them, it never varied. Besides, what other explanation could there be? He was born to be the question on which the rest could measure themselves and then stretch their lives.

It seemed to be a destiny they shared--Ancil Murdock and Sarah. Their lives were questions, and that's what joined them for good or ill. The townsfolk, those who whispered her name, Sarah, along with their judgments of her, came to her door in tears or with faces white as the bones they begged her to cast in their behalf. She gave what she had when she chose, and she gave it freely. But she'd never set out to be anyone's answer.

In her fifty-four years her body had changed form but slightly. Her teeth yellowed and wore down from the grains and nuts, and the cords in her neck protruded. Her skin, though, had stretched itself more tightly over her bones and when she saw her reflection in the window of the grocery in Cold Creek, it was not that of a women softened by age, but a body made of parchment and sinew with jade eyes and still red hair.

That morning after the big storm she had opened the door of

her cabin on a world toppled by wind. James Olson's barley lay trounced by the feet of giants who must have been playing pick-up sticks with the branches and twigs tossed from the trees. She took a deep breath and stretched. Then she saw the blue hat. Yarrow, Yarrow, she mourned. I suppose you took the girl away from him too. She untangled the hat from the thorns and set it on her head. No sense letting a good hat go to waste. If Yarrow turned out anything like Lily, she never would come home.

~~~

Sarah had never glimpsed an angel, but she knew how they'd surrounded her since she was a girl. Devils too. They danced sparks in her hair on winter nights, whispering in her mind. She fought them off all the while her mother died.

My sweet girl, her mother reached and touched her face.

Sarah knew what it is to run. She ran from Guardian Angels Orphanage in Minneapolis where a judge put her after her mother died of TB. She no longer can remember much about the place, just red brick walls and big dormitory rooms and nuns with scarce faces and lowered eyelids who could never take a mother's place. She stayed two weeks eating liver dumpling soup and blood sausage before, on a night with no moon, she slipped past the curtained bed of the snoring nun, and out the door that locked conveniently from the inside. She'd be on her own. She knew the rule: any child who can't appreciate the blessing given her in living at Guardian Angels, doesn't deserve to spend another night, warm, and sleeping among those who are wiser and more worthy. If you run away from here, no one will come looking for you.

She followed the Mississippi River north, always holding to the country roads, stopping outside towns so small they had nothing but a general store and a clapboard church. She gathered small things along the way. Feathers. Weathered bones of small animals.

Bones slip easily from the cord on which they're strung. They fall on a wooden table with a sound like milk teeth scattered. In moonlight they glow because they have absorbed the oils of a woman's skin. At first Sarah cast them only for herself, their patterns difficult to enter. Why am I here? she asked the bones. Will I find love? Is there a purpose to my birth and death? What am I to do? The voices in her mind laughed, but she would not stop the casting of the bones. Laugh all you want, she told the voices, I am here. I'm only asking why.

Little by little she learned to leave her body and enter the pattern of the bones. In this pattern no edges exist, nothing begins nor ends. Atoms whirl and separate, universes open to infinity. She entered the pattern of the bones and walked among the stars into the mind of God where she learned there is no 'why,' but only the velvet dark of being.

In cafés where she washed dishes for food, she spread the bones on the table and tried to see the pattern in them. People stopped to look. They asked about the bones. They asked her to find a pattern for them. Dancing, singing and casting bones, this is the soul's way. Everything has pulse. Feel. Listen. Hold the bones. She feels the pulse of the person in front of her; she feels it with her soul. Those three, the bones, her soul, and the pulse of the other person's being mingle. When she listened carefully to that pulse, she heard the truth. It happened every time.

Often they gave her money for the insights she took from the way the bones lay.

Touch and go is what it was. She waited on tables, collected garbage, cast the bones--anything for a few dollars. Then once the Mississippi ended, she turned west. She bought an acre of land in North Dakota between three farms.

~~~

Marcia Murdock found her first. Sarah was nineteen years old. She saw the door was ajar when she returned from gathering raspberries by the edge of the field. The older woman sat at the wooden table in a ray of sunlight that sharpened her face and put fire in her eyes. She smiled, but Sarah read something almost sinister beneath the smile that put her on guard.

"I see you built a shack on my land." The woman separated each word just enough to cause each to drop on Sarah's ear as a warning. Marcia Murdock was a beautiful woman then. Good bones. That's what people say of beautiful women. She looked carved, chiseled by a master artist.

"The county assessor says different." Sarah replied.

The woman lifted her head in a pose so that Sarah was made to see the best side of her face, the eyebrow that she raised above that inscrutable eye. "Do you intend to live here?"

"As I started to say, the state owned this acre between the farms. I bought it." Sarah's voice stayed calm and steady. A strong voice. Resolved.

Marcia Murdock, deciding to make the best of her lapse of attention regarding the land, hired the girl to entertain her friends with prophecy. They paid Marcia dearly and she kept the greater portion of the money in a strong box hidden in a large wardrobe. Sarah gave but the skin of truth because truth's wild depths cannot be purchased with gold, but only with a willingness of heart. When she cast the bones she saw in the faces of the questioners either greed or longing. To the greedy she gave a fortune like the gypsy they expected her to be. To the desirous she gave hope and an invitation to visit her in the woods. The one chosen by God is not often the one this world notices at all.

Over the years the people brought Sarah whatever she might need. If she fell sick, Doc Johnson soon was knocking at her door. If Swede Munson chopped a cord of firewood, he brought her a bundle. Even Joseph Olson once carried a big sack of flour on his shoulder and let it drop onto her wooden table. She saw the fissure in his eye. The sorrow. This was after Lily left. "You knew her," he mourned, his face in his hands. He was a man whose words resisted his thoughts. She read the bones for him and saw patterns of ripe fields drying to ruin in an unremitting sun.

For all of them she, even now, thanks Marcia Murdock who, in the end, got the lesser benefit from the deal she made. Who knows but that her strong box still is hidden, locked, in her dank wardrobe? The people came to Sarah. She took no money. They let her travel in their eyes.

~~~

In his own house Sarah first met Ancil Murdock. He was but sixteen and not yet enchanted by Lily St Germaine. His mother clung to him, fondling him with words. She pulled him toward her. This is my son, my handsome boy, Ancil. Kiss me Ancil. He backed away. Sarah felt his disgust and then his fear like a beetle caught in a honey trap. His rejection triggered his mother's anger. Little Bastard! She spat at him. He said nothing. He walked away.

He came to Sarah in the woods. She cast the bones and in their pattern saw an empty universe. "You will seek in dark places," she told him. She wept. He wanted her to tell him more but there was nothing more to tell. Not yet. And they were both of them too young to know the depth of affliction, the extent of anguish in such things.

He brought ducks in autumn which he shot as they landed in the backwash of Cold Creek. He brought partridge and grouse, and later in November, venison. His gift was for the hunt. In the breath or the eye or the manner of flight he felt the point of vulnerability, and his aim was sure. Sarah felt no squeamishness about such things. In winter he brought rabbit white as the snow, and she dressed it out and served it up for both of them in a stew.

~~~

Leaves in summer cast a green light and she directed Ancil's gaze to the ever changing play of brilliance and shadow. They sat together on her porch. Not a porch, really, just planks nailed down across the front, a kind of enlarged stoop to keep rain from running under the door. He leaned, tipping the chair so only its back legs touched the wood. Maybe he was thirty by then. His chest heaved large and muscular.

"No one ever loved me, Sarah," is what he told her after a long silence.

"Not your mother?" she asked, even though she knew the answer he would give.

"She loves herself and her money. She doesn't even love her land, just the amount of land she owns."

"And how is that different from you, Ancil?"

"She substitutes money and possessions for herself."

"And how is that different?" She pressed him. She could feel the resistance in his mind.

"I needed her."

"Is there no one who needs you?"

"No one at all."

The green light played across his face, emphasizing its angles, deepening the sadness in his eyes that contrasted with the hard lines around his mouth.

"I hate her," he said, "for holding everything so tight."

"And Lily?"

"Lily's nothing to me now. Lily is just air I'll never breathe again."

"And James?"

He darkened. "James is a little bastard and can go to hell!"

"Hell? And isn't he already there, and been there these many years, ever since you raped his mother?" The words were red-hot coals in her mouth that she spit at him. She hoped to burn him with them. She meant to wake him up by searing him with the truth.

He laughed like the devil. "Shit!" he sneered as he pushed the chair back. It squealed, wood on wood. "The whore wanted it!" He knocked the chair over as he got up. He left it toppled on her porch and strode off into the woods without looking back.

~~~

She cast bones for Ancil Murdock and he told her his story in fits and starts, little pieces here and there tucked between venomous bursts of hate. He left to her the task of stitching all of it together, or else he didn't care one way or the other. A person can come to detest his life with such focus and intent as to seek its destruction, not only in his own body, but anywhere he sees its reflection. Weakness, violence: he found them equally detestable, and rarely allowed himself to experience the one without the other.

He had her by the throat one night. He'd surprised her in her sleep, jerking her from bed and throwing her onto the floor. She felt the planks. Slivers of wood cut from this very land forced themselves through the thin cotton of her nightgown and into the backs of her legs. Once his hold on her stopped breath altogether and she began the slow motion flight into unconsciousness, she actually welcomed the ragged splitting of skin, that small pain, possibly the last sensation of her body. She smelled his dead fish smell. She looked into his eyes and wasn't afraid because it had been years since she'd feared death.

Everything dies. It's the way that God let's go of what's become a hindrance so we can expand. So we can grow. She didn't fear him; she detested him. She detested the overt violence she felt exploding from the weakness of his decomposing mind. She kept her eyes on him through all of it.

"Don't look at me, witch! Close those green cat-eyes or I'll close them for you, you piece of shit!"

Through the window she could see the moon full and silver as God's eye. And then she didn't see anything.

She woke, probably a moment later, gasping for breath and hearing Ancil's wails. His hand caressed her hair and face. "Sarah, Sarah, Sarah," he cried. Her throat felt like a twisted foot and no sound could come out.

Who am I? She would have yelled at him, and did manage to say, finally, when her voice managed a croak. "Who are you trying to kill?" He was up off her by then, snorting, sniffling, weak as a worm. "You'll not kill me!" Words like fingernails on slate. "I'll have my rifle cocked the next time, Ancil Murdock, do you understand my meaning?"

Later he said he must be the devil's spawn, that his mother had been right. He never could get himself around the thought that underneath her fawning, his mother despised him.

"Her nature was quicksilver," he told Sarah one autumn afternoon when she walked beside him while he hunted the ruffled grouse. "She constantly changed shape towards me. I never knew what to expect." His shotgun seemed a part of his arm.

"She dressed me in those ridiculous costumes. Velvet. Can you beat that? Velvet girlish pants and jackets, and she took me with her to her high and mighty Presbyterian church. They laughed. The other children. What would you expect them to do? They laughed and I fought them and the clothes ripped on the gravel in the church alley. When she found me, ripped and bloody, it was the clothes she mourned. She took the velvet in her hands and turned it over and rubbed it and then shook it in my face. 'Why you little bastard!' She called me that over and over—Bastard, like it was my given name. 'Just look at what you've done. You mean, ungrateful boy.'"

Ancil continued on in a flat voice. "She called me bastard from the time I could remember. And when I argued, pointing out my father, she just laughed and said, Little do you know."

"What if you are?" Sarah asked him. "What difference would it make?" She'd always held, regarding Ancil Murdock, that while evil certainly ran in a strong current through his character, it had not eroded him completely. The pattern of evil in him was strong. But it had not yet consumed the whole man.

"Every difference." He lifted his shotgun and aimed it at a red squirrel that scolded them from a tree branch. It tumbled from its perch and landed with a thud. He kicked it off the path. "I'd be nobody," he snarled.

She kept her silence. She didn't ask him why he killed that squirrel, since she could feel the hollowness of Ancil Murdock in herself, just as if she'd cast the bones and seen their patterns intersecting. She felt his hollowness at the little point of bone between her breasts that she'd always thought must be there to protect her heart.

A few years later Ancil brought news of the world. He spread out the Sunday Grand Forks Herald on her table and pointed at the headlines. Such information slipped through her mind leaving barely a trace. Wars, politics, stocks and bonds. She didn't know these things as others know them. She didn't vote or need much money. She did know war, of course, because she could see it in the casting of bones. She saw the patterns that contradict. She saw how life is blocked and how it shrivels. She saw the fragmentation of minds, the hunger of the spirit, the crazed soul that will do anything to end its dark suffering. She had looked into the absences. She had come to believe that the pattern in the bones is recognized by contemplating the something that is not there. She read the bones as others read the stars or ponder ancient writings. And she couldn't help thinking that whatever human beings do, all the anxious striving, is simply the expression of an aching in the heart of God. Maybe even wars and every other kind of violence we commit upon the world are but an exaggerated reflection of God's struggle to see his own face.

She held the bones in her hand, letting them drop, one by one, onto a cloth she'd woven from linen, silk and wool threads. She always scattered them slowly, never knowing the hell she would enter in the pattern that they took. In Ancil's patterns she'd begun to see twists and turns and dead-ends and love cut off and raging anger mixed with lust. She'd seen patterns in his bones that seized her heart with such anguish that she'd thought herself trapped in his tangled spirit, and when she emerged she wondered for a time if she no longer should be his seeker, because there was in him so little left to find that was not already damned.

On that day before he went to war, she cast the bones and entered the complete emptiness that often was Ancil's pattern, the desolation of winter in stark Dakota fields.

Once at the beginning of winter, and just at twilight when the snow and sky defied division, she had watched a five-point buck come out of the woods and stand listening, alert against the endless sweep of land. A horned god. Ruler of this frozen world. He pawed the white ice that locked in earth whatever might remain of grain or tubers. His breath, great clouds of steam. His agonized cry, afterwards, when the earth refused to yield to him, spoke of something in Ancil Murdock that she could understand. And so the two of them continued on.

She wondered from time to time, though, if we are greeted on the other side of life by the many fragments of God's body. She wondered if Ancil Murdock would be there when she arrived, and if he were, she wondered if he'd know then the secrets that through all his life on earth, he couldn't fathom. She wondered if God would whisper what would not come through her own clenched teeth—that even from the wicked among us God gleans something good and gives it to the world. Maybe God does, and maybe God doesn't. Who was she to say? She also considered that such as Ancil Murdock might be placed by God upon the path we walk as an obstacle to be eliminated. She considered using a knife. She considered turning upon him with his own gun.

The time Ancil came back from France with a German Luger that he kept displayed on the wall of his mother's house and brought to Sarah's cabin to fondle while she cast his bones, the arrangement made no pattern at all. Nothing she could enter. Just a chaos like that in the Bible before God breathed spirit into the dark waters of nothingness.

~~~

After her mother, whom Sarah loved by blood and need, she loved Lily St. Germaine. She loved her and thought the winds would leave her be, would let both of them root themselves like vines root at the feet of giant elms and twine like rope to the topmost branches. Even the pattern of the bones entwined, and she told her: Lily, there's no separating you and me.

The gypsy and the nun—such were the images that flooded Sarah's mind when she first laid eyes on her. Young. Both of them so young. She like a willow with muted color, and Sarah as she'd always been, sumac flaming in the sun. She thought herself the gypsy and Lily the nun, but according to an irony the years had taught her defines this earthly life, Lily ended up the gypsy, didn't she?

"We'll pick wild raspberries," she told Lily when she came into the cabin, even though she could see in her a determination woven of sorrow and strong as the web a spider spins. She set her satchel on the floor beside the door and stood there, her hands hanging at her sides like something no longer part of her. A little breeze came through the window and troubled the hem of her skirt.

"I'm leaving, Sarah." Her voice like a door slamming.

"You just come sit down," she told Lily, pulling a chair out from the table. "You just give yourself a little rest and then we'll pick some raspberries. There'll be plenty of time afterwards for you to decide what to do."

So far Sarah didn't know what had happened to her beyond her experience with Ancil, something that would have been enough to bring her to the cabin again. She hadn't heard of the words that Joseph spoke, nor had the soft tissues of Sarah's brain been seared by the image of little James standing with clenched fists in the middle of the Olson kitchen. Sarah stood by the chair, but Lily didn't move. Only her skirt moved, and had it not been for the breeze that day, Sarah would have thought the two of them were transported into a still life painting. "Lily?" she said and reached out towards her.

Lily fell towards her and she caught her in her arms. She felt the way breath catches and rips like cloth snatched from a hook.

"Come with me, Sarah. I don't know if I can do this by myself."

"Shhhh." She tried to calm her. She hummed then, as softly as she could, vibrations of her voice joining the pulse of her weeping.

"Maybe you don't have to go," Sarah said.

It seemed Sarah's lot in life to be bound by distance to those she loved, by staying when they say they need to go, by letting her own life be an iron stake driven into the ground of their origin. When they came back, if they did, she would be the magnet drawing them.

When she quieted, Sarah took from a shelf two baskets she had woven from bark and the strong grass of the fields, and placed one of them on the table in front of her. "We'll pick wild raspberries and talk," she said as though she knew what was best. "And afterwards you can either stay or go."

Lily followed her into the woods sticky with midsummer heat. Mosquitoes like puffs of black smoke lifted from the grass wherever they stepped, and they waved them away from their faces. It will be like this wherever you walk, Sarah wanted to say, but knew it wouldn't matter. Little irritations rise up anywhere. A woman alone on the road has lost her soul and has no choice except to find it or die.

"The raspberries grow just beyond those big trees and that patch of stinging nettle. Keep your skirt close to your ankles and kick the nettle aside with the sole of your shoe."

She demonstrated. "Here, let me go first," Sarah said. "I'll make a path."

Sunshine in the little field where the wild raspberries grow dried the grass and kept the mosquitoes away. Lily and Sarah sat on an old log and ate the raspberries they had picked while Lily described the events that loosened her roots and then tore her away from Joseph and even from her little boy.

"Shouldn't you stay and face him?" Sarah responded after a while of sunshine and fresh berries. The wild berries were small, no bigger than the tip of a little finger, but had a flavor so intense that each one was worth ten of the tame ones.

"Joseph or Ancil?" Berries had stained her lips. She had a smear of red on her temple where she had brushed away a stray lock of her hair.

"Both, I expect." Sarah held her basket balanced on her knees. She kept popping berries into her mouth to keep their conversation light, knowing Lily was wild that afternoon, skittish as a doe that looks at you but bolts the minute you move towards her.

"I can't." She looked away, out over the field of wild oats.

"Why not? What would happen if you did?" It came to Sarah of a sudden that she yearned to keep her there, hold her, not let her run off as she had once run off. All sorts of thoughts entered her head. The thought—she can't go alone. This one is too fragile to go alone. The thought to cast the bones for her. The thought to read them such that she would have to stay. Looking sideways she could see Lily's thin wrist and her hand still with a wedding band on her finger. She felt the heat of her body. It was all she could do not to reach out, grasp her wrist, hold her back.

Lily didn't say anything, just kept looking away.

"It's best that I go," she finally said so quietly that Sarah barely heard her. Then Lily took the antique wedding ring from her finger and placed it in the gypsy's. "Take this back to Joseph," she said.

"But, James…" Who could believe that she could leave that boy?

"He'll be better off, Sarah. I'm no fit mother. He'll have Adeline and Joseph."

"Don't be a fool, Lily." Sarah touched her arm, and she flinched but didn't look, not even then. "Ancil Murdock is not your fault. I swear, someone ought to shoot that man! And Joseph's acting like a child."

"I can't face either of them."

"Why? What frightens you?"

She looked at Sarah straight on. "That the entire thing is my own fault, and because of that I will lose everything," she said. "At least if I go away I'll still have some fragments of myself. Maybe at a distance from this place and those men I can see more clearly how my own bits and pieces still can fit together." She stood up from the log and her basket of wild berries fell from her lap onto the ground. "I just wish you would come with me."

The magnetism of that plea almost uprooted Sarah. She could see herself setting off, one foot in front of the other, all around the world if need be. To stay with Lily. To be with Lily. What else was there? To care for Lily. For the space of a breath nothing held her and she floated upwards from the ground like a milkweed seed set free. But only for a breath. Even without the bones she could see the pattern, the weakness in Lily's plea. And she had to put it to herself honestly: would she betray her that way? She would not. They stood up. Sarah took Lily into her arms, finally, and kissed her raspberry stained lips.

"Where will you go?"

"Somewhere. West. As far as possible." She lifted her hand to Sarah's face and laid her palm against her cheek. Then she turned away, toward the creek. Sarah watched her go, keeping herself steady, rooted where she stood. She thought those would be her last words, but where the creek turns and converges with a little stream she turned once more to look. She waved and called back.

"Wherever I end up."

Afterwards Sarah continued to rise early, like a nun, summer and winter, in order to be there before sunrise when morning first dims the stars. She took a deep breath of it, the newness of it, sharp as a steel blade in winter, and in summer cool and smelling of grain. Whatever gave her this gift of life, she thanked that one. She joined her voice to the song of the mourning dove that returned each spring. In winter her voice whispered a litany of fire after she laid the logs in the black stove and blew on kindling to coax the flame. Her cabin aged, but it served. Over the years she plugged the cracks between logs, gathered windfall firewood from what the woods provided her, kept a garden, and for what she could not produce herself, she traded the casting of the bones. Isn't that the way of nuns? Trading prayers for goods. Her prayers were in the language of the bones.

And when she cast them for herself, the pattern falling on the cloth resembled a road she traveled within her mind toward a destination she couldn't conjure. It was the road that Lily traveled. She called down that road, Lily! hoping she could hear. But the way was tangled and the earth absorbed her voice.

The years tamed her spirit. She tended her herbs and flowers in summer and read the bones, although the spirits in her mind kept a silence that would have felt strange to her in younger years. The patterns dissolved long ago, leaving only the soft chaos like the last moment of twilight over Cold Creek. Still she could read the bones, seeming to have words for others that she could not find for herself. Odd consolation for all that had disappeared. Still she sang, her voice deeper, songs that had no words.

9

Redwing first visited old Ancil at the Murdock place just after Hannah got lost by the cottonwood. Sometimes she couldn't stand it, looking at Yarrow, at her puckering skin and the places where hair hadn't yet grown. Yarrow didn't have eyelashes anymore and looked disgusting. That was the truth. Even though she was Hannah's mother and needed Hannah's care. Even though she was pretty once. Even though she saved Hannah's life and kept her from looking the same way. Or maybe fire chooses its victims in ways no human understands. Maybe there was nothing, even now there could be nothing that Redwing or Hannah, either one, could do to change a thing. Redwing often had such thoughts, despite her determination to win back her mother's love with goodness. When these thoughts came, bringing with them feelings that belonged rightfully to Hannah, Redwing needed to get out of the house.

Nobody liked her Uncle Ancil. Yarrow said she wouldn't give him the time of day. And Gran called him a snake. But what could be so wrong with him? Redwing had wondered this on the day she was walking along the fence that separated the Murdock farm from the Olson's. That day she had left the house because Yarrow was sleeping and Redwing felt more discouraged than usual, both with Yarrow and with her own life. If Hannah had been there, she might have been lonely for Wanda and for the way things used to be. She might have been mad. Just really in a fury about everything. She might have wanted to yell at Wanda for not jumping out the window. Why did she do that? She might have gone so far as wanting to kill Yarrow for turning out ugly and useless and silent. Such feelings could never be allowed. Only without feeling could Redwing be good and strong enough to do what was needed to win Yarrow back.

The fence stretched to the woods where old Sarah lived. Redwing remembered that Hannah saw her years ago, before Yarrow took her away. Maybe the fortune-teller would come down the path toward the road and she'd be singing. Maybe Redwing could visit her in the shack and learn how to tell fortunes.

Instead of the fortuneteller, Ancil Murdock showed up at the fence.

"Well, well." he had said, his face completely serious. "Yarrow's girl."

Redwing had squinted her eyes, clenched her teeth, and drawn her lips into a straight flat line in an attempt to appear foreboding.

"What's the matter?" The corners of his mouth turned up just a little bit. "Cat got your tongue?"

"No," she said, but she didn't turn away.

"Do you know who I am?" he asked.

"Ancil Murdock." Everybody knew who everybody was, even if you'd never spoken to them. Besides, didn't he remember how Hannah met him at her Grandma's funeral? Of course she knew who he was.

"Right you are, Missy. Ancil Murdock. Your great uncle."

Why did she go to him? She wondered that sometimes, afterwards. The solution might have been as simple and commonplace as that he spoke to her. He smiled. He read passages to her from books he snagged by the spine with his forefinger and let fall from the highest shelves into his hand. Passages from the classics—the *Iliad*, and the St. Crispan's day speech from Shakespeare's *Henry V*. He combined the poetry of his books with his own stories from the war in France. He showed her his uniform and a pistol he took from the stiff hand of a German soldier at a place called Belleau Woods.

~~~

Great uncle Ancil carried his rifle so it pointed toward the ground. It was late summer. By then Redwing must have been fourteen. James had harvested the barley and stubble poked her at every step. The breeze lifted the chaff along with the dust of the prairie, covering her sweaty skin that itched something awful, an itch that grew almost intolerable under the brassy North Dakota sun.

Ancil was teaching her to hunt prairie dogs. It was target practice with a real payoff because they should be called prairie rats the way they bred and messed up the prairie and endangered the horses that might break a leg in one of their holes. They popped their little heads up to sniff the wind and Ancil would take aim. It would be unsporting to use a shotgun even though it could make their heads explode like tiny red volcanoes. He always chose to use his twenty-two.

"There's one!" He shot. It fell. "They're so dumb they deserve to die."

Hannah would have said Uncle Ancil was the dumb one, but Hannah wasn't there. A good thing. Hannah would have cried. She would have turned around and walked home, all that way, alone.

"Now you." He handed Redwing the rifle.

"Keep both eyes open. Use your aiming eye. Line it up, sight to head, and pull the trigger."

A little breeze loosened the scent of cut grain and lifted chaff off the ground, swirling it into her hair. She pulled the trigger.

"You hit it!" He reached over and squeezed her shoulder. "Good Girl!"

She followed after him to inspect her first kill, but it wasn't dead. The bullet grazed it, stunned it.

"Shoot it again," he ordered.

She could see right into the prairie dog's little eyes.

"I don't think I can," she said.

"You have to. It's your kill and you have to finish it off." He recited the rules of the game.

Redwing heard Hannah's voice inside her mind, "Turn around and go home," but she pulled the trigger anyway.

~~~

Old Ancil, when he breathed into her face, smelled like rotten fish. His nose hooked down, the beak of a chicken hawk. He sat in an alcove of his big house and smoked cigars while he read his books. The walls on three sides of him were covered, floor to ceiling with books, except for one window, and that was grimy with cigar smoke. Also the lamp—grimy—its formerly cream colored shade gone to a sickening yellow-gray.

"Come here, girl." He motioned with his hand.

"Call me Redwing." By then she must have told him that a million times!

He cackled.

"Redwing, then. Come on over here, Redwing." He slapped at his bony knee. "Come and sit. I'm not going to hurt you."

"I'm too old for that," she told him straight out.

She had seen what hawks can do, swooping from the sky, claws extended. She had seen the baby rabbit squirm and heard its terrible cry. She had watched the hawk on the strong, curved branch of the cottonwood, tearing at the flesh and sitting afterwards so full it couldn't fly and didn't need to since it was the largest bird around.

One summer afternoon when the crickets had set up a din in the ripening fields and the hot wind stirred the prairie dust and deposited it on her damp skin, she sought out the relative cool of Ancil's study. He'd pulled down the window shades to protect himself from the radiant heat, and the light, suffused through the canvas, had the color of old photographs. In the corner of the room an electric fan with unbalanced blades clicked in irritating rhythm as it moved air that reeked with the odor of his stale cigars.

"Hot enough for you, Missy?" He brought her a glass of iced coffee thick with cream, just as if she were an adult, and pushed aside a pile of books in order to set it in front of her on the dusty coffee table. She was sitting on the sofa that once must have been quite stylish, but by then it was frayed. The carpet had been worn threadbare, and several of the inverted tulip glass lampshades were broken or missing altogether.

"You go ahead and drink this coffee; it'll do you good—put hair on your chest." He paused next to her, resting his bony hand on the top of her head. She felt his fingers picking and then running through her hair. "Straw," he commented. She smelled his fish-smell as she always did when he came too close.

Even with all the cream, her coffee tasted bitter.

"How's that coffee, Missy?" He gave her his hawk glance.

"Fine," she said. "Good."

"There's something I have that you might like to see." Ancil said, getting up from the sofa and reaching up for a red leather box that he'd placed in front of a row of books. He brought it back to the sofa and sat again beside her. He released the lock and opened it. She saw that it was filled with pictures. He picked up one of a young woman in a long flowered dress.

"Your grandmother," he said. "Lily Ste. Germaine."

"This is my Grandma Lily?" She bent to look at the image more closely, but the photograph wasn't quite clear, and the woman's face blurred a little, no matter how closely she held it to her eyes.

"A real beauty, that one," he said as he let her hold it in her hands. "This was taken before she married your grandfather. See how she holds her head? So high? You resemble her a bit."

"Where did you get it?" She asked, already hoping that he intended to relinquish it that day and give it to her.

"The lovely lady gave it to me herself. Too bad about her," he said.

"What do you mean?" She ran her fingers over the image as though, by some sleight of hand, she could draw the woman's features out from their photographic mist.

"Turned out like the rest." He took a deep breath and reached into his pocket for a cigar, licked it, and bit off the tip.

"By running off to the circus?" she asked.

He laughed. "That's a good one!" He lit the cigar and exhaled a bluish plume of smoke. "No, young lady, not by running off to the circus. By being a liar and a whore like all women are prone to be."

"What's a whore?"

He just kept laughing.

"Can I have it?" She asked him after they'd rummaged together among the photographs and his cigar had been reduced to ash.

"And what's that, Missy?"

"My grandmother's picture. Can I have it?" Because she ought to have it. Because what was her grandmother to Ancil Murdock? A whore. A thing that made him laugh.

"Not on your life, Missy." He took it from her hand and then must have seen that she looked stricken. "Well, maybe when I die. You can have it when I die."

~~~

Old Ancil spit blood through lips the color of the clay in Cold Creek. He ground the metallic red mucus into the dirt under the heel of his boot.

"Harden yourself, Redwing," he'd told her in October of 1951 when they practiced with shotguns on ruffled grouse. "Separate the animal from its life before you pull the trigger."

Ancil cleaned his deer rifle in the Murdock's living room. He blued the barrel and rubbed it with a soft flannel cloth.

"We'll hunt the woods along Cold Creek. Herd travels the creek this time of year. Who knows? Might even get a shot at that old witch squatter."

"Why shoot Sarah?" she said.

"Damned woman, cheating us out of land rightfully ours." He snarled and bared his teeth.

"You could drive her off. Scare her or something." The girl only said this because it was what she knew he wanted to hear. Actually, she still wanted to see the fortuneteller close up, maybe even talk to her.

"I might yet, Missy." He coughed again and spat in a tin coffee can set beside the sofa. "Damn!" he said.

"Please call me Redwing," she said.

He laughed without mirth and rubbed the rifle barrel.

"I'll call you what I like. Maybe I'll call you whore, like your grandma. How'd you like that, Missy?"

If a deer appeared at the thicket's edge, if it stood there, still, in her rifle's sights, if she saw a quiver in its flank, or if it lifted its regal head, could she harden herself? Would she want to? Hannah used to feed the deer dried apples from her hand. James taught her this, silently, standing as he always did, like a tree at the field's edge. Deer came to him. Then he put the apple slices into Hannah's hand. She felt the soft lips of the deer. She looked into the large eyes. She remembered the small eyes of the prairie dog.

Hannah was buried. James forgot to look. Yarrow turned in on herself. Wanda turned to ashes. Ida turned to blood. Only Ancil Murdock dared to tell the truth.

Uncle Ancil motioned. The deer had emerged from the thicket. They lifted their rifles. The deer stood motionless in their sights. The doe turned her head and looked straight at the girl, but she had become a hawk. She and old Ancil, both of them were hawks, and she kept her eyes open as she tried to close her finger hard against the metal trigger of the gun. But she couldn't make her finger move. Ancil shot. The doe's knees buckled and she fell.

~~~

Yarrow heard the door slam behind Hannah.

"I see you're back." She whirled her chair to face her daughter and her voice broke around the edges. The girl had been gone all night.

"Where were you?" Yarrow called after her, swinging her chair around again.

"Do you care?" She turned away from her mother, opened the door of the fridge and grabbed a bottle of Coca Cola.

"You're my daughter, Hannah, my only daughter. What do you mean by asking that?"

"You have Emily now."

"And I can't care for her alone." Emily was three and walking, getting into everything. Yarrow had to keep her confined to the playpen for safety's sake when Hannah wasn't home. "Where were you? I needed you."

"Uncle Ancil says you don't." She faced Yarrow. "He says you can walk if you'd just get up out of that chair. He says there's not a thing wrong with you."

"Ancil? You were at Ancil's?" Her voice trembled.

"He invited me."

"We don't go to Ancil's, Hannah, you know that."

"He's just a sick old man. Why can't you be kind to him?"

"And what does Ancil know of me, anyway?" Yarrow ignored her question. "Ancil hasn't even spoken to me since before I left for Red Pine. Hardly talked, in fact, since before I married your father. Who does Ancil think he is, pronouncing judgment on me?"

"People change." The girl knew she sounded like a smart aleck and that her mother probably wanted to throttle her, but impatience was rising in her against her will, a bitter flow of words across her tongue, pushing against the back of her teeth, and it would not be contained.

"I don't think so," Yarrow said and the girl heard the flatness in her mother's voice.

"I think they do," she said as she rummaged in the kitchen drawer for a bottle opener.

"Ancil despises us," Yarrow reminded her.

"He likes me."

"More's the pity then," Yarrow's voice turned from flat to hard, and her daughter didn't answer.

Then it was as though Yarrow exploded, as though she refused to believe that her daughter could speak that way to her, her mother. The next words burst from her like vomit, like a poison the body refuses to hold any longer.

"Who the hell do you think you're talking to? Let me tell you this, young lady! I just hope you come to your senses before ..." She paused tangled in what she had intended to say, the words twisted around in her mind, her thoughts a thicket. "If he hurts you, you can just forget about getting sympathy from me. You're on your own, you hear me? On your own!"

"Fine!" The girl's voice broke on the word because of the sob that smashed into it from behind. "And will you please call me Redwing!"

"I absolutely will not!" Yarrow yelled.

Hannah turned on her heel, slamming the door like a rifle shot behind her as she ran from the house.

~~~

"Did you ever love anybody?" Redwing dared to ask him on one of those last days in 1954, when the pure sun of early winter cut in a slant through the curtains and divided his skinny body right down the center.

"Your grandma Lily," he rasped. "And after that I never saw the good in it."

That was the day he gave her the deer rifle and enough bullets to kill the entire herd over and over each hunting season until she died. That was also the day he gave her the faded picture of her Grandma

Lily. "Here. Take the damned thing!" He threw it at her. He'd had it under his pillow. She bent to pick it up off the floor and wondered how love reaches the point of damnation. She brought both home and stowed them in her closet, the gun way in the back, behind some clothes of Hannah's from before she lost herself under the cottonwood tree.

But when winter held its deepest sway and rainbow-colored dogs hounded the brittle sun, she took the rifle out again, loaded it and went into the snow-covered prairie alone. She aimed it at whatever she saw as though enchanted by death. She imagined herself blowing a white rabbit all to kingdom come. She pretended to shoot the head off a red fox. Although her tears blurred the animals in her sights, she told herself she wouldn't feel a thing. The crack of the rifle shot, hollow across the plains--wouldn't this become everything to her? At night she lay in bed and thought of it, this cracking of the world, this only thing that's real.

One day, in the woods, she saw the fortuneteller. She hid and watched her gather sticks. She pointed the rifle at the old woman's head, just because she could.

Afterwards she dreamed she was a rabbit, a fox, a poor woman gatherer of firewood. She dreamed her own head exploded in slivers of bone and a shower of blood. The next time she sat beside the cottonwood she put her mouth over the barrel of the rifle. She felt the slight catch of her tongue as cold attached flesh to metal. It wouldn't let her go. If the gun exploded, even by accident, she would be the rabbit, fragments of her skull forced into the tree behind her. Would Yarrow notice, then, that she was gone? Would James? She no longer thought of them as mother, father. They belonged to Hannah, not to her, and she felt Hannah stirring beneath her in the frozen earth. She watched the brittle sun angle across the sky. Her clothes had frozen to the ground by the time her body's warmth finally released her tongue from the rifle barrel.

Unable to discover a magic to break the enchantment, she began to seek death out, picking at the bones of animals half eaten by predators. She practiced pointing the gun at her heart and leaning on it. She did this until she stopped hearing Hannah's whispers on the wind.

10

Ancil woke coughing blood. Horrible! Disgusting! A death sentence. During the war they coughed like this from the mustard gas. Coughed up their lungs before they died. Ancil's company came upon a whole platoon exposed to the damned stuff. They'd marched a couple hours before they felt the burning in their eyes and the sore throats, and they knew, of course. They knew what they were in for. Next came the yellow blisters under their arms, around their eyes, in their groins. After that, the vomit. The medics strapped them to their cots because of the flailing, the crazed dying they endured. Horrible. Eyes blind, stuck with ooze. The swelling of their throats, their voices rasping prayers to a deaf God. The choking. The gagging. The suffocation. Finally, after a week of that, the death.

It had been the war. But hadn't all of life been like that for him? Even as his own life drew to a close he'd rather not endure the stinking of the bed, and often wandered down the stairs to spend his night among his books. It was better, anyway, if he sat upright even to sleep, when sleep could come. Years of books. Hundreds of them. Probably thousands now. His mother called the place his den. It was a den of sorts, a place for the wildness in him to rest and be contained. He could be different there.

He still had his first book, a Reader. He still remembered deciphering the words and becoming lost in a rhyme. His mother preened. My boy can read, she bragged to all her friends, and so young. She didn't know that when he was lost in a book he escaped her power. She bought him every book he wanted. He still had them all. *Arabian Nights. Tales of the Brothers Grimm.* By the time he was thirteen he was well into the classics of world history and literature.

War. Sex. The eternal conflict between evil and good. At fifteen the philosophers. Hegel's dialectic.

The smell of his books. The combination of leather, dust and smoke. The sight of them. A red leather spine called to mind a phrase. Dante's "When I was within, I would have flung me into molten glass to cool me, so immeasurable there was the burning." (Purgatorio, XXVII. 49)

Is there a hell, he wondered. And if there were, what part of him would go there? Surely no just God could send him there in his entirety. He couldn't say what part of him a God would most appreciate. Might not Lucifer be best loved for his audacious challenge? Power values power. In the hunt Ancil sought the strongest prey.

The girl could be a crack shot if he could have gotten her to shoot at something that moves. She chose targets that couldn't die. See that little red stone, she said to him, and shot. The stone flew up from the ground. Must be heredity! Her problem with killing wasn't one of skill, and it wasn't really nerve. It was synthesis. A philosophical problem. A Hegelian problem. Join with the animal, he told her. Look it in the eyes. Breathe its breath. Know its thoughts. Know its next move. Feel its heartbeat in your chest. And shoot.

"But I'd feel like I was shooting myself," she had said.

"You got it," he replied.

"I can't shoot something whose heart beats inside my own chest," she argued.

And he told her that's the only time you can. It's the only time.

Death posed a question to him. This question was a hole. It was an empty place inside him. It was gaseous. It had always been there. He thought he had courage, but this was something he wouldn't face.

~~~

When he started school he tore up his little velvet waistcoat and tossed the scraps out behind the pig pen. He wore work boots to school and smelled like the barn. He walked his little sister, Agnes, to the old one-room schoolhouse every day until their mother made her quit school. He kept close to her, knowing that his smell caught in her throat and made her gag. Knowing he had this power over her, the power to move her in ways she could not control, pleased him. Agnes had a pouty mouth, a flat nose that looked like someone broke it, and hair the color of dusty wheat that stuck out from her head like the straw in a robin's nest.

"Don't you ever comb your hair?" he'd ask her. He pulled her in underneath the railroad loading platform during school lunch hour. The year had turned round to April and the snow had melted early.

He'd grabbed her and forced her against the damp bank of earth, feeling her heart that beat faster than his own, and the emptiness her woodsy smell always brought to the pit of his stomach. Sunlight through cracks between the boards in the loading dock drew lines on the hard dry earth where they lay. A line cut a slash across her body and ran on to divide her face in two sections. She put her hands down at her sides, palms flat on the cool ground and leaned against the bank of earth that formed the sides on which the platform was built. Dirt everywhere. A bit of light coming in through the culvert on each side, and those lines, but all the rest just dirt, just as if they were buried in it, she and this dirty boy, sister and brother, together.

He laughed. He lit an old cigar he'd found, dragged smoke into his mouth and then blew it in her face.

He lifted her dress and undershirt. She shivered as cool breeze brushed her tiny nipples. He reached over and pinched her left nipple like fire on a match, quickly, as if to quench it, make it sizzle as he extinguished it.

Then he pushed at her and she fell backward onto the ground. He crawled on top of her and held her hands against the dirt.

"Okay, you asked for it!" He sneered and closed his mouth over her tiny bud of a nipple. His teeth bit like a lizard's. She didn't make a sound.

~~~

The doctor told Ancil he was much worse. The time might be shorter than he originally thought. Outside the leaves blew off the trees in gusts of wind, and he remembered those times, those damned times he called for his mother and she didn't come. He called in the dark, in the night, out of nightmares, out of the blood of sleep and the horror of all he'd seen so young. "Mommy, Mommy," he called toward the room where she slept. "I didn't hear you." She always told him at breakfast when he asked where she had been. "Mommy needs her beauty sleep," she said. "But I was afraid," he whined. "Don't whine," and her voice scraped down through the top of his head like a file. "I don't like a little boy who whines."

He was about five years old. His mother's face looked down at him. She smiled. She was beautiful. She was wearing a red flower in her hair. She was telling him he was her own, her Ancil. He was in love with her. He took hold of her hand, put her finger into his mouth and sucked. She said he was her good boy. He was the only one she loved. She said, "You are my little man." He thought about his father. "Now that daddy's gone," she said, "you are my only little man."

The smell of his mother when he buried his face in her laundry hamper among her cast off clothes gave him his first erection. He went to his sister, Agnes. Why was he angry? Agnes's tiny body smelled of damp wood under autumn leaves. She cried when he tried to get himself into her and the sound of it drowned out his mother's voice taunting inside his mind. So he went back to Agnes. She was little, just a little girl. The more he went to her, the more he hated her and the more he wanted her to cry. He wanted to hear her telling him to stop. He wanted her to say "you're hurting me, Ancil." And those words made him want to hurt her more.

He remembered Agnes each time he and Hannah hunted grouse. He smelled the child-smell of damp wood under leaves and he remembered.

Lily had wanted him. Delicate Lily. She married Joseph for safety, but she wanted him. Ancil could have made her rich. They would have had such children. James, if Ancil had had his way, would be living in this house, farming land that would have been his true heritage, instead of that dwindling land of his that he'd never had the sense or else the daring to expand. When James and Yarrow came back from their little excursion and Yarrow told Agnes she'd married the boy, Ancil had laughed himself sick wondering what kind of little six-toed monster the two of them would produce. The joke was on him. Nothing wrong with Hannah.

Lily wanted him. But she ran away.

The Murdocks bought up land during the dust bowl years. Wasteland, they called it then. Wasteland worth a million as it turned out. They bought out Lemke's and Helmer Anderson. Old Helmer wanted to stay on and work for them, a tenant farmer, and so he did. Said they gouged him, but his was an empty complaint. People choose and live with what they choose. Ancil's mother wouldn't touch either the Ste. Germaine's or the Olson farm, nor would he, later, when the Murdock land was all his. Why would he? What's left of both will come to them eventually through the slow evolution of generations. Marcia Murdock, to Ancil, to Agnes, to Yarrow and James, to Hannah their mongrel daughter. Their mixed blood.

~~~

The one time Ancil left the farm it was to go to war. 1917. For two years he'd collected reports from the Front. Clipped them from the Chicago Tribune, the St. Paul Pioneer Press and from the New York Times. Essays, some of them, from America's best modern writers. The sinking of the Lusitania in 1915, the Brusilov Offensive, the Tragedy on the Somme, both in 1916. If you were a man you went overseas. He enlisted in the Marines—one of the "devil dogs," and ended up in France. Belleau Woods. It was the sixth of June, 1918.

A one-acre patch of woods here, a five-acre patch there. In between, the oat fields. Open. No shelter. They carried only carbines and bayonets. Grenades attached to their belts. The officers had side arms, but Ancil wasn't an officer. They advanced in a V formation from the cover of woods out across the field and the German machine gunners opened fire.

All the years since then, whenever he told the story, he made himself out to be a hero. That field was as close to hell as he would get until he died. Most died right there. The Huns riddled them. Ancil's position fell toward the back of the V, and he watched them fall. Heard the screams. Saw bodies explode, red stumps of arms and legs, eyes hanging from their sockets.

Before he'd left Cold Creek, before he saw all this, his mother had come to him in the den.

"Ancil?" she said.

He put down the newspaper. It had a post written by E. Hemingway. He looked at her. She still was beautiful then, if a son can see a mother's physical beauty. He thought he could. Beauty covered her thin, tepid soul like the death mask of a saint.

"Don't go, Ancil," she said.

"Don't be ridiculous, Mother. Anyone who's a man is joining up to fight this thing," he told her.

"You aren't cut out for it, Ancil," she said.

"You think not?" He curled his lip. He scoffed at her.

"I know you, Ancil."

He picked up the newspaper and ignored her until she turned and left the room.

In Belleau Woods that day in June he threw himself on the ground and covered his face with his helmet, hoping that the men, as they rushed around him, would think him dead. Most of them did die. Maybe all of them died. No one remained to call him a coward. After the battle he wandered the fields with the medics, looking for survivors. He picked up a German Luger off a dead Hun and brought it back with him as evidence of his heroism.

He came home to the women, to his mother, to Sarah, and to Lily, all of whom seemed to sense what he'd become.

~~~

He took Hannah deer-hunting. Or it would be more accurate to say that she took him. He was so weak he could only sit in the blind while she thrashed about through the trees to scare up the prey. War or no war, he'd never shot a man. Deer now, that's a different story. Every hunting season he would get his deer.

He dreamed the creature that year. Large. A buck with eight points. He was in the middle of the creek, standing in water to his knees, and the buck was off to his right on a rise of land. It was night and the moon seemed caught between the creature's antlers like a crown. Then Ancil was sitting with the water flowing over his privates that seemed frozen with the chill of it. And the buck had come down to the creek to drink. He stood so close that Ancil could look him in the eye. Finally Ancil lay in the water. He was a giant leaf, fallen. And the buck stood above him. Ancil's eyes opened from under the water, and he saw the buck with the sun just beginning to rise behind him.

As usual he got his deer. Not the eight point buck from his dream, but fine enough considering it would be his last. As usual Hannah refused to pull the trigger even though she had a fine doe in her sights.

~~~

His father lay in a pool of blood the morning they found him in the ditch, thrown from the wagon, crushed by farm machinery, barely breathing. Ancil could see it still. The team of horses broken loose, one of them down, tangled in the gear, too tired by then for more struggle. "You go." His mother held back. She imagined the worst. It was the worst. She pushed him forward from her toward what they could see of clothes, his father's clothes, and what still lay within them. She pushed him forward and when he clung to her hand she bent his fingers back one by one to free herself. "Go," she said. "Tell me what is there." He felt her hand on his back, pushing. He heard a low gurgle from the throat of the downed horse, its struggle momentarily renewed by the sense of their presence. Under his feet the gravel of the road, slipping beneath the soles of his shoes. He felt smaller than a pebble, than a blade of grass. He had just turned five. He saw the pile of clothes and the body inside, twisted, a tangle of arms and legs. His mouth filled with tears and snot. "Daddy?" He tried to call out to him, if it was him, but his voice stuck inside. Five years old. What was she thinking? He turned around in the road. She stood there, her hair loose from its knot, hanging in her face like tiny snakes. "Go, Ancil," she called out. "Find out if Daddy's hurt. Find out for Mommy. Be a big boy for Mommy." Ancil heard the crunch of gravel. He heard the movement of each leaf on the tree. He got to his   father,   and   his   father   was   alive.

"Daddy?" Ancil crouched down next to his father's head. His knees had scabs on them from a fall the day before. The scab on his right knee broke open and began to bleed. The head lay in a pool of blood. The left leg bone had torn through his good pants and gleamed red and white in the morning sun. "Daddy?"

Ancil reached out and touched that face. His father opened his eyes. "Who are you?" he said.

"Ancil. I'm Ancil." The name tore itself out of his mouth. "Your son," he said.

His father took a breath that rattled. Then he said, and all of Ancil's life he never stopped hearing the words, "I don't have a son. You're the bastard of that fucking Henry Olson."

~~~

Towards the end Ancil was on morphine. Visions. Showers of blood and fire. The silk of a woman's cunt. The infinite eye of the stag. A whirl of stars. Fields of oats that extended forever. Numbers falling into a box. Millions of numbers. Death standing in the corner of the room. Interconnecting circles. The stars falling from the sky. Fields turning to ooze under his feet. Eyes melting. His feet disappearing in the mud. The air around him molten glass.

He watched his books. They appeared to live. It was the morphine. The books turned inside out. He remembered whole lines of text, not always as written. Consider the Lily of the field.

Lily, he thought. If you had stayed I might have been saved. You might have saved me. As it is, I'm on my way to hell.

Hannah asked him if he had ever loved.

"Lily," he told her.

But he didn't love her. He wanted her. He'd never loved anything, not even himself.

He was nothing but a hole.

Ancil watched Lily come from a long way off, that day, so many years ago. Desire uncoiled its snake and turned to lust. He watched her cross the field toward him. He stood behind the large elm they had plowed around all those years and never taken down. He adjusted his position as she advanced. Belleau Woods and she his enemy. He didn't question it. Women use themselves that way, he thought. Women only seem fragile, only seem beautiful, only seem desirable. Women create desire and desire softens us, dissolves our strength. He thought these things as he waited for her behind the tree, so near the fence. You went to France to find the enemy, he thought, and she was always here, living here, right under your nose.

He stepped from behind the tree and let her see him. He wouldn't let her make him soft, not this time. Not now. Never again. He stood like the power he was. He felt his manhood swell, huge and hard, a weapon against all that ever made him small, all that ever made him whimper and turned him into a mama's boy, a simpering idiot. He let her see him standing with his legs spread wide, his arms crossed on his chest, his chest thrust out. He knew himself to be Nietzsche's Superman, the Colossus, Satan himself.

He can't remember what she said. He felt the slightest softening at the sound of her voice. He would not allow the coward to arise. Not again. Never again. He took her down.

He smelled her scent. It made him wild. He heard her pleading. His anger exploded onto her, to hurt her, to quell her power. He saw her tears and his instinct was to put out her eyes. She would not make him soft. No woman ever again would soften him. He tore her clothes. Her pleading hardened him. All his strength concentrated itself into his sex and he thrust it into her. She closed against him and he thrust harder, tearing at her, feeling the wet, smelling the blood. They warred and he won. He looked into Lily's face and she was no longer Lily; she was all of them. Her face changed shape and form right in front of his eyes. Every woman he had ever fucked. Every woman, right to that moment, who'd raised in him the snake of lust. Finally, Agnes. Finally, his own mother. He fucked his mother there in the field as he thrust his sex into Lily over and over, pounding himself into her, grinding her into the earth with his anger and disgust. Vanquishing her power.

He stood above her afterwards. Even then he wasn't spent, and he shook his sex in her face. He left her broken. A lily twisted and crushed and rubbed into the ground.

He expected her to come back. He expected one day to open the door and there she'd be. You are the only one who understands, she'd say to him. You are all that can touch what's wild in me. You are my dark god.

She never returned.

Even her son could not draw her back. Ancil would never see her again.

In her place was Hannah.

~~~

One day Redwing came to take him for a walk. He got the shotgun out. He told her that he could maybe get himself a white rabbit and see once more before he died the bright red of a rabbit's blood staining the new snow.

Ancil Murdock had stepped spryly that winter day, almost as though his sickness had been cured. His face, though, kept the look of wet clay. Redwing could almost not remember when she'd seen color in his skin other than that found beneath the dead leaves of Cold Creek. She'd gone to read to him, expecting him to be holed up in that awful-smelling room of his, but he'd been waiting by the front door with his gun.

"A grand day, my beauty!" He'd said to her, and she noticed that his voice still rasped with the illness. "I'm well, today, Missy, well as I'll likely ever be again, and it's you I choose to accompany me on my last hunt. Rabbits. White snowshoes. They're near invisible against the snow." He'd taken her arm with one large hand and held his shotgun with the other.

A shining day is what it was. Frost laced the bushes and trees, and the sun, always angled low in winter, shone through the crystal prisms that cast a soft lavender color across the landscape. She walked with him, watchful, thinking him old and frail because he was gaunt from cancer. His hair had turned white. His cheekbones protruded and his nose hooked down toward his chin. She watched his chest heave and rattle with each breath he took and heard the hissing as the air escaped him. They left the plowed road by the hedge of bushes that lead toward the fortune teller's shack. "There's rabbits hidden all over around here," he'd said. They stopped so he could load his shotgun.

"We'll just sit here and wait."

They pushed back into the bushes. It would be a blind, and warmer, too; a kind of shelter, though the day had been still and the sun a brittle light absorbed by frost and snow that covered everything.

"I'm not old, you know," Ancil had said. "I imagine I must seem old to you." He sounded wistful. "So young you are."

What could she have said that would have changed the future? "It must be hard for you to be so sick," is what she had said, words that seemed innocent and even caring at the time. Perhaps she ought not to have sounded caring.

Ancil had reached over to her and cupped her chin in his gloved hand. "So like your grandmother you are—my Lily."

What could she have done that would have turned him away right then. Where had her imagination been? She had felt spellbound by him and the fear she would begin to feel had not yet risen in her belly.

"You're so ripe." he'd murmured, leaning toward her, and she felt his hot, stinking breath on her face. "I could have taught you so many things." His hand slid from her chin to the top button on her coat. "There are things, my little beauty, you should learn from a master, things about being a woman, things about how to please a man, things I could pass on to you." Now his face seemed to collide with hers, features of youth and age dissolving into each other. The smell of him sickened her. She felt his hand pulling at the buttons of her coat.

"Stop!" She pushed at him. "Stop it!"

He pulled his face back and laughed. "Aha! A little spitfire!"

Just then the rabbit appeared from behind a red thorn bush, pure white against the snow, almost invisible.

"Shhh..." Ancil reached for his shotgun. He whispered, "Here. You shoot it. This one's yours." He thrust the gun into her hands.

"No." Redwing looked straight into the rabbit's eye. The first thought that came to her was "Emily." But in an instant that Emily-thought spun out to include herself, and then seemed to encompass everything. But the way she saw it that day was that without the rabbit in it, the world would collapse in upon itself and disappear. "I can't do it," she said.

"Can't?" Blood shot into Ancil's clay-gray face. "What the hell?! It's a goddamn rabbit!" The rabbit startled, ears alert, and then hopped back into the thicket. "Damn it all anyway."

"It would have been wrong." Her voice sounded thin. She could already feel the thread of bile rising hot from her stomach into her mouth.

"And who are you to talk about wrong?" Never had she heard a voice so cold. "You little bitch. You think you are so good, coming over to my house, reading to me, walking with me, talking nice. You have no idea what you are, do you?"

Maybe she could have left him there. Right at that moment, as the sky began to be overcast and the hoarfrost drifted from the branches of the trees, she might have simply walked away. If she could be as wise, even, as the rabbit. But instead she said to him, "I don't know what you mean."

He seemed to uncoil right before her eyes, "Well then, Missy, maybe it's time you found out. I have a journal," he snarled as he shook a bony finger in her face, "and the whole story's there except the part I'll finish writing this afternoon. Maybe the whole world should know who you really are and the fucked up family that spawned you."

She shivered. A wind was coming in with the clouds. The temperature fell. She clenched her teeth and tightened her gloved hands upon Ancil's gun.

"You're acting crazy." It was the last time she would plead with him.

He snorted. "I thought you might be different," he said and the corners of his mouth turned down in disgust, "but you can't even shoot a goddamn rabbit."

His voice drilled itself into her mind. The words fractured all that had begun to be firm in her young self. He told her that she actually was his own spawn, that her father was his bastard son and a soft-headed idiot led about by women. He reminded her that her mother was his sister Agnes's child and another of his bastards. "So what does that make you?" He laughed until he began to cough up blood. He spat it out onto the snow. "And Yarrow! Ah yes, consider that queer you call your mother. You know damn well what she is. A butch cripple who made a laughing stock of your father. She's no real woman at all."

Words possess a power to undo a life. Her teeth began to chatter. She felt so cold.

"And that new one—what's she called? Oh yes. Emily. Baby Emily, bastard of a bastard of a bastard. That kid's bloodlines are so fucked up you might as well call her a monster." He fumbled in his pocket for a cigar and a match. He'd begun a new paroxysm of coughing and spitting blood. Smoke. He needed the soothing smoke.

Redwing stared at him. He lit the match and she saw the flame in front of his face. He had the power to bring the whole Olson family down in flames, much more destructive than those she once saw murder Wanda. Wanda burned and died. Hannah's family would be condemned to a lifetime of fire that could not be extinguished. She watched Ancil light his cigar and felt a corresponding flame inside her that melted the paralyzing cold.

At that moment the rabbit reappeared. Ancil threw his match down into the snow. "Shoot it!" he hissed. "Show what you are. Shoot that rabbit."

She stared into his eyes that looked dead and cold. He wasn't a man at all but a great snake. She stood and lifting the shotgun as he'd bid her do, aimed at the rabbit. The limb of the thorn bush arched above the rabbit's head and tiny red berries hung against the white of both rabbit and snow. "It's too beautiful," she thought and, almost by instinct, swung around to aim Ancil's shotgun directly at the cigar he held between his thin lips. She paused only an instant, but it was long enough to see the surprise in his eyes and something else—a suggestion of relief, even of gratitude. He hated himself. That was his affliction. And in the instant that she saw this in his eyes, she also saw the shadow on his face of all the other afflicted ones--Wanda and Yarrow, Ida, James, the lost Lily, all of them, even Hannah. Then she felt his heart beating inside her own body, and she made the choice. "All of it is too beautiful."

She dropped the shotgun into the snow at the feet of Ancil Murdock and turned towards home. She walked away. She walked along the creek until the snow began to fall again, a soft heavy snow that covered everything. She did not turn back and was not, therefore, a witness to the way he watched her go. She didn't see him drop to his knees. She couldn't know about the tiny spark of possibility her words lit in his heart. She didn't hear the deepening rattle of his breath, his gasps for air, she would never imagine how as his vision dimmed the rabbit reappeared and sat just outside his reach. He tried to call to her, to tell her how white he saw it now, how beautiful, but he had no voice. He fell.

By morning he had disappeared beneath the snow that wind blowing in later from the west would harden into drifts.

11

Such a winter hadn't hit Cold Creek since the one that began with the Armistice Day snowstorm of 1940. Snow, snow, snow. It fell sometimes as much as twenty-four inches in one storm, and afterwards the temperatures plummeted to minus forty degrees. Prairie wind sculpted the drifts. One day the hen house completely disappeared. Snow curled up and over the top of the Olson house and James shoveled a tunnel to the barn.

Some time went by before anyone realized that Ancil Murdock was missing. The news trickled out like water melted under an ice dam on a roof. "*In extremis*," the doctor shook his head while drinking coffee with the fellows at Tom's Café downtown where the plow cleared the streets every morning. "You could see it," offered an old-timer. "He didn't strike me as a man who'd do himself in, though." And another: "Could've got caught in the storm. Likely Buck Miller will find him come spring." And another: "A fellow that sick couldn't have gotten far."

Sheriff Buck Miller called off any search until spring. No sense losing more men looking for a dead body in such a wide expanse of white. They all were certain he was dead. How could he be anything but? Spring would come soon enough, and in the meantime Ancil Murdock was in cold storage just the same as he'd be if they found his body now and brought it into town.

Redwing stared out the living room window at the snow. It put limits on the world. Drifts covered the back windows completely. Outside the living room snow came up to the windowsill, and frost designed the lower half of the glass. She focused on the fall of individual flakes from sky to ground and tried not to think of Ancil, frozen and buried in the woods. Ancil and his gun. She wanted no one to know she'd been there. She couldn't understand the choice she made, nor could she forget the vision of the afflicted ones. It troubled her that suffering could turn to hate. "I became as hateful as he was," she admitted to herself, and the admission caused a shivering she couldn't control.

Now she became a servant of both Yarrow and Emily, doing whatever she could to keep the house tidy and meals on the table. They needed to conserve. She assigned herself the task of managing the root cellar, seeing that the winter vegetables did not spoil and go to waste. The plow came by every three days and James used the tractor blade on the long driveway from the house, but still the drive to down for supplies could be dangerous in the sub-zero temperatures and the constant threat of another storm.

Hannah would have done better now than Redwing. But despite her mother's hopes, Hannah was gone and couldn't be called back.

In the ceiling of Hannah's bedroom closet was a square frame of wood around a hatch opening into the attic. No one had visited the attic for as long as Redwing could remember, and possibly never since the house had been built. Redwing stood looking at it. Would the wooden cover over the hatchway slide away if she pushed it? What was on the other side? Probably an empty room hung with icicles, but you never know. The house had been here for generations. If she had a ladder...

The pantry stepladder would work. She lugged it up the stairs, pushed her clothes aside, and positioned it in the closet. She climbed until her head almost touched the hatch covering. She raised her hands and pushed. The cover was stuck. She struck it with her fists.

"Hannah?" her mother called up the stairs. "Are you ok?"

"I'm ok. Just trying move something."

"Don't hurt yourself."

"I won't."

Another strike and the covering gave way. Redwing slid it aside. A draft of chill air hit her face. She grabbed her winter jacket from the clothes rod, threw it onto the attic floor, and hoisted herself up.

Frost covered the beams and she picked up her jacket and put it on before beginning her exploration. In the light from grimy windows on either side of the large space she saw that the attic was not empty. As she neared the window on the east side she saw that what she first thought were stacks of wood or cardboard leaning against the wall were actually paintings. Turning around she could see similar objects stacked against the west wall. There were scores of them. Realistic. Surrealistic. She lifted one of them at a time up to the light. Some paintings were on canvas, some on wood. The prairie at sunset. A Janus figure of one man with two faces. A torn blue dress hanging on a bare tree limb. A nun with closed eyes. A detail of a woman's breasts seeping blood. The sneering face of Ancil Murdock—younger, but definitely Ancil. A spider on a windowpane. Upon each picture the artist made a paint slash, blood red. So many more, and all signed simply, *Lily*.

On the west wall she had hung just one painting, that of a small boy. Redwing looked at it closely. It must be her father. It must be Lily's tiny son whom she had left standing alone in the middle of the kitchen when she went off on her journey. Attached to the painting was an envelope. Redwing removed it, opened it, and unfolded the stationery.

My Darling Son,

Someday curiosity might lead you to this place. I hope so. What I am about to do to you is unforgiveable. A mother must never abandon her child, and I would stay with you if there were any way for staying to be possible. I would take you with me if I could, but to uproot you from your safe home with your father and grandmother is unthinkable. How would I take care of you? I've imagined holding your little hand and starting down the road together, but the dream is just that—a dream. The road will be long and the outcome uncertain. I know that both of us could die on a journey such as this. So I have left you because I love you and there is no other way.

By the time you find this, if you find it at all, you might be grown into a man. I hope you will have found happiness. Please pray for your mother, that she might have found peace and healing from the terrible wound she will inflict upon both of us this day. I pray this for you and will pray every day for the rest of my life.

My plan is to turn my face west, west and north where the

mountains meet the sea. On the map I found a small fishing village called Port Townsend. I will try to find work.

My heart is breaking.

Your mother,
Lily

~~~

Spring came late, melting rapidly when it came, swelling the waters of Cold Creek, depositing fresh black soil on the fields. Buck Miller and his deputy found Ancil Murdock's body alongside his gun on a rise of land in the woods." Poor bastard." he spoke like a benediction over the body and then to everyone he met in town.

~~~

Redwing sewed a few small things into a piece of blue cloth to wear on a cord next to her heart. A stone from the banks of Cold Creek where the cottonwood stood. A silver ring from Yarrow that no longer fit. Six kernels of barley from James' field. A curl of Emily's hair. She included photographs of everyone except for Wanda whose every image went up in flames. The faded photograph of Lily Ste. Germaine she wrapped in cellophane for safety.

Redwing felt a steel winch attached to her heart and it pulled at her in ways that reminded her of Hannah and threatened to tear her apart. She had to go west to Port Townsend. If Lily Ste. Germaine could be found, if Redwing could bring her home again, all that had been ripped apart in her family could maybe be knit together. If Gramma Lily would come back home, then all that had been severed, as the cat had once torn the bluebird from its life and severed it from its babies, could be restored and made to live. Redwing felt appointed to this task. Called to the end of the world where mountains rose out of the sea.

As pale light brushed across the night just before dawn she went to each of them where they slept and watched them, forcing the image of them into her mind, telling herself to remember. No one woke. In the dimness Yarrow looked whole and without scars, beautiful as the day she left and took Hannah into a different world.

Redwing didn't dare touch her, not even to brush back the strand of hair that covered her closed eyes.

Emily's little body curled like a snail's shell. She was sucking her thumb. Just for a moment Redwing thought to take her. Wasn't she hers? Her baby? Who else had sung her lullabies? Who taught her how to talk? Who fed her and put her to bed and woke her up and soothed her when she was afraid? Right from the beginning, the day James brought her to the house and put her on Yarrow's lap, Redwing knew that no one could love her and protect her like she could. But Yarrow would need a baby now that she was getting well again and Redwing had gone away. Besides, Redwing didn't know if she was capable of love without Hannah. Emily must stay. She bent over her and kissed the top of her sweet head. Then she felt a tugging at her roots and a spurt of determination that leapt from her belly up into her head. She turned and left the room.

Dew hung on the bent ends of grasses all across the field to the creek. A meadowlark broke her song and feigned a ruined wing to lure the girl from her nest in the grass. Redwing made an arc around her because there's no sense in frightening a creature without need. She had left the rifle behind.

"You rest," she told Hannah by the cottonwood. "I'll take care of it." Not knowing what she meant, but watching the sun spread itself all over the swirling waters of Cold Creek. She plucked a long hair from her head and tied it to a branch as a sign.

I'm gone, she thought as she turned from the cottonwood tree and followed the creek the way opposite from the road running out from town. She didn't want them to find her and they would search the road first. Trees lined the way between the farms along the path the water cuts. They sheltered her.

She followed the creek, keeping herself hidden, and arrived at Sarah's cabin as the sun crested the tops of the trees.

~~~

Redwing couldn't tell the woman's age. She saw the way she stood, hands on her hips, legs spread wide under what looked like three skirts of colors that put together jolt you. Her men's work boots gave her the look of a gnarled tree, one that wouldn't be moved.

"Better come with me." The old woman reached out to let the girl take her hand.

"I ran away from home," Redwing said, straight out so as to keep a secure footing.

"Ummmm." She tapped her pipe against her hip. "Must be a family trait. First your gramma, then your mama, now you. Must be in your bones."

"I can't say, Ma'am. I never knew my gramma."

"Lily. Went off to save her life, that girl did. Never came back." She put the pipe in her skirt pocket and sat, knees up, her skirt a valley between them. She gave the ground in front of her a little pat as though to say, sit down.

"Did she tell you where she was going?" Redwing sat. She leaned her elbows on her knees and held her chin in her cupped hands.

"Oh, she told me all right. She laid her burden in my heart and mind for safe keeping, and keep it safe is what I intend to do until my grave. Nothing moves me from my promises. Not even death can move me. Not that there's much temptation."

"People must not have asked because they all thought you were crazy."

"I like you, girl," she managed to say between spurts of laughter. "I like you a lot."

"What is it they call you, girl?" They walked side by side towards the shack. The sun leaned toward the tassels on the barley.

"My name's Redwing."

"What kind of name is that? That's not your name. That's an Indian name."

"I know. It's what was left when Hannah wouldn't come back from the old cottonwood." She was thinking how maybe she shouldn't leave the farm. Maybe she ought to sit beside the creek under the tree where Hannah lay. If she sat there long enough, watching the creek run toward the river, maybe Hannah would wake up.

"Names. They're links, you know. You drop your name, you have to look for it 'til you find it again. Can't get into heaven without your name!" Sarah tended to walk with a long stride, like a man, her boots stomping down the stinging nettle that grew along and sometimes in the path.

"Mine's under a cottonwood tree." Redwing spoke quietly, as though it mattered not much at all whether she would hear.

"You dropped your name under a cottonwood tree?" Sarah said it matter of factly, as though dropping your name under a cottonwood might be the most normal thing for a girl to do, considering....

"Yes, by Cold Creek where the cattails grow. But I don't want to go back."

She tossed her wild hair. "A name is never where you dropped it, girl. We can't go back--ever. When you drop your name, it's forever after out in front of you like the Bethlehem star or a red leaf on the river. You have to run like crazy to keep up. Makes you a wanderer. Other things can make you wander, but dropping a name does it faster than anything else I ever came across."

"Nothing was left of me but Redwing, and then everybody needed her." Like a confession.

~~~

"You're a young one." Sarah smoothed a light green chenille bedspread over the old couch in her one room cabin. She'd been comparing Hannah to her grandmother at the time she left the farm, also to her mother that night of the rainstorm when she took off for Red Pine.

"Not so young."

"Younger than you suppose, though not too young for going." She fluffed a pillow and laid it at one end of the couch, smoothing its flour sack cover with her hand.

"Why do we leave," Redwing blurted out, "the women in my family?" It was Gramma Lily who left. It was Yarrow. Now herself. But maybe it was all one leaving, just spread out over all the women and all the years.

"You don't know?" Sarah looked her right straight in the eyes.

"I guess I don't know for sure." Redwing felt words coming slowly, one by one, as if each of them popped up singly from the bottom of a muddy swamp. "I thought I did. I feel it though, like a magnet's pulling, and I can't stop myself."

"That might be all there's to it." Sarah sat on the couch, hands folded in her lap, studying the girl's face. "Magnetism. The drawing of a life that could be ahead of you--the gravity it makes. There's also that opposing force, that thing behind you that you can't abide.

"Lily's the magnet. It's my grandma who's calling me."

Sarah never told her not to go.

She took out a strand of beads carved from bone and put it over the girl's head. "Wear these. Lily will remember them."

"Bones?"

"I cast the bones for Lily." She drew a circle with a stick on the ground. "I could do it for you, too, if you want."

Redwing nodded. Curious.

"First, go deep inside and find your question."

"What question?"

"Any question that makes a hole in your mind. Go to the place in yourself where you feel empty. That's the question."

"What if it doesn't have words?" The girl's mind wandered out to where Hannah lay under the cottonwood tree.

"It doesn't need words." Sarah shook bones inside their leather pouch and they made a clicking. Then she closed her eyes and cast the bones on the ground. They scattered, small bones, some broken, gray bones, ivory bones, making a pattern on the earth.

"What do you see?" The girl herself saw nothing but bones on dust.

"What I see is dark and cold," Sarah spoke in low tones. "A song I used to hear I can't hear anymore. I feel like I would give my life to fall asleep just one more time listening to its melody."

"That's Hannah!" Redwing blurted out before she could think better of it.

"Hannah, is it?" Sarah opened her eyes and looked at her.

"Once she was me. That was my name. Hannah's who I used to be."

~~~

The creek curved through trees and thickets where raspberries grew. Sometimes she walked in the creek rather than beside because water was the only clear path. She sang to keep out the murmurings of Hannah. She had thought she'd stay buried, but it seemed like

Sarah had used her bones to start digging Hannah up. "I buried you," Redwing told Hannah right out loud.

"Why?" Hannah seemed to murmur in the voice of the creek over stones and through long cattail stems. "Why oh why oh why oh why..."

"To keep you safe," Redwing explained.

"But the song of my life--it won't be free."

Redwing told Hannah what she herself wanted to believe. "When I sing it, you'll sing it with me." But what you've buried stays that way until you dig it up and how can that be done? What would remain of her? And how would she be changed? She'd been a weeping child when Redwing buried her. All those tears. What if tears could act with earth to melt skin and muscle? What if all that remained of Hannah was bone and a murmuring voice? A child's skeleton shining under the rich black soil.

At night she curled up beneath another great cottonwood, knowing she could find no real protection there, but having no longer the need for such things. She slept and, in her dreams, became Hannah, her hair like the tangled roots of a tree in the rich black Dakota soil. Gypsy beads decorated strands that hung next to her face, and when she shook her head the beads rang out. "Song of our lives," she sang in a mumbled voice. "Forever free..." And her song was a thickness like underground streams that you only sense but never hear really. Then slowly, slowly, so that the happening kept its secret until nothing could deter it, the great black expanse of earth surrounding her that was, in fact, the essence of her turned to oil, to a great thick flood in which she could not but flow.

Redwing opened her eyes to the sun breaking the horizon. "Hannah," she whispered, and would have cried but had learned how not to do that. Instead she reached up and plucked a leaf from this tree, so like the one under which Hannah slept back at the farm, and she scribbled her name on it. "Hannah." Then she set it floating west on the waters of Cold Creek toward a destination still hidden and far off.

After she lost sight of the leaf, she hurried faster, not even stopping to eat. The woods thinned and she saw fields that stretched to the horizon. Her beads clicked against each other as she ran toward whatever lay ahead.

On the third day she arrived at the big river just above the forks. She followed the river into town and sat down at the counter of the Riverside Café.

The waitress put out her cigarette, squinted her eyes and looked the girl up and down. "You look like you haven't had a good meal in weeks! And I expect you don't have a dime. Right?"

The girl had only the beads, and she laid them in the open hand of the waitress in trade for a grilled cheese sandwich and a bottle of Coke.

12

Nothing ever again had felt as sweet to Yarrow as Hannah's little mouth around the nipple of her breast. Such a long time she had waited for her, waited for James's seed to take root. Waited, feeling barren. Waited, wondering if her mothering of him had ruined her for conceiving her own child. Now Hannah had turned into a young woman, but back then, her baby hands cupped the smooth skin of Yarrow's breast, her eyes sought the mother's eyes without fear and with total reliance. The milk is for the baby, Yarrow told James back then, when he turned to her in the night. Without words he rolled over to face away from her and went to sleep. Soon Yarrow had fastened herself so completely to Hannah that she lost all awareness of his need. Twice a week he satisfied his instincts on her, swiftly, she supposed to keep from troubling her too much, and the few times she wanted some connection of sex with love, even as little as the mention of her name, he couldn't give it.

After the fire her breasts became dry and webbed with scars.

Hannah was lost.

Emily cried.

James worked the land, and if he watched for her to return from the emptiness where she lived, Yarrow was not aware of his gaze.

The fields crackled with early summer heat the day that Hannah left for good. Yarrow recalled it afterwards. She recalled the haunting song of Old Sarah, almost not heard on the still air. She had made little of it. She was used to Hannah's disappearances. She was used to hearing the old woman sing as she walked the road to town. That day Yarrow did the little tasks she could. Shelled peas that James brought in from the garden. Used the railings to prop herself up along the kitchen counters where she made soup and sandwiches for their lunch. He didn't ask where Hannah was. He ate his soup. He spooned it up into his mouth without a word, making little slurping sounds, lifting the sandwich to his mouth and biting clear into the center of it. Emily jabbered, breaking the silence, and the sound of her voice reminded Yarrow of crickets in the fields. "Don't dawdle," she said to the child as she played with her food, fishing peas from her soup and lining them up on her sandwich plate. James finished in five minutes, said thanks, and went back to the fields. Emily and Yarrow lay on the downstairs bed and took a nap. Inconsequential things. Daily things.

And all that time Hannah was running away.

Next day the men went out. Yarrow heard them calling for her.

"Nothing." James said that evening. He had his head in his hands. "We didn't find a thing."

He didn't blame Yarrow. He took Emily on his knee. She was four, the very age Hannah was when Yarrow had taken her from him in the middle of a summer night.

~~~

James turned off the radio. Hannah had been gone a month. Emily slept, curled on his goose down sleeping bag that he'd folded into thick softness before he put it on the floor between Yarrow and himself. Yarrow reached down and touched Emily's face, so like his, and she thought how motherhood is wider than what our bodies can offer us, wider even than our minds. She thought how motherhood only begins by stretching our wombs; it ends by stretching our hearts to accept and even treasure things we would have thought could bring nothing but death of dreams. The stretching goes as far as wounds and the scars that cover wounds. It stretches far and deep as to that child hidden deep inside oneself, in the wardrobe of the past.

"Tell me about Wanda." He looked clear-eyed straight at her. It must have been Ida who opened him that way.

"Are you sure, James?"

"I know she meant a lot to you, and to the girl."

Her heart still clenched each time he couldn't say her name, or Hannah's name. But he could say Ida. He could say Emily. Even

Wanda he could say.

"I didn't know I'd find someone like her, James. When I left here all those years ago, I wasn't even thinking what I might find."

"I'm not accusing you of anything. I just thought if you could talk about her…"

"She stays with me, James. In my mind. She talks to me all the time."

"Ida too. I feel Ida just that way." He leaned back in his chair and stared off into the distance.

"Ida talks to me, too," she said.

He chuckled. "They live with us, I guess. Maybe I could meet that Wanda of yours."

Yarrow talked for what seemed hours. The moon moved across the sky. She told him everything, all the funny things, the tender things. She told him about town's boycott of the café. He took her hand and held it in his larger one. His fingers felt warm.

"You loved her."

"Yes. Completely."

"You slept with her."

"There was a freedom in it, James, and a naturalness I can't describe."

"Something I couldn't give you."

"Something I don't even think I could receive until Wanda opened me to it."

"Do you think you could ever love a man again?"

It startled her. She looked into his eyes and saw a longing there she'd never seen in him before.

"I don't think of love that way, James. I can't see it as confined like that. Maybe love goes where it is called."

"To me? Could it come to me?"

"Do you want it?" She felt the pulling of taut skin over her breasts.

"You don't know?"

All she felt was what remained after the burning. All the loss. The scars.

"I've never been sure. Not ever."

James lifted her from her chair and carried her to her bedroom.

"I'm ugly," she whispered as he began to remove her blouse.

"You can't be ugly to me."

Yarrow closed her eyes when he uncovered her breasts. She felt his warm fingers trace the webs of scars. She felt his tears fall on her skin. Then she heard him murmur, "Yarrow, Yarrow, Yarrow," and she realized that this time his love was different than before.

In the middle of the night Yarrow awoke to Emily's cries.

"Mommy, Mommy. I had a scary dream."

"Hannah?" She called. But Hannah didn't answer her, and she remembered that Hannah had gone.

"James?" He must be upstairs in what used to be their bedroom, but he could always sleep through anything!

"Just a minute, Emily. Mommy's coming."

Yarrow sat up in bed and willed her legs over the edge. She felt her feet touch the floor. She wavered a bit when she stood up, her legs were so weak, but with the help of James's railings, she made her way upstairs to her little girl.

"I had a scary dream." Emily whimpered.

"I know, honey. But it will be okay. Mommy will sing you to sleep."

As Yarrow sang her lullaby to Emily, she realized that the song of her life was, at last, forever free.

When the little girl slept again, she made her way slowly across the hall into the room where James slept alone, the room where Hannah was conceived, the very bed where Ida received James's seed and Emily came to be. Love is so much larger than we imagine. Yarrow slipped beneath the covers and curled her body into his.

"Yarrow?" He called her by her name and it wasn't difficult at all.

She put her arm over his shoulder and touched his chest. "I'm here, James. I am here."

13

"You've got a nice place here." Redwing told the waitress as she handed her the bone necklace. "I pretty much grew up in a café over at Red Pine, Minnesota. My mother and this other woman, Wanda, ran the place."

"You don't say." The waitress turned the necklace over in her hand. It was a big-boned hand, chapped red from lye soap. "You look pretty young, honey. Your mom still live in Red Pine?" Probably the waitress was somebody's mother herself. She had a tired look about her eyes, the look of somebody with two full-time jobs. She'd done her hair up in a net, oily like she hadn't washed it that week.

"Not anymore." Less said, the better, Redwing decided and started to slide off the round counter-stool.

The waitress caught hold of her hand and pressed the bone necklace back into it. "Honey, you go ahead and take your necklace. It's way too fine a thing to trade for grilled cheese."

The necklace felt warm as a living thing in her palm. She closed her fingers around it. "It wouldn't be right," she said to the waitress, "just eating for free. Isn't there something I could do in payment? Some little job you need done?"

The waitress smiled and the lines around her eyes crinkled, softening her broad angular face. "You're a good girl. What're you doing here in Grand Forks? You're not running away or something, are you?" A bead of sweat traveled from her hairline toward her right eye and she wiped it away with the back of her hand.

"I'm just on my way to see my grandmother." Redwing's mind

skidded on the words. She hoped she wasn't telling the waitress a lie by making it sound as though her grandmother lived in a little house just down the road, by making it seem that she had a letter in her pocket, written in trembling script, inviting her to visit.

"Your grandma live close to Grand Forks?"

"It's a ways away."

"Well, I hope you're not planning to hitch-hike, honey. That's dangerous. And no money? Are you sure your mom and dad know where you are?" A strand of her hair had escaped from the net and was plastered with sweat to the side of her face just in front of her left ear.

Redwing stood up. "I just thought you might have a little job for me. Dishes? I could wash dishes. Wait tables. Cook, even. Wanda taught me to make wild berry pie."

"Well," her mouth puckered, like a goldfish tasting the inside of the glass bowl, as she scrutinized Redwing's face for more information. "There's always dishes." The water glass clicked against the chipped crockery sandwich plate as she piled them together. "I guess it wouldn't hurt if you was to go back in the kitchen and ask Max—he's cooking today—ask Max to get you set up at the sink. Afterwards I'll give you a little extra. How's that? Help you get to your gramma's?"

"Thanks, Ma'am." Redwing slipped the bone necklace back over her head and around her neck, and she turned toward the double doors that led to the kitchen.

PART THREE

14

The woman holds the hollow bone from an eagle's wing between the thumb and forefinger of her right hand and hears the eerie sound as it catches the breeze coming off the Strait of Juan de Fuca. She has looked up from arranging the bones on her wooden table to watch sunset tint the mountains the color of a Malayan garnet. She moves to the open window of her house and breathes the cedar scent. Wet cedar in bloom. Who would have thought cedar trees bloomed? But of course they do. All living things flower at least once. Evenings like this she sees it, understands. She raises her arms and breathes again. Jagged peaks the color of apricot, root beer, and spring roses, change with the slant of light and jut into the sky like the bones of the most primitive, the first of all the gods.

She runs the fingers of her left hand through her short, spiky hair. Gray hair now. But it could be any color nature offered. She would tint it with blackberry juice before taking her drawings down to Port Townsend where Jason at the Cedar Mountain Gallery would tease her about being old. Old woman, he would say, who do you think you're fooling? And he'd laugh. He loves her for it, though, her eccentricity. Always on the edge of the circle. Always at the point of highest velocity, barely grounded, about to spin off into space.

And she isn't old anyway. Only sixty or so, but the turns her life has taken would make anybody's head spin. No wonder she chopped off her hair and dyed it purple! And all the people she's been! Goodness! Who could keep it straight? Who would want to? Now they call her Bones. Jason calls her Bones when he isn't calling her Old Woman. But it was Lily she'd been born. Lily Ste. Germaine of Cold Creek, North Dakota. A long time ago, that was. A long, long time.

~~~

Forty years ago as Lily Olson, she took egg money she'd saved over several years and paid the train fare to Seattle. From there she went by steamer towards the Olympic Peninsula. The day had been clear as the steamer made its way into Port Townsend Bay, and a well dressed, older woman standing beside her on the deck pointed out the array of snowcapped mountains that circled the town, from Mt. Baker on one side to Mt. Rainer and the Olympics on the other. She also warned Lily about the town's reputation--a history of brawls and shipwrecks, saloons, prostitutes, shanghais, murders and suicides. "The respectable folks lived up on the hill, and the rapscallions congregated down on Water Street. Things are better these days, but you'd still do well to head directly up Taylor to Washington Street, then make your way to the intersection of Blaine and Pierce. There's a Father Klein at St. Mary Star of the Sea. He's new and beset with division among a dwindling congregation. But he's a good man who inherited his difficulties. A compassionate man. He can probably help you find work and a suitable place to live."

Rapscallions, she thought after they docked and she made her way down Water Street towards Taylor; she didn't intend to get tangled up with any more of those. The street looked better, more prosperous than she'd been warned, but it wasn't a place for living, only for passing through.

Both the church and rectory were as run down as Lily felt, and she wondered what Fr. Klein might have done to deserve such an assignment. She adjusted her dress, smoothing the wrinkles. About all she could do on the trip was to brush it, get the dust out. She knocked on the door.

The unreadable eyes of the priest who opened the door

unhinged her a bit. "Are you needing something, *Fraulein?*" He spoke with a thick German accent.

When she recovered her voice, Lily introduced herself and explained that she'd been directed to the church by a kind woman who shared with her the passage from Seattle. He nodded and invited her into the draughty house, motioning to a worn horsehide chair where she sat.

"Are you Catholic?" He inquired, sitting down in a wooden rocker that squeaked when it felt his weight.

"I am." She didn't want to tell him everything. She didn't want to mention North Dakota. "I was educated by the nuns."

"*Sehr gut!* You could work at St. John Hospital, maybe?"

"I don't know, Father. Might there be something with less people? I'm looking for a more quiet life than hospital work can offer." She paused. It came to mind that she was behaving as though she could have any kind of work she wanted. What naiveté. She didn't have that sort of luxury. "Of course, I'd be happy to find any work at all. I'm sure I would have the skills for some sort of work at the hospital."

He stuck out his bottom lip, pulled on it between thumb and forefinger, thinking. "Mattie Brodie. The solution ends up right in front of me." He rocked forward and looked straight into Lily's eyes. His own lost their protection, and she could read in them a curious combination of gentleness and determination. "You'd have to ... *erleiden* ...how you say?" He called towards a closed door. "Katherine!" The door opened from the kitchen and a young woman wearing a blue apron appeared, wiping her hands on a dish towel. "My niece," the priest explained, then "Katherine, how you say *erleiden?*"

"It would be 'endure,' Uncle. Or maybe 'suffer'."

"Endure. *Ja.* It would mean to endure the loneliness, to endure the distance, to endure the *exzentrizitäten* of an old woman." He'd refocused his attention on Lily and away from his niece who returned to her kitchen. "Can you do that?"

If she could endure Adeline Olson, she figured she could endure any woman. "I think I can," she said.

~~~

The priest told her about Mattie Brodie as best he could--a widow, a member of St Mary's before his time, and now barely surviving on her land above Discovery Bay. Once a week someone from the Legion of Mary made the trip up to her house, bringing supplies. Lately they'd needed to clean house for her, at least a little, as the arthritis had stiffened her into near immobility. "It's the constant chill," he confided. "I feel it coming in my own poor bones."

If she wanted to try it out, she could spend the night at the home of a Legion of Mary couple, and accompany them the next day to meet Mattie.

~~~

More like a wren than a woman, with a stooped body, and hair that had never quite turned gray and was the texture of dried grass that has curled in the sun, Mattie stood in the doorway of her house. Lily and the Legion of Mary couple, Fran and Ted, could see her already from a turn in the rutted dirt road, and she became more distinct as they closed the distance. The Ford truck swerved and bounced. The higher they had driven, the more visible the Olympic Mountains appeared above Discovery Bay. Lily caught her breath. Oh, to paint that!

"Well, I'm old, you know," Mattie responded to Lily's "How are you?" after having been introduced. And then she giggled, not like a girl so much as like a woman who had experienced all life had to throw at her and now found the whole mess hilarious. The parishioners carried supplies into the house and set them on a kitchen table made of what looked to be the wide leafed maple at which Lily had marveled on her way up the hillside. Mattie toddled to her woodstove to make tea.

"Here, let me help." Lily rushed to her side. The old woman walked with her legs widely spaced for balance. She wore no shoes over her heavy wool socks, and Lily suspected that if she had any at all, they must be specially made because her toes were a mess of twists and bumps frozen in place by arthritis. Her hands, too, gnarled knuckles with brittle sticks for fingers, looked incapable of lifting anything at all, much less a cast-iron teakettle.

"I'm old. I'm not dead." Mattie giggled again. Then she

motioned to Lily to go ahead and help. "You're a good girl," she mused, pointing out a china teapot -- "my dear mother's" -- and a tin of tea leaves.

The four drank tea and discussed arrangements. She didn't really need Lily, Mattie told them. And when both Fran and Ted fussed over her, saying how kind Father Klein was to think of her this way, and she was getting fragile since her late husband went off to heaven, and what would she do if she were to need to go outside for something and fell, then was unable to raise herself up again, and there'd be no one close enough to hear her cries. What then? Why she could just die there, lying on her back, staring at the sky.

"Wouldn't that be nice?" Mattie tilted her head, looked at all three of them with soft eyes.

"And what about Lily, here?" Fran said. "Why Mattie, you have more room than you need, and this poor girl has no one and nothing. She needs a bit of time to get her feet on the ground, and a place to stay while she does it, and a good work to be doing, for an idle mind, as we all know, is the devil's workshop."

Mattie turned to Lily. "I can be crotchety." But her eyes were a summer rainfall.

"You probably have reason."

And the agreement was reached.

Mattie no longer climbed stairs, so Lily could have the second floor to herself. There was a bedroom up there and a storage room. "Nothing here is very big, except those mountains, the trees, the land, and the bay. You can see all that just fine from upstairs." A few years earlier, Mattie had begun to sleep in a small room off the parlor. She and her husband had built it for the nursery. "Seems not like this lifetime we built it," she told Lily. "Seems like it was a dream time when we thought it was all just part of being married. We thought the babies would just come. They came early and blue and soon dead, all three of them. When I sleep there now I feel them all around me like little angel spirits watching."

~~~

Lily had no angel watching. Her angel stood in the middle of the kitchen back at Cold Creek. Whose way was easier? She wondered this the next day during Mattie's afternoon nap when she'd gone outside to explore the paths that cut through the property and along the ridge above the bay. It wasn't all that many days ago that she'd left her angel son. Not that many days since she'd felt the assault of Ancil Murdock on her body and her mind.

She dropped to her knees alongside the path and scooped up the delicate carcass of a wren. All of it was there, collapsed in on itself, sun-dried, feathers glued to bones with tough remnants of blood and flesh. She examined it carefully. Nothing broken. A storm may have opposed its flight, or an eagle in mid-air. She imagined it snatched in the talons, struggling, then the release, the fall when the wings wouldn't work, the chirping and flapping in the dust, then death. Sweet. A release from the effort, every single day, to soar, to meet whatever dwells higher, and never, never an end.

Later that day she cleaned it, separated bones from feathers, laid it on the porch railing in the sun where all that essence, everything left over from the striving, bleached to a startling white. She checked on it every day, and time passed.

Upstairs in the storage room a table made of fir stood by the window overlooking the bay. She began to draw bones, whatever she found. Wolves. Bear skull. The pelvis of a black-tailed doe. She arranged them—pure, ivory, the color of milk-teeth under her pillow, of diamond willow driftwood under the moon—on a slate-colored rock or on velvet or on rich black dirt. It could take hours, days.

She arranged the bones on the table. Predator with victim. Coyote and rabbit. Eagle and wren. Here was the jawbone of a cougar intersected by the femur of a fawn. Light slashed into shadow, the gleam of bone around the absence of flesh. Who was victim now that both are dead and all that's left of each are the gleaming jewels of what they were and didn't know until too late? She moved the coyote's skull so that the hollows of bone catch the light through the window, light off the bones of earth, those mountains of gods, the Olympics. She passed the rabbit's fine bones through the coyote's absent eye, through the cave of skull, into the hollow that once held brain. It was a kind of intercourse, wasn't it? These would be erotic drawings, because there was a bit of that, wasn't there, in every death?

She'd seen the way they stand before each other, victim and

predator, eyes locked, entranced. She watched one evening. It may have been this cougar, this very fawn. She had held her breath to see them caught in that moment as lovers are caught just before their lives change forever. It was the moment of surrender to inevitability or what seems one's destiny. It was eternal terror and love.

Nights, after Mattie was asleep, Lily contemplated bones. Skeletons of eagles, wings outstretched; of a hummingbird, its bones like thread, its translucent skull. She stared at them until her flesh evaporated, until her eyes disappeared, became hollows in her soul, until she heard their scream of life, until she became that scream.

Sharp lead. Thick vellum paper. Paper was the flesh of birds now, of wolves, even of her own self. On paper she put down whatever can remain. She traced the scream in contours of bone on the receptive surface. She pressed and her mark remained.

~~~

Winter came and Mattie worsened, taking to her bed. The Legion of Mary volunteers came up the hill only when the roads dried out, so supplies needed rationing. Mattie ate like the wren she resembled. Though the house had been well built, the chill crept in and firewood dwindled. Lily piled quilts on Mattie; she killed an old hen and made enough soup to last a week. More food, firewood, some aspirin and a bottle of brandy arrived with the church volunteers on their next trip, along with more drawing paper and pencils.

"Lily and I make do," the old woman told them when they inquired. "We're indebted to Fr. Klein and the parish for your help." She motioned to Lily to get money from the cupboard. She paid for the supplies; the trip and time was a charity she was willing to accept.

"What is it you do with all that paper?" Mattie asked. It was mid-January and the church volunteers had just left to get back to town before dark. Lily had propped her up in bed against a colorful quilt and several pillows.

"I do a bit of drawing of things I pick up along the path."

"What things?"

"Oh, bones and things."

"You're an artist?" Mattie's eyes twinkled.

214

"Oh, I wouldn't say that. My mama would have liked to be an artist, but her life was cut short. I did a bit of drawing in school, and a little bit afterwards, but just for myself. My papa used to say the arts could be a good hobby for a woman, but we shouldn't set our hearts on it. It takes too much time and energy just to survive." It was the longest explanation of anything personal she'd given Mattie so far.

"Could I see a few of your drawings?"

Upstairs Lily sorted through the drawings on the table. Not this one; not that. Most of them seemed too revealing. What sort of eye did Mattie have for the subtleties? Weren't they just drawings of bones? But she knew they weren't only that. She selected the hummingbird and the bear skull.

"Ah..." Mattie exclaimed. "Very stark."

Lily said nothing. No one had looked at her work like this since she was a child with Sister Irene.

"Have you ever worked with color?"

"In school. Also a bit before I came to Washington. I did think of using plants like water color. Blackberries in season. Rhododendron petals. Seaweed. I wasn't sure."

Mattie lifted her hands from the top of the quilt. Her fingers pointed every-which-way. "Just look at these hands." She mused more with fascination than with sadness or anger. "These hands also used to paint the living things around this house. A hobby of mine, just like your papa said." She giggled under her breath. "Just imagine, dear. Both of us with a secret lifeline to what's beautiful." She motioned towards the kitchen. "You go into the pantry, Lily. At the back you'll find a little cubby hole that leads under the stairway. Just open its door--there's no lock. All my things are back there. Paints and brushes, an easel, whatever you might need."

"Oh Mattie, I couldn't..."

Mattie shook her gnarled hands. "And what will happen to it all if you don't use it. Can I paint? I can't even hold a brush. Please take them. If you use them it will be as if one of my angels lived and grew up with my own gift inside her. It will be like I was part of you, looking through your eyes, painting the beauty and starkness with your hand. It will be like not really dying when I die."

Lily nodded. She went to the pantry, lighted the kerosene lamp, opened the little door, crawled in under the stairs and drew out all that Mattie said was there.

~~~

The next few weeks Lily spent more and more time caring for Mattie who seemed to become littler every day. She ground aspirin and mixed it with honey to make it more palatable. She tore old sheets and towels apart to make diapers when she realized how difficult it was for Mattie to be propped on the bedpan. She heated rainwater on the woodstove and washed her. "That feels good," Mattie said as Lily lathered her hair and rubbed her scalp. She oiled the woman's skin which had become thin and dry as parchment.

Mattie told stories while Lily sat beside the bed and followed the woman's emotions by looking deep into her eyes. "Who will I give these to, if not you?" So Lily learned of the trip West from Maryland to join a man she'd never met. She learned of the tears, the strangeness, the surrender to duty, and finally the first glimmerings of love. "He waited for me to love him." She patted Lily's hand. "You know what I mean, don't you, dear?"

Over the years, letters from the East stopped coming. Then the babies died. She described each one. Two boys. One girl. She held them, dead though they were. She rocked them, counted their fingers and toes, sang them lullabies. She wept so when Francis (that was her dear husband: Francis Brodie), when he took each small body from her arms and buried them under the big maple where the broad leaves could shelter the tiny graves from the rain.

She drifted on Mattie's words, a river of words, a lifeboat of words bearing both of them up.

"Now I know only you, dear Lily, and the folks from the church. If I could live longer, I'd tell stories about you, but it has to be the other way around, I'm afraid."

In March the coughing began and Mattie asked for Father Klein.

"Don't you need a doctor?" Lily had been collecting the greenish brown sputum, wiping it from Mattie's lips. "It could be pneumonia."

"Of course it's pneumonia, dear. I need Father Klein, not a doctor. Tell Fran and Ted when they come up tomorrow. Tell them there isn't much time." She began coughing again, deep, tearing coughs, strong enough to turn the old woman inside-out."

Lily knelt by the bed and took Mattie's hand. "Don't leave me, Mattie. I just found you. Please Mattie, don't die."

The old woman ran her twisted thumb along the edge of Lily's hand. "We all die, but we don't really go away. My angels are here, and my Francis, too. I'll be with them. We'll keep you company. You'll be my daughter and I'll watch you paint the beauty."

Lily leaned down and kissed her forehead.

"Remember, dear. It isn't just a hobby."

In two days the priest knocked on the door. He wore a green stole over his cassock and carried the holy oils and the blessed sacrament in his case. Lily showed him to Mattie's small room, and he said "Bless you, Lily," nodded to Mattie saying, "I've brought the Viaticum." Then he closed the door behind him.

~~~

The day after the undertaker drove out to the house to collect Mattie's skin and bones, Lily hiked up into the Olympics. She took a backpack with food, paints and brushes. She continued to hike even after the logging road ended against a thickness of trees on one side and a sheer drop of yellowish rock on the other. A path led alongside a stream that plunged thousands of feet right in front of her into a chasm of Douglas fir. She grabbed the trunk of a young hemlock, got a good foothold in the rocky ground, and pulled herself up the steep incline into the forest.

She followed the stream as it afforded her a source of pure water. With Mattie gone she found her mind right back at the farm, taking the first step into wilderness. She ate blackberries and her hands became stained by their blood smeared together with her own. From time to time she cried out into the thick canopy of cedar, hemlock and fir. Her screams attracted eagles that landed on the topmost branches. If she saw Ancil Murdock standing in her path right now, if she saw Joseph, she'd have the words. Mattie gave her the stories of her life, and now she'd have the courage to tell her own, say her own words. But Joseph and Ancil were far from her, disappearing into the prairie soil, as she climbed high above them into mountains rising like teeth out of the ocean.

Her fingernails broke on the rocks as she climbed. Several times she was certain she would fall, tumbling a mile down, tangling with vines, cracking her head open, spilling her brains. She would be food for wolves if there were wolves here. Wolves and ravens would clean her bones.

A bobcat crossed her path and sat not twenty feet from her, staring like some Egyptian god. She stared back. There was nothing left in her but the thick emptiness of grief, a gravity pulling her into the wild.

At the end of the day she came upon an abandoned log cabin and took shelter there. Rain slashed through the giant trees and wind bent them. By nightfall the rain had turned to snow. She wrapped herself in her sleeping bag and huddled on the narrow wooden bed. She shivered. For the first time since leaving North Dakota it occurred to her that she could die after all—that running away, in itself, could cost her life.

The immense silence of snow settled on the mountains.

In the night she thought of Sarah surviving on the prairie in winters more severe than the snows of this one night, and loneliness enough to last a lifetime. She took her courage from memories of Sarah, and her tenacity for survival from cords of love binding her to James. All of them, lost to her now. Even Mattie--lost. Heartbreak combined with anger. She had swallowed her anger and would spit it out on vellum paper in the form of bones. All the betrayals, all the loss, every abandonment including her own, the affliction of her very being-- she would lay everything down like bones to be cleansed by the storm.

In the morning she started down. The cabin had been right at the snow line, and she soon emerged onto a path dried by the sun. In mid-afternoon she found a cave. Lily crept inside. The stones under her hands and knees were slippery with condensation and cold. Her eyes burned. My eyes will explode, she thought, if I don't cry. I don't want to cry. There's no reason to cry. I'm alone here; nothing has happened that has not been constant almost all my life. Maybe this pressure of tears is my life beyond memory, beyond everything. Her hand encountered a sharp stone in the floor and the tears come at last as the stone tore the flesh of her palm. She drew her knees up to her chin and clasped them in her arms. She rocked with her tears.

Her head throbbed from the crying. She could not move; she was too weak. She slept in the cave and dreamt only of a dark room and a knocking at the door.

~~~

Someone had tacked an envelope to Mattie's front door. Worry scuttled through Lily's mind. She put down her backpack and went inside, laying the envelope on the kitchen table. Then she sat in Mattie's old rocker and looked at it. It could mean anything. Just open it! her mind ordered. But what if she needed to leave this house? Where would she go? But, of course, she must leave. It occurred to her that she knew nothing of Mattie's financial situation. The letter lay there, having what she felt sure would be the answers, but she needed to let it lie until she was ready to know.

She returned to the porch and brought the backpack inside, unpacked it. Put the sleeping bag upstairs in the storage room, laid paint and brushes on the fir table by the window. Her waiting took the form of sketching an envelope held in the beak of a wren. She then opened a tub of red oil paint, took a fine brush, and made a mark in the corner, as though she'd pricked her finger and the blood dripped onto the paper in the shape of a wing. Only when she was finished could she go back downstairs to where the answers lay.

Her name was written on the front, Lily Olson, in an angular hand. She used a paring knife to make a clean slit at the fold and then drew out a folded sheet of St. Mary Star of the Sea stationery. Her eyes scanned the short note. He wanted her to meet with him at the rectory as soon as she could.

The next day the sun gleamed off the bay, and Lily hiked down the rutted road from Mattie's to the main road leading into Port Townsend. She kept walking, but it wasn't long before one of the other bayside people gave her a ride and dropped her off in front of the rectory. Fr. Klein's niece met her at the door and led her into the parlor where she'd met with him on the day she arrived from Seattle. He motioned for her to sit, once again, on the horsehide chair.

"We missed you at Mattie's funeral," he said.

"I'm sorry, Father. I was overwrought. I'd grown close to Mattie, and her death undid me."

"Such things happen, though most people find *trost,* their comfort, in prayer." His face looked gentle.

"I went into the mountains, Father. Maybe prayer is what I did there. I'm not sure I know what prayer is anymore." Right now her empty heart felt as close to prayer as she ever was likely to come, but she didn't tell the priest about the scream inside that wanted to come out, that wanted to go somewhere, to someone. And maybe that someone was God. But maybe it was just Mattie, or her mother, of even her little son.

"Our Lord also went to the mountains to pray," the priest responded. "Prayer, it does not always feel like prayer. We pray best, I think, when we do not know that we pray at all." He reached over and took her hands into his. "I'm sad with you that our dear little Mattie has left us. She loved you, too, *Lilie Liebes.*" He reached to the table beside his chair and took from it a file of documents. "The day I brought *Viaticum,* Mattie asked me to write down a Will to file at the courthouse. She signed it, and I witnessed it. These are the documents. All of her possessions she has willed to you, Lily. The house, the land, you own it all. She called you "daughter" and told me there was no one else. You loved her well."

~~~

The years passed and Lily painted. She kept a garden and Mattie's chickens. She was both thrifty and resourceful with Mattie's money. Sometimes she made the trek into the Olympics back to the cave and descended through a tunnel into its womb-like chamber. She brought her kerosene lamp because what she required of herself needed light. She brought paints made of earth's pigment. She came crawling, like the ancients of the caves at Lascaux, and she painted by firelight. She painted on the bones of earth. She gave these bones the flesh of her mind, the flesh of her heart and soul. She covered the bones of earth with the body of her life.

Her mother was there, not as she was in life, but as she inhabited Lily's mind and haunted her with a longing expressed in a high pitched scream. The scream echoed in the cavern as though the cavern were the woman's larger skull.

She painted her son, standing as he stood when she said

goodbye. Never should she have been a mother. Poor James. Hadn't she done to him exactly as Aimee Ste. Germaine had done to her? For all he knew his mother had died as surely as hers. Her own mother stripped from Lily, as from herself, the abundance of life, the fullness, the nourishment she had needed to endure. But even as she thought these things, she saw the image of another mother whose arms were open. It was Mattie, and infinitely more than Mattie. Her body was the night sky filled with stars; her belly was the cave itself and Lily an embryo within her. This mother was gestating her, taking her back into her body to bear her into a new and different birth.

~~~

Port Townsend grew, Fr. Klein returned to Germany where he was executed during the Nazi regime for his aide to the Jews. Lily wept, though it all made an ironic sense. She still could sense his hand on hers, his acceptance of her without question. She painted his arthritic hands, cupped, holding a Dakota meadowlark, about to take flight.

Sometime during the next twenty years, Lily began to sell her paintings. Early on Saturday mornings she caught a bus on what was now Discovery Bay Road. She carried a large deerskin portfolio and rested it on the floor in front of her knees all the way into town. If it wasn't raining she set up right at the corner of Tyler and Water Streets where any locals or occasional tourists were sure to pass. Most didn't stop. She wore hiking boots from army surplus, and men's fatigues even in summer. At noon she pulled the camouflage shirt over her head and sat on the bench in her men's undershirt, letting the sunshine tan her bare arms. Sometimes she sketched shells. Mostly she watched the sailboats and ferries on the strait.

The locals raised a hand to wave. They stopped to talk.

"How ya doin', Bones?" She allowed them to call her that. The name fit her now more than "Lily" did. They knew her by the absence of all she used to be.

"Can't complain."

"Any new pictures?"

"The skull of a black bear."

"Looks like an eighth continent."

"I call it Sanity."

Most of them owned at least one or two of her drawings; a few had framed them and hung them on their porch or in their garage. It wasn't for them that she'd applied herself to seeing what most cannot see.

"You should put more color in these drawings, Bones, besides that red swish of yours. A little variety. Some leaves. Some grass. Maybe the mountains in the background with a sunset or storm clouds. Something active. Alive."

"I appreciate your advice." The paintings she still hesitated to sell. She stored them in Mattie's room where the angels could stand guard.

"Bet you won't, though."

She leaned back and grinned. Her teeth hadn't seen a dentist in ten or twenty years.

If she sold a drawing then she bought dinner at the Belmont. She sat on the balcony where she could feel the wind off the strait. She ate their clam chowder. Mt. Baker and especially Mt. Rainier appeared much farther off. She pondered how perspective changes things.

Afterwards, if it got too late for the bus, she walked up the hill, nodded at the man with the long beard who sat in front of Aldrich's Grocery, and turned left onto Laurence. The night was cool, as the nights were always cool here. Just before the street dips down toward Kearney she turned on Scott and disappeared behind a thicket of wild roses alongside an abandoned house. The side door stood ajar. A cat scurried past her as she slipped through into an empty kitchen. She almost stepped on the dead rat lying in the middle of the floor. Resourceful cat. She lifted the rodent by its tail and flung it into the thicket. Then she climbed the stairs which were painted, alternately, black and red, and went into the front room, the one with the bay window and what once was a window seat, now a simple ledge. She sat down and loosened the laces on her boots, setting them neatly against the wall. Moonlight through the sooty windowpanes mottled both window seat and floor. She lay in it. She took a bone rosary from her pocket, held tightly to the cross and first bead, and she closed her eyes.

~~~

For twenty years she thought the rape had been her fault. Until she saw the cougar kill the fawn, she hadn't even called what happened to her by that terrible word, rape. She knew the man. She trusted him. She'd thought rape must be violent and swift, but he moved deft and slow. In her dreams his muscles glow, his eyes are hollows filled with gleaming. His hand upon her face had set her trembling, like the flank of the fawn as she stood entranced. Her mind said no, but her body didn't move. He stopped her in an open field, but there was no escape. He entered her like teeth.

~~~

"So you just up and ran away, then."

The old man made it into a statement rather than a question. The woman, Bones, sat beside him on the sidewalk in front of Aldrich's Grocery. For several weekends she had stood in front of him, staring at his face. He was porcelain. She'd never seen skin stretched so tightly over bone. His closed eyelids could hide insanity or a drugged mind, but she rejected those possibilities. Instead, his eyelids covered brilliance from a different world, a higher realm. She felt sure of this because his face was the perfect image of bliss. If only she could draw him. Maybe she could, in fact, draw him, his bones, his skin of such translucence it barely could contain his light. Like her, he was ragged, and like her, it mattered nothing to him.

She sat beside him and closed her eyes. She began, slowly, falteringly, to tell her story, and when she was finished he said, "So you just up and ran away."

"I ran, yes, but I never thought of it like that. Not away. I was running toward something that got lost somewhere in a distance so complete I might not ever find it. I had to try though. Don't you think I had to try?"

"And did you? Find it?"

"No." Then Mattie came to mind. "Some of it, maybe." She could see a luster of it in the old man's face or under his skin, in the bone of his skull. Something that could not quite be concealed by the muscle and skin that covered it."

"It is quite strange, don't you think?" she asked the man, who stared past her as she formulated her thought, "how our faces aren't our own?" It occurred to her that we never see our faces, not even with a mirror. We can't see the contours in the same way as the one who observes us, so it's almost as though her own face had been given to her not for herself at all, but for this man or for anyone who might care to look.

"Will you let me draw your face?" she asked him.

"Do whatever you want."

His name was Tobias, and she drew him Saturday evenings before she walked the remainder of the way to Scott Street and the empty house. She drew him like the most refined of bones, the most brilliant. Bones polished like fine ivory. Bones gleaming with a luster difficult to capture in the touch of her graphite pencil on the thick paper. She drew him as she would have drawn a god, and she failed. Afterwards she carried his image back up the hills and pinned him all over the walls and stared at him by every kind of light—by the dawn and twilight, by the clear noon light and by the muted light of storms. He was the perfect creature. He was the beauty rising out of sorrow, and she could not capture him.

"Did you find what you lost?" he asked her at summer's end.

"Maybe it's gone forever," she told him.

"Maybe you've had it with you all along and you just forgot," he said.

"Or covered up...."

"Like bones. You always talk about bones."

Her mind whirled. She was dizzy as though standing on an Olympic cliff. She was right on the verge of knowing.

"Yes. Yes, like bones. They remain, don't they?" she said.

"They do. Maybe they're what keeps the secret," Tobias said, and she took it in as if he held the key to knowledge kept hidden always.

"Secret?" She barely breathed the word.

"The one we don't really want to know."

~~~

She gathered her tools and left the cave. Outside a wind was rising off the strait and the leaves of the alders had turned gold in the valley below. Her masterpiece, in a cave, where no one would see. It never would be sold.

Oh well, selling her drawings hadn't been her intention. It just happened one day twenty-five or thirty years ago that the thought came to trade drawings of bones for food or clothes. Then ten years ago along came that art dealer from Seattle, visiting Port Townsend, noticing her drawings where she had them stacked on the picnic table down on Water Street. Lily had been counting her few coins to see if she had enough for chowder at the Belmont when she suddenly had a hundred dollars and her last ten drawings on consignment in a gallery.

What was she going to do with a hundred dollars? The paintings sold in the Seattle gallery, and then what was she going to do with thousands of dollars? The art dealer banked it for her and Lily made a will leaving all of it to James and his descendants. She wondered suddenly if ever he'd found those early paintings in the attic at the farm. Maybe not. No one had come looking.

The sun set as the full moon rose. No need to hurry. These paths were so familiar now that she could be blind and still find her way home. The cougar, the bear, the lynx held no danger for her anymore. She'd become as wild as they. She'd lost her fear. She bent to something gleaming ivory on the ground.

~~~

Lily sat at the maple table in the kitchen. Another winter had passed and just down from her the wild rhodies were blooming pink all through the woods. She smelled their sweet scent mixed with that of the heavier cedar. She watched an eagle drift on updrafts, so close she could see the white of its head and tail, almost close enough to look directly into its eye. For a few moments she flew with the eagle in her mind as if between herself and the bird existed a symbiosis impossible to deny.

All winter she'd felt pregnant. How odd. Her hair white. Her body having gone through the change years before. Still and all, she contained a life in her that struggled to be free. It put her in mind of James. It bothered her that he might not know.

She rose from the table and shuffled among papers arranged neatly on shelves in Mattie's large pantry. She selected a piece of white paper, not thick like vellum but thin like parchment. With a pencil she began to draw the bones of an eagle, and under the finished drawing she wrote:

Dear James,
This letter, although perhaps you don't remember me, is from your mother...

15

Hannah, who still thought of herself as Redwing, found her way to the world's edge. She traveled by her thumb, often feeling invisible, disappearing as she used to feel her father might someday disappear. Once she arrived in Seattle, in 1957, she lived on the streets, sleeping in churches and abandoned buildings until she had the money from odd jobs for a ferry to Port Townsend.

She settled there. Her grandmother could be anywhere close by, and she began immediately to search. To make ends meet she hoped to work the ferry run between there and Whidbey Island. The Port Authority told her she wasn't qualified to direct traffic, being a girl and all. But she persisted. She went back to them again and again. Remembering Raggedy Lily, she wore heavy boots and men's work pants, jacket and cap. They finally gave her a try. She and two men directed cars coming onto the ferry carport, first to the center, then right, then left portals to keep the ship balanced. On the other side they signaled the same cars off, down the gangplank, onto the Seattle terminal. She thought maybe she would get lucky and the work she did would actually be a key to answer the questions so deep inside she still hadn't found the words for them.

Some mornings, early, the fog drifted heavy onto the waters of the strait and the ferry entered the belly of that ghost. Redwing stood in the ferry's gaping maw, holding the heavy chain that secured the carport, and gazed out into the swirling cloud and onto the choppy water. Even in summer the wind had a chill to it, but in winter it could sting your eyes enough to cause tears. She got used to it. She prided herself on her tolerance. It's nothing, she told the men who asked her wasn't she cold? Didn't a girl like her need a warmer job? It's nothing when you grow up in North Dakota, she told them. You ever spent a winter in North Dakota? Forty-below. It never gets that cold here. She watched gulls appear like spirits through the mists and land on the waves. They pecked at seaweed churned up from the bottom. They caught bits of bread tossed from the upper deck. Their cries tore through the sound of waves against the hull and the chug of the ferry's engines. The captain sounded the horn as the ship neared the port of Seattle, and Redwing felt the vibration of that sound deep in the core of her belly. No place on earth could be more unlike home than this.

She felt herself a spirit stretched between two shores, swirling and lingering like the fog, something without substance that could dissolve in a beam of light and disappear. She clapped her hands together in their heavy gloves to warm the tips of her fingers. Her nose looked no redder than the noses of the men who worked alongside her.

As it turned out, she directed traffic on the ferry, back and forth the entire winter, shivering in the lash of wind, the sting of sleet, standing against it in the prow, practicing the discipline of nature. And on days of sunshine she stood in the panorama of mountains, barely breathing, torn on those bright peaks. Torn, yes, but somehow also settling down, making for herself a home at the edge of things. Each day she searched the faces of women who came on and off the ferry. She searched the faces of women who walked up and down Water Street. How could she recognize her grandmother even if she did see her. All she had was a faded picture of a young woman. How much might she have changed. She might have been the woman who walked past her that very day, the one with gray hair bound neatly in a bun. She'd even asked, "Do you know a woman named Lily Olson?" and the woman shook her head. She smiled but didn't say a word.

Terrible images also came to mind during the ferry crossings: of Wanda outlined by flames, of Ancil dying in the blizzard with all the suffering of her world in his face. How could a world go so awfully wrong? Back and forth from Port Townsend to Whidbey Island, every day, clear weather or foul, she seemed to have dropped fragments of her childish hopes and horrific memories into the deep waters of the Strait of Juan de Fuca, and she seemed to watch them sink, becoming smaller as they disappeared from sight.

She began to ask at the stores along Water Street, at restaurants, of people coming out of the churches, the thrift shop, of people who lived on the street or in one of the bunkers at Fort Wardon. Do you know of a Lily Olson? This is her picture, but she'd be in her sixties by now. But people shook their heads. "Never heard of her." Are you sure? She said she was coming here. "When was that?" Thirty years. "That's a long time."

Redwing had rented a room in a rooming house. On the second floor, she had a small window from which she could see the water. On the windowsill, chunks of glass. From glass, stones, driftwood, rust-colored bits of curled bark from the madrones, she fashioned artistic designs, mobiles that she hung from the ceiling and that moved sensuously in the sea breezes. Even in winter Redwing often kept her window open, especially at night, in order to smell the salt and sense the closeness of the ocean. She lay in bed and concentrated on gratitude for the simplicity of her life. She read herself to sleep by the light of an old brass lamp with an amber-colored shade that warmed the whole room with its light and cast shadows the color of worn bronze. She read what she could pick up at the second hand bookstore downtown for a dime or a quarter. She mined the stories for a clue to life's suffering. The closest she found was a novel called *Grapes of Wrath*. She'd read a bit and stop, closing the book. Her heart raced and she breathed deeply of the salt air. But she always opened up the book again, hoping somehow by the blessed arrangement of the words on the page to discover a meaning in all the affliction. She clasped Sarah's beads in her hand as though they were a rosary. It was the only way she could fall asleep.

Broken sea-glass hung on the madrone tree outside her window where the salt winds could catch hold of it as they blew through the sound with the tide. The glass was old and well polished by the sand. Only the more recently broken bits glittered in the infrequent sun. The older bits gleamed from within their satin patina like rare jewels. She walked the beach after winter storms had uncovered the cast-off remains of human habitation transformed by the constant tides. If the ocean can do this to cast-off glass, she thought as she collected the fragments, maybe it can transform anything. It might be for that I came here. Maybe she could drop anything into the Pacific Ocean and it would come back to her changed. Transformed.

At first Redwing stored the sea-glass in jars to keep on her windowsill. But feeling the glass together like that, piled, one fragment upon another, some fragments hidden in the dark interior, she felt troubled. She sensed a desire in the glass, an accumulation of spirit, requiring freedom of space. One afternoon when the agitation in the glass reached an intolerable peak, she emptied the jars on her dresser. The sun shone brilliantly that day and the relief she felt as light found its way into the core of each broken shard simply had no words.

As though her life depended upon it, she began the task of wrapping each fragment in fine steel wire until she had several ropes of sea-glass in various lengths, some as long as four feet. She took them downstairs to show Ardis, her landlady, to ask if she could hang them in the tree. She found the woman in the kitchen kneading bread dough, a rhythmic callisthenic resembling a dance.

"Like Christmas decorations?" The woman held up a three-foot rope of the sea-glass. "Heavy stuff," she commented. A dab of flour powdered her cheek where she had pushed back strands of her graying hair.

"I suppose. But up all year. To catch the sun, when there's sun."

"Regular little artist, aren't you, Redwing?" She handed the rope back and resumed the kneading of her bread dough. "Can't see as it would be a problem. You go ahead, honey. Probably start a fad. First thing we know there'll be sea-glass hanging from all the trees in the neighborhood."

The smooth skin of the madrone accepted the hooks she used to fasten the sea-glass ropes and the tree itself seemed to her to stand with more assurance afterwards upon the bluff above the water. Sounds of broken sea-glass woke her each morning. The sea-glass madrone tree rang in the wind like an enormous wind chime.

On a Sunday morning just before Christmas she splashed cold water on her face, pulled on jeans, a thick knit sweater, her hiking boots, and the waterproofed slicker she wore on the ferry, and was outside in less than five minutes. She wouldn't have needed the cold water. Mist wet her skin and made corkscrew curls in her hair.

The receding tide had left the narrow strip of beach wet and filled with driftwood from a winter storm. She heard the slap of waves, sounding more like lake than ocean. Just past the point, though, tides at their highest always crashed against the bluff, undercutting the land and unearthing the roots of trees. On this day a mist, almost light rain, swirled with the wind and obscured the water.

The tide was not yet far enough out for running, or even for walking an uncluttered path. Someone else seemed to be up early and had climbed over the giant remains of old growth cedar and Douglas fir, some of it logged and escaped from its moorings, the rest torn up by its roots in the violent winter storms. She was seated on one particularly large specimen, wedged deeply into the sand, and flaunting roots that extended twice her height. The woman was staring out to where the mountains could be seen on a clear day. Hannah waved and yelled a greeting, but her voice tore apart in the wind. It could have been her grandmother. Any woman in her sixties in all of Port Townsend could be. If Lily Olson wanted to be lost, all she had to do was change her name. Hannah knew all about that.

At one point on the beach the shoreline turned to create a cove accessible only at low tide. Here the bluffs towered above the water and were pocked with loose stones, making the land uncertain. Even when she craned her neck to view the top of the bluff, she could see no houses, for every house built there would risk the eventual and inevitable crumbling of the land. The cove gave the impression of total wilderness. Redwing sat on a spruce log and watched a blue heron fish the shallows.

~~~

Later that same winter, one afternoon in Seattle, she stopped in a small art gallery on the waterfront. Among watercolors of lighthouses, oil paintings of ships and crashing waves, and elegant boxes crafted from the burls of the Washington broad-leafed maple, Redwing came upon paintings and pencil drawings of bones.

"These are evocative," she commented to the gallery owner, a woman dressed in khaki, a red wool scarf, and hiking boots.

"Yes. I get those from a supplier on the peninsula. They're done by a woman, a hermit of sorts, who has a place above Discovery Bay. Quite compelling, don't you think?"

It made Redwing think of Sarah. And in some strange way the

bones evoked what she could only call ghosts. Wanda again. Ancil, of course. And something of Hannah's father as he was when she was still a small child. Standing in the field at sunset, a dark tree or maybe a bone against the fading light in the sky.

"What's the artist's name?" Redwing asked.

"She signs them, 'Bones,' along with that signature mark of hers. You'll see it, small or large, on all her works."

Redwing saw it but scarcely dared believe. The mark, its color, began to flood her mind. She knew that mark.

She bought a delicate piece titled 'Winter Blackbird' and hung it in her room back in Port Townsend. After that it was the last thing she saw before turning off the bedside lamp at night, and the first thing she looked at in the morning. A silver pine reaching from the mountain into the sky, the bird's stark bones resembling a shadow on snow, and beside them a simple streak of red.

~~~

Every morning and night as Redwing stared at the painting her determination to find her grandmother increased. The paintings must be Lily's. They each had that red streak, that blood mark that characterized the work she'd found in the attic. They also called those other paintings to mind because of the stark style, though Bones's work was, if such could be achieved and apparently it could, more stark even than Lily's. But also more transcendent. Lily's work had ached with a kind of emptiness Redwing knew only because of what she'd felt when Wanda burned, when she walked away from Hannah, when she'd walked through the snow away from Ancil's dying body, when she kissed the sleeping Emily goodbye. The work by the mountain woman, Bones, had a simplicity of spirit that drew Redwing into the emptiness as though it were a place of endless being into which she might be able to surrender everything and find, maybe for the first time, the freedom to love it all completely.

Ardis stored different kinds of oatmeal in large green glass jars on open shelves attached to the kitchen walls. Irish steel cut oats. Scottish oats ground fine. Traditional Quaker oats. Redwing chose the Scottish oats and put the heavy saucepan on the burner. A cup of water, a pinch of salt. The finely ground meal of oats joined the boiling water and she turned down the heat and covered the pan before she measured coffee grounds. In ten minutes she had sat down at the table and was eating creamy oat porridge with pecans and tart dried cherries and drinking strong coffee as she stared out the window at the early morning fog.

Just as she was finishing, Ardis scuffed into the kitchen wearing her bathrobe, her hair done up in a scarf to cover a scattering of pink curlers. "Mornin'," she mumbled.

"G'morning, Ardis." Then, "Hey Ardis, you've lived here a long time, right?" It suddenly seemed to her that this woman might be of help in finding Lily.

"About all my life." Ardis poured herself a cup of coffee and sat down opposite Redwing, and lit a cigarette. "Thanks for making the coffee. I really need it this morning. Been working all night on a dream. Darn thing had my brain spinning."

"Dreams can keep you awake for a long time afterwards."

"Yeah." Ardis took another drink of coffee.

"Ardis?" It suddenly occurred to Redwing that the woman might know something about her grandmother.

"Yeah?" She sighed and looked at the girl through heavy eyelids.

"Have you heard of an artist, a woman who calls herself Bones?"

Artis looked up sideways and cocked her eyebrow. "Isn't she that one lives out along Discovery Bay? Inherited the old Brodie place, I think. Spiky hair? Color of blackberries? Keeps to herself a lot? She used to sell her drawings down on Water Street. Haven't seen her much lately, though."

"Could be." Redwing controlled her excitement. "I bought a painting of hers in Seattle. Where exactly is the old Brodie place?"

Ardis got up to refill her cup. "Don't know exactly. All I know is that you'd probably need to drive out along Discovery Bay Road, and her place would be off to the left and up into the hilly part. Probably her road's not marked. You might try the courthouse. Don't they have maps of people's property? I think they probably do." She snuffed out the butt of her cigarette on her saucer. "You must really like that painting of hers to go through all this trouble."

~~~

"I took you for a boy." Bones stood in the doorway holding a pot of boiling water.

"I suppose I might have looked like that from a distance," laughed the girl, though it was Bones herself who looked mannish with her spiky hair and solid, muscular body.

"May as well come in then. I've made tea." She turned and disappeared into the half-light behind the door, and Redwing followed her. It wasn't Lipton's tea. It had a sweet odor, like flowers. "Leave the door open; let the air in." Not like North Dakota, the screen doors, to keep out mosquitoes. "I watched you coming up the road." She set a plate of oatmeal-raisin cookies on the rough wooden table. "Don't get many visitors."

Redwing looked around the house. A black iron woodstove, lit. It must always be chilly up here. The kettle on top of the stove, steaming. Three windows, open to a cedar scented breeze. Wooden chairs, a plain maple table, an old rocker--nothing cozy.

"You live alone here?"

"Yes."

The woman poured a strong tea, flowery and the color of whiskey cut with water, into china cups and set them carefully on the rough wood table. "Nice bone beads." She touched Redwing's necklace, lifting it slightly then letting it go.

"Thank you. A friend made it." Redwing lifted the fragile bone china cup to her lips, sipped the tea and then set it again on the saucer. A delicate clicking sound. She let her eyes wander again. Images of bones drawn on vellum covered the far wall of the cabin. So this IS the famous Bones, she thought and gestured towards them. "I'm pretty sure I have a drawing of yours. You titled it Winter Blackbird."

"Oh?" The old woman was studying her face

"Yes. I found it in Seattle. A gallery."

"I've never gone back there, to Seattle. There's a fellow in Port Townsend takes care of those things for me. I see a bit of money now and then."

"So you're Bones?"

"It's what they call me. And you?"

"I called myself Redwing for a lot of years, but my real name is Hannah." The name slipped off her tongue and fell onto the air like a red leaf falls upon the water.

"A good name." Bones continued to examine her face carefully as artists tend to do.

"You think so?"

"Like mountains, the H on either side shelters the Anna."

Hannah laughed. "That's amazing," she said. "I've thought that too. I used to draw my name that way, the H's shaped like mountains on both sides."

"Anna," she said "is grace. A nun told me that. A dear friend from my childhood."

"Grace between mountains. I like that."

"A good name. Mountains and plains. H like the mountain winds over the prairie of Anna's grace."

"You talk like a poet." Hannah or Redwing, she no longer felt sure, took a drink of tea. "I know those prairies well. I used to live there."

"Not much of a poet." Bones said, picking up her cup. "Not much of anything at all, though I was once an old prairie dog myself. Care for more tea?"

As though an invitation had been in place since the beginning of time, Redwing continued to climb the dirt road to visit the woman. Often she stayed there on her days off, sleeping overnight in a sleeping bag laid on the floor.

"I wish I'd visited Port Townsend while you were there," she told Bones. "Ardis, my landlady, says you've sold your drawings on the sidewalk down by the old ferry dock."

"Stopped doing that two years ago. Must've been before you arrived in the area. Anyway, all my good work ends up in Seattle now. I do get to town almost every week, but without the drawings, who'd notice me?" Redwing looked into the woman's dark eyes. How could she have missed her? And yet she knew, if she were truthful, that she probably had passed her on Water Street and never given her a second glance. An old woman in army fatigues and an eccentric hairdo. She tried to remember whether anyone she'd ever known had turned out to be exactly what they seemed.

As the weeks piled one atop the other, Redwing followed Bones on trails the woman herself had carved through thick forest. She listened to her sing into the vast distances over valleys that plunged thousands of feet toward the Hood Canal and Dabob Bay. She waited for the woman to speak, to reveal who she was, whom she once had been. Bones took her down slick rocks beside a waterfall to a stand of mountain hemlock, a place, the woman said, inhabited by black bear. Perhaps they'd find a skull. Perhaps the bones of wee creatures. They carried back-packs in which to store the bones. They came upon an eagle, rotted in upon itself, wings still spread six feet from tip to tip.

"I wish I knew why you came here." The two women, young and old, sat together on the porch of Mattie's house watching the midsummer sunrise. Redwing questioned Bones. The old woman's hand rested on top of the hand of the younger.

"For silence. It became necessary for me to gaze into the silence." Bones rubbed her thumb across the top of Redwing's hand in an absent-minded sort of way, intimately, as though the young woman's flesh were an extension of her own.

"My father used to rub my hand like that." Redwing told her. "I think he did it instead of talking. He must have thought the touch, along with his silence, would tell me everything he wanted me to know." She touched Bone's fingers, exploring them, her index finger learning the shape of the old woman's thumbnail. It could have been her father's thumb, smaller and older but similar in shape.

"Did it tell you?" Bones asked. She didn't take her hand away but let Redwing continue to explore.

"Maybe not," Redwing said in a whisper. "If it had, I probably wouldn't have run away." Suddenly the woman's touch felt unbearable. She drew her hand away. She stood and faced the mountains. "Maybe I didn't know how to hear him."

Bones said nothing for a long time. An eagle cried, eerie, long, echoing off the mountains. "We both ran away then," she finally said.

"But you were looking for silence." Redwing told her. "I was leaving it. I wanted understanding, acceptance." She paused. "Forgiveness."

"Not just silence. I had a wild thing in me. It would have destroyed everything. It destroyed my marriage." She paused again, looking out at the jagged peaks. "I needed to find a place large enough, wild enough, to contain me. I didn't want to destroy my son."

"You have a son?"

"A little boy." She laughed. "Goodness. He's old now. Forty-some... I've forgotten."

"Where?" Redwing turned to face Bones. She could feel the tingling of her skin where the woman had rubbed her hand.

"It doesn't matter, dear. That life is gone."

"It does matter. It matters to me."

The old woman's eyes looked directly into Redwing's own. "I don't know if what I left or what I've lived here is necessary for anyone but me. For me there was no other way. All these years. All the bones...."

Redwing found herself remembering clouds on a North Dakota horizon. "That's what draws me to you. The bones. The silence. And the mountains. I've loved mountains, the idea of mountains. I used to look out over the prairie and pretend to see them in the outlines of clouds. Once I looked through my father's binoculars and saw the mountains of the moon." The two landscapes began to join for her, the prairie and the mountains, the Anna and the double H of her name. Hannah.

The woman went on as though she hadn't spoken. "I came as far as I could. Past here is the land's end. When I see these mountains I know that beyond them is the ocean. The cavern in the bone of earth. Creation's eye."

"Didn't you ever want to go back?" Redwing asked her. "What kept you here all this time?"

"The emptiness. I imagine that was the attraction. And stark bones, these animal spirits. These mountains, bones of earth entranced me. There had to be something, something at the core of it all. Some jewel at the center. I couldn't leave until I'd found it."

"So when you draw bones you really are..."

"Searching the emptiness."

"In the world?"

"And in myself. Maybe even the emptiness of God." Bones reached her hand to Hannah's face and smoothed back a strand of hair. "Maybe I was looking for forgiveness, just like you."

"Did you find what you were looking for?" Redwing asked her.

"Three times. Three times I came close."

"When? Where?"

"The first was in the love of Mattie, the woman who owned this house and opened her heart to me. The second I found in the face of a beggar I tried to draw. My pencil became a nail driven through my heart into his and on through his into the center of the universe. Though I attempted it again and again I could never capture the beauty of compassion in that face. And now I see it again in you, Hannah. You simply came up the road. But now you're part of me. In you I think I can see what became of all I left behind."

"You called me Hannah."

Bones reached out again and touched her hand, lightly rubbing Hannah's skin with her thumb as she had done before.

The younger woman watched the movement of the old woman's hand against her skin. She held back tears.

"You need to go back to him." Bones said.

"And you? What about your son? Don't you need to go back?"

"This is my home now, Hannah. And you are all I need of going back." She smiled, continuing to rub her hand, so lightly, with her thumb. "And you, dear Hannah—you are all he needs of me."

Hannah realized she had known most of the summer, but was afraid to say it. What if she had been wrong? Just dreaming up a fantastic thing to answer her needs? But the woman's touch on her hand--Hannah couldn't ignore what she was feeling, but she needed one more confirmation. She lifted the beads up and over her head. She held them in her hands and offered them to the woman.

"These really should belong to you." She laid the necklace in the woman's hand and put her own hand over the top of the bones as though to hold them secure.

"Sarah's beads," the old woman murmured.

"You knew." It was a question as well as a statement, but mostly a statement, an acknowledgement.

"I knew the minute I saw them that somehow you must have come to me from Sarah and from James."

"You're Lily." Hannah whispered.

"My mother called me Lily after the Lily of the Valley growing beside the house."

"And your little son is James?"

"My son is James."

"My father."

"Yes, Hannah, I suspect that's right."

"I've been looking for you all my life."

Bones smiled and took her hands. "No dear. You've been looking for Hannah. That's what you've been doing."

"Yes." Her voice shook. "Hannah. The Hannah I buried by the creek."

Hannah let her room go, quit her job on the ferry, and stayed through the summer with her grandmother. Bit by bit she told her story. Cold Creek and Hannah underneath the cottonwood. How Yarrow ran away during the summer storm. Of Wanda and the fire that took her life and left Yarrow and small Hannah so changed. She told her about James and Ida and the baby Emily who became like her own. She described old Sarah, her song, and her casting of bone. In low tones she told the story of Ancil, his gun, and the way his face melded with the faces of all afflicted ones just before he died.

Her grandmother listened. She polished bones and listened, and afterwards she sometimes sang to Hannah, holding her and rocking back and forth like a grandmother would. "We do what we can," she crooned. "We look suffering in the eyes until we find the beauty hidden in its emptiness."

She smoothed back Hannah's hair. She lifted Sarah's necklace of bones and rubbed them between her thumb and index finger. The oils in women's hands had polished the bones so that they gleamed like fine ivory. Sarah, Hannah and now Lily Ste. Germaine.

The leaves of the alder turned golden-brown and fell. The morning Hannah packed to descend the mountain the two women sat together again, holding steaming cups of coffee and, as was their ritual, they watched the sunrise.

"Life sets us moving, Hannah. Things happen." There were tears in Lily's eyes. She blinked them back. "Your mother is lost or your best friend is burned to death. You are raped or ignored or your existence is denied by those you most need to recognize you."

"It's a betrayal."

"An abandonment."

"An affliction."

"But you were brave, Hannah. Ancil Murdock tried to take you down, as he took me down, and you refused to let him destroy you. What you did, what you saw in him, you saw for all of us."

"But I ran away."

"Life ran away from you, and so you ran away from it. Am I right?"

Of course! She was right. One way or another it's what we do. And the only way back home is to reach the end of the world and go beyond it. "How do we stop? Do we have to run forever?"

"Until we forgive ourselves for everything we couldn't be. Until we get to the shining bone of what we are that's hidden within everything we hoped for. In that moment we've come home."

"Wanda did it by fire."

"Everyone has their way."

The old woman, her grandmother, reached into the pocket of her jacket and pulled out a letter and a little leather bag of bones.

"Give this letter to your father when you get back to Cold Creek." She said. "He has the best of me in you. And as for the bones—you keep them. In return for Sarah's beads. They might speak to you. Sarah will sense if you have the ears of soul for it. She'll teach you if you want to learn."

"You won't come back with me?"

"I live here now." She gave Hannah a hug. "This is where I ended up when I stepped past the end of the world."

Hannah left her that day. She took with her the letter, the bones, and a rolled piece of vellum that her grandmother asked her to give to Sarah. "She'll understand," is all Lily said.

The story isn't finished, Lily thought as Hannah turned to walk down the road. They'll think it is. They'll exhale their relief as though they hadn't let themselves breathe for generations. Everything, finally, they'll believe has found its place, is in its place. But Sarah would tell them that the bones say otherwise. Nothing stays the same. The pattern of the bones changes every time someone scatters them on the earth. In an instant, everything can be transformed.

She wouldn't be surprised if Sarah were getting set to leave Cold Creek. Sometimes she can see it in the bones—how her old friend will go down the road singing and playing her flute. She'll wear a funny hat she's found somewhere and carry her little bag of bones attached to her belt. There's a certain freedom of movement a woman has to have.

It will be late summer and the barley ripe. She'll wave to dear James in the fields with his new combine—he'll be harvesting barley. It's all there in the bones. That's what Sarah will tell Hannah before she leaves. Pass it on, she'll say. Tell Emily. The answers don't matter; it's the living that counts.

Sarah will walk the roads again, following the current of Cold Water Creek, and her old hair will crackle in the late summer wind. She'll walk the distance to the world's end, and that's when she'll see Lily coming towards her. The two of them will be wearing hiking boots and their skin will be brown as the bark of the old cottonwood tree. They'll be laughing and won't be too old for running to meet each other.

"Are you going home?"

"I'm there already, Lily." Sarah will say as she takes her friend's old hand. "We're both already there."

~~~

Hannah wore the little bag of bones around her neck on a leather thong. It bounced against her as she walked. She left her Grandma Lily and went down the mountain. She had thought all she needed was to find her. Then she thought that only if the two of them went home together could things be right, but that turned out not to be true. Hannah would return to Cold Creek alone. She would connect the going and coming back. She could already feel them giving way to one another.

You become a pilgrim, she thought as she walked ever farther from Lily. You wander to the end of things, even to the mountains of the moon. There you polish your spirit like the bone of earth, your vision like sea-glass. It can take years, a lifetime, but finally you recognize in everything as in a mirror what you went into the world to find: the face of anyone you've ever lost, and now you recognized that face. It is your own. It is Hannah.

PART FOUR

16

Emily leans out over the bank of Cold Creek and watches her face turn to liquid. A liquid girl, adrift with leaves and flecks that shine in the morning sun. She is waiting again under the cottonwood tree where she has gone each day for years, except for times that blizzards swept across the prairie sculpting waves of snow over the rolling land.

It is early spring. The day is warm and smells of linden blossoms and turned earth. She leans back against the old cottonwood and scans the horizon beyond her father's fields, and beyond the fields of the old Murdock place. Her Grandpa Harris joins them now for holidays since Uncle Ancil and old lady Murdock died. Farm fell into wrack and ruin, as the girl's father never tires of muttering when he thinks that she's asleep and cannot hear.

"Hush, James." The girl hears her mother from the other room.

"We're well rid of them."

"Still and all…"

"My grandmother, God rest her, never trusted those Murdock's."

"I'm a Murdock, James."

"There was something, Yarrow, about that Ancil when he was

alive. Something just not right."

"And it's over now, isn't it? And even if it weren't, is it ours to judge?"

"He schemed until he got everything."

"And what did it benefit him? Poor, empty and old before his time. And the way he died. To my way of thinking, that squares the book on it."

I'm not a child anymore, thinks the girl as she watches thunderclouds mass where land disappears into sky. She begins to hum and then to sing the lullaby she knows will bring back the scent of the little mother and the feathery touch of long ash brown hair that falls, covering the smaller girl's face.

"Blow, blow, the grasses blow," Emily sings in an alto deep and complex for one so young, the timbre of old trees.

"Song of our lives forever free,
Will bring us home, far though we be."

The sound comforts. It flows inward. It is like warm milk.

"Hannah's making her own life," her mother tells her as she combs Emily's black hair and braids it in the French way. "I suspect she went off and joined the circus just like your Gramma Lily. And when a woman runs like that she won't come back on her own. It takes a mighty power to bring her back, something she can't control. Maybe even it takes God. You'd best stop watching for her the way you do. You'd best stop singing that song. Why, my Hannah, she actually could be climbing the mountains of the moon by now; it's been that long."

Even from the mountains of the moon the little mother could return if she wanted to. If she remembered who she was.

I will never run away, the girl promises the cottonwood tree and the redwing blackbird that balances on a cattail. Never, she tells her reflection in Cold Creek. The thunderclouds fill the sky and tremble with lightning. The girl runs toward the house, and because she's suddenly in such a hurry to be home, she doesn't notice the young woman walking up the road, bent into the wind.

YARROW'S LULLABY

g-e-g   a   g   b   g   a
Blow, blow, the grasses blow,

c   b   a   g   e   a   f   e
Wind in our hearts, child, singing low,

g   e   g   a   gbg   a
Song of our lives forever free,

c   b   a   g-e   a   f   e   e
Will bring us home, far though we be.

ABOUT THE AUTHOR

Christin Lore Weber is a prize winning multi-genre author. Her first novel, *Altar Music,* (Scribner, 2000) was named an **LA Times** Best Book of the year 2000, as well as being chosen for **Publisher's Weekly's** "First Fiction," and the Independent Booksellers "Booksense 76." *Gypsy Bones* is her second novel, and the first book she has published directly as an e-book.

She lives with her husband, author John R. Sack, on Sunshine Hill in the Pacific Northwest.